Matthew's Run

The Terra Prime Series

Book One

Terry A. Hurlbut

Published by Conservative News and Views.
https://www.conservativenewsandviews.com/.
Cover by Andrew Dobell - Creative Edge Studios.
www.creativeedgestudios.co.uk.
Printed in the United States of America.

To Andrea

Contents

Chapter 1

Colors. Lines. Geometric figures. And then, distortion, as if the vista before him was some kind of watercolor on quicksand, and some giant suddenly decided to stir it. He tried to run, but he couldn't. Although he could sense he was on his feet, the belt around his waist held him fast to something. Something he couldn't see but was solid enough to hold him.

And Lieutenant Commander Matthew Morrow USN had known no other environment for ... how long? He couldn't tell. Was he dreaming? He must be. This environment made no sense as a real one. His batteries were fully charged; he knew that much. If he could just get free of that annoying restraint, he could run so fast no one could catch him. But how? His limbs would not obey him. And *where?* Everything around him reflected change—and always the same kind of change. No landmarks of any kind. No sun, either—just bright light or darkness, on an endless cycle.

He couldn't make out the words floating to his ears or see the faces of the people speaking, but he could definitely hear two distinct female voices nearby.

As he continued trying to force his eyes open, he listened to the female voices, one dubious and one decidedly scornful, though without the context of the actual words, he knew not what they discussed. Then suddenly, the voices fell silent.

And a minute later, with equal suddenness, everything went dark. Totally dark. But *now,* he could open his eyes.

Without thinking, he opened his metal, airtight eyelids and focused his eyes—one of the few parts of him that were still real and original to him—then, he just stared. He waited for the scene to change yet again.

But it didn't.

Finally! I am awake! And alive? he smiled. *Wonderfully, gloriously alive!* What a relief! And how wonderful to look at solid objects again!

The low light came from fixtures in the overhead. And not more than five meters away were ... bulkheads! One in front of him, two to either side—and he was standing in an alcove set into another bulkhead behind him. And he could also see at his feet: a deck! All were as solid as any such features of a ship. *Or in a building on a planet surface,* he reminded himself.

As soon as he thought about it, he used his other senses for clues.

The muffled sounds that had so confused him—because they never did quite fit together with the ever-changing vista he had lived with for so long—were gone.

Though his ears were his own, his hearing wouldn't be what it was without some of the best hearing aids ever invented. He listened and observed everything around him intently.

What's that smell? He breathed deeply. Though he only had half his smell receptors, the other half were artificial, and his artificial lungs had never failed him. And, they felt natural enough.

The next thing he noticed was the girl. Human, Caucasoid, with a hint of Middle Easterner, 175 centimeters tall, weighing maybe 50 kilograms, well-proportioned, with dark hair and green eyes, aged approximately 25 standard years. She wore Navy undress whites. He read the nameplate, COHEN, over her right breast. Her accouterments and insignias identified her as a sublieutenant—specifically, a "nursing officer" with a psychiatric specialization. She was reaching forward with her right hand—of course … His on-off switch under his left armpit.

She started to withdraw. Without hesitating, he reached out and took a firm grip on her wrist. With his other hand, he reached for the heavy, restrictive belt around his waist and unfastened it. "Not so fast," he said—in Standard, based on human English. "I want to talk to you."

The woman tried to jerk her wrist free. "Ow!" she cried out. "You're hurting me! Let me go!" She spoke with a primarily British accent, as Matthew did.

He loosened his grip—not enough to release her, but enough, as he hoped, to stop whatever pain he was causing her. "I apologize," he said. "I intend no torture, Sublieutenant Cohen. But I have some questions, and I require you to answer them. "

As he spoke, he processed what else he was seeing, hearing, smelling, and "tasting" in the air. He'd been standing in an alcove, a human-sized, human-outlined cavity in the bulkhead behind him. Incongruous, that, given the three-meter-plus overhead—but such overheads always struck him as too high. *Though, an Elf would find the overhead perfect.* That heavy metal belt he'd just unfastened had been charging his batteries. He was in a hospital room, except someone had removed the bunk that once stood here. The gravity was the same as on any Naval ship—or any United Systems installation, on any member planet. Total gravity manipulation made that possible. He found the air polluted, with the signature smell of Sol d— "Earth" in Standard. And, judging by his receptors, the pollution was significantly worse than his last shore leave on this world.

Before him, the woman's eyes widened—then narrowed. Her heart, which had been racing, slowed to a steady beat. Likewise, she took one easy breath, then let it out.

"I trust you have recovered," he said aloud. "Now then, let's talk. But don't lie to me. I'll know immediately. If you doubt that, consider this," he went on to recite her vital signs to her. Signs he "read" just by watching, listening, and feeling. That made her eyes widen again. But when her eyes narrowed, she managed to look pleased. *Now, why should that be?*

"Now," he said. "First, tell me the date."

"The date?"

"Yes," said Matthew, willing himself to be patient, "today's date."

Without missing a beat, she replied, "Em-jay-dee-en two-oh-four-one-oh-nine."

What?!? MJDN204109? He'd expected a much later date than the date of his arrest, but not *fifteen years* later! Was she lying about that? No—her vitals checked. So did her easy confidence.

"All right," he said at last. "That late date at least *partially* explains the extra pollution I smell. But the exact date raises another question. What are you doing in a room with a patient probably diagnosed with acute paranoia, on a sleepy seventh-day afternoon?"

"How did you know?" she asked in evident surprise.

"Oh, come now, Sublieutenant Cohen. I can calculate day-of-the-week from any modified Julian day number as easily as an organic can subtract one date from another to get an interval of days. Surely, you know that."

"Tell me, Commander Morrow," she said, and Matthew could tell she was willing herself to be calm, "Have you any limit to your capabilities?"

I'm asking the questions here, he almost said—then stopped. She wasn't mocking him. On the contrary, she was genuinely interested in what this man-like creature, who held her by the wrist, could do. He still didn't know whether he could trust her (after all, they'd just met!), but a little judicious sharing might be in order.

All those considerations, he processed in a few thousand clock cycles. "I might be limited in one thing: I never could 'make small talk,' even with fellow officers," he said truthfully. "But I do know this: I am on Sol d, and specifically in Bethesda, Maryland, Nuevo Aztlán, United Nations. I assume this is Bethesda Naval Hospital.

"But, though I can tell whether an organic is lying to me, I *cannot* read one's mind … nor discern the motives of that squad of *whoever* they were who arrested me without explanation, brought me down with what I can only assume was a hand-held electromagnetic pulse device, attacked me by stealth even to have a chance to use said device, and have held me in I don't know how many places of confinement, without ever doing me the courtesy of informing me of the charges against me—for fifteen years. Nor do I know why my commanding officer would ever consent to my receiving such treatment, in total violation of the Uniform Code of Military Justice. If Navy brass were looking to create a *model* for acute paranoia, they've done a first-rate job. But, *why?*"

"I do not know," said the girl. "I've never seen those parts of your medical or service records."

"Why did you awaken me?" Matthew asked. The time for directness had clearly arrived.

"I don't suppose I could convince you that I did it by accident?"

"Don't be absurd," said Matthew with finality. "I know you're not the only person who came to see me. I heard two voices before you awakened me. Yours, and that of another young woman who spoke to you with a slight hint of scorn—as if she were challenging you to finish what you had started."

And then it hit him. "In point of fact," he said slowly, "you don't even have clearance to enter this room."

She gasped—then shut her mouth and actually *smiled*. "You have me there," she said.

"That still does not answer my question. But it *does* tell me you awakened me deliberately."

"Commander," she said, "you still have me under a form of restraint. Obviously, you want something from me. Would you mind telling me what that is?"

Was she trying to gain his trust? "First," he said, "information. Basic, everyday information about what life is like on Sol d and in the Six-o'clock Quadrant. Of course, I don't expect you to supply that, so I'll have to experience it myself. To that end, I want the layout of this floor and this building."

"In other words," she said, "you want to escape this ward. Do you, then, trust no one?"

"I commend you," said Matthew. "Whoever trained you for this sort of work trained you well. You are trying to gain my confidence. I, on the other hand, merely require your cooperation. I shall have to leave the mystery of your awakening me for later. For now, let it suffice that, when you start something, you have to finish it. And you are *going* to finish it.

"So here are my terms. You will render me any and all assistance in escaping from this building—and in acquiring certain materials I will need to repair my wired and wireless networking interfaces.

"In return, I will keep you alive and feed you well. I will release you only when, and *if* I can make good an escape from Sol d itself, or at least join any community of intelligent beings whom I can trust. And under no circumstances will I molest you in any manner.

"But if you cannot accept those terms, I shall have to render you unconscious and continue to hold you largely in that state until you *can* accept them—fully. Do you understand?"

He waited. He didn't have *quite* the fabled and infinite patience of a machine; his brain was still organic. What sort of person had he been before Dr. Erich Frankel had given him this fine body? He stood at one hundred, ninety centimeters tall, with short brown hair, which Dr. Frankel had given him. His skin was faintly golden, his eyes blue. He would guess that any organic being with his build weighed around ninety kilograms—but of course, he weighed much more—considering the heavy titanium inside him.

An adult body—but had he even *been* an adult? His memory did not know. As a point of fact, he had never given the matter the slightest thought until perhaps a year or two before his arrest. But now he must find out—or die. His present surroundings told him that much—if nothing else.

But his patience, though not infinite, was vast. Why not? A clock cycle, for him, was nothing more than a hyperfine transition of cesium 113. And he knew from experience how long to wait for an answer.

She gave her answer right on time. "I accept," she said, her dignified tone matching the look in her eye.

"Thank you," he said. One last test: he released her wrist.

She took a few seconds to massage her right wrist. "Nothing broken, anyway," she said. "Now let me see—they did leave printers in all patient rooms. I've heard talk about re-establishing something hospital administrators once called Central Supply, but just talk, so far. Now let's see if this printer even works."

…*Why wouldn't the printer work?* What had happened to Navy logistics that the surgeon-in-charge would even *think* of re-establishing a centralized storeroom for medical supplies? And had the civilian economy suffered similar deficiencies?

"Two elastic bandages," she said. A few seconds later, two bandages popped out of the printer bay.

"Why didn't you merely requisition a corpsman's or hospitalman's uniform?" he asked.

"Are you kidding?" asked the girl. "A req like that would raise all sorts of red flags, especially from this room. Now—won't you please sit down? I'm going to wrap up your face so no one will recognize you, so long as they don't get too close. Don't worry—I'll leave eye holes for you."

Of course, he could have done the job far more quickly and efficiently himself. But letting her do it kept her occupied. It also allowed him to measure her sincerity.

She took five minutes—again, longer than he would have taken—but she did an excellent job. As if she had as significant a stake in his escape as he had. He could still see but no longer recognized himself in the mirror on the rear bulkhead. But something about those bandages was a little off. *What was it?*

She'd done a smart, professional job, all business, and yet … He couldn't put his finger on what was not quite right.

He looked over at her as she held a finger to her lips. Then, as he waited, she opened the door a crack.

Then she waved at him to follow.

He did.

They stepped out into a deserted passageway. Of course, that desertion was temporary. He could still hear the buzz of an occupied deck all around him—though he guessed the girl couldn't. She led; he followed. Until he knew more of the layout, he could do nothing else.

All good so far…

"Excuse me," said a man's voice. "But how did that patient get his face disfigured? He belongs on the plastic service, not here."

"A recent admission," the girl lied, remarkably smoothly.

"No one notified Security," said the man, who wore a uniform Matthew didn't immediately recognize. His eyes narrowed; he *did* recognize it, and that shocked him all over again. Not Ground Patrol whites, or Marine greens, but an all-black uniform, *the same uniform that squad had worn when taking him down,* fifteen years ago. The man before him sported the chevrons of a sergeant, like a Marine—yet not. "Let me see that man's armband."

The girl could have cried out for help and denounced him to the guard. Or warned Matthew—or tried to, anyway. Instead, she just stood where she was while Matthew reached out with his left hand…

…and took the guard's sidearm. With his other hand, he took the guard gently but firmly by the throat.

The guard was at least sensible. He said nothing as Matthew transferred the handgun to his right hand and put his left hand on the Sergeant's throat. His extra circuits made him almost ambidextrous. But he still favored his right hand, as he always had, even before … becoming *this*. Almost idly, he noticed that the girl simply waited for him, making no attempt to escape or to summon any form of assistance.

Taking his hand off the guard's throat, he ordered, "Walk toward the hoist. Softly and calmly, if you please." He jerked his head to the girl as a signal to follow.

The guard took three steps. Then Matthew stopped him with a grip on his arm. "I said *toward* the hoist," he said. "You are walking away from it."

"How did you…"

"I know a hoist when I hear it," said Matthew. "Now turn, and move."

The guard did so.

The hoists were exactly where Matthew had placed them. Three sets of hoist doors greeted them. To the girl, he said, "Call it."

She never got the chance. Instead, all three hoist doors opened. Out of each stepped eight-person squads of obviously well-trained soldiers, with long guns drawn and leveled. They all wore the same all-black uniforms, and varied in rank from a buck private to a color sergeant. And they looked to Matthew like petty tyrants, not Marines.

This could get nasty. Most of their weapons were standard-issue-directed-energy weapons. But the Color Sergeant carried a weapon ending in an array of parallel square-plate antennae. Now, that had to be an electromagnetic pulse weapon. Against that, he would be helpless. Except for one little thing he could deploy now that he was alert…

He reached for the girl and held her close to him. He felt her tremble, heard her gasp.

The disarmed Sergeant broke, dived, and rolled away from him toward his colleagues.

Then the Color Sergeant spoke. "Put down your weapon," he ordered, "and surrender."

"No," said Matthew.

"I said, *put it down.*"

"Go ahead," said Matthew. "Shoot."

The girl trembled even more. Out of the corner of his eye, he saw her eyes widen.

"Why, you … all right. You have ten seconds to comply, and then we *will* shoot."

Matthew couldn't see the girl's eyes, but he knew her heart was racing faster than ever.

"…Nine. Eight. Seven. Six. Five…"

"Are you people *crazy?*" the girl cried. Her shock was as obvious as it was genuine.

"…Four. Three. Two. One!"

And the lead Sergeant fired.

As the shot flashed, Matthew watched triumphantly as the determined faces of the black-clad guards changed to expressions of shock. An electromagnetic shield—like a force field on a personal scale—blocked the pulse from the Sergeant's weapon. Matthew smiled as he watched them all scowl at him, and instantly, all the hoist indicator lights went dark.

Matthew had a hard time remembering some things, like where he'd learned to erect a body shield. Ah, yes, he remembered now—it was on that fateful mission against the cyborg raiders from the Hive in the Twelve-o'clock Quadrant. The Hive had perfected the technique of shielding against directed-energy weapons and EMP weapons. And these Hive raiders had foolishly tried to disaffect him. Instead, he had "stolen" their shielding skill, and never imagined he'd have to use it—until now.

The lead Sergeant bellowed a scatological oath.

A corporal cried out, "What the Five is he, a Hive raider!?"

At that last word, several DEW beams struck Matthew's body shield at full force—and glanced off it. Matthew had decidedly had enough. He hardened the shield so it would not merely disperse the energy but reflect it. Half the section arrayed against him, and killed themselves or one another with reflected beams. The smell of burning flesh permeated the air around them.

"Now," said Matthew to those who still stood. "*You* put down *your* weapons." He raised his handgun to make his point.

Several weapons clattered to the floor as the remaining soldiers who had held them raised their hands.

"Now," he said even more sternly, "hit the deck and lie on your stomachs with your hands over the backs of your heads."

They obeyed.

He released the girl, who now stared up at him, her eyes wider than ever. Through that little drama, she had suffered neither scratch nor burn—for the body shield had protected her, too. Now he turned to her. "Pick up that long gun ending in the square plates, and bring it to me," he ordered. "And be sure to collect at least one DEW weapon for yourself."

Without any further instruction from him, she selected weapons whose owners hadn't had a chance to fire them. *Good.* She even checked them for a charge. The EMP gun she handed him didn't have a full charge, but was still good for maybe two more discharges. She also handed him a DEW gun that was fully charged. Then, she took time to don a gunbelt, holster a handgun, and sling a long gun over her own shoulder. "Anything else?" she asked, smiling.

"Take the female guard nearest your size to another room and relieve her of her uniform," he said. "You," he then turned to the first Sergeant he had encountered, "strip off your uniform. Quickly. The rest of you: don't move if you don't want to suffer any further casualties."

"You'll never get away with this," said another surviving corporal.

"Tell that to your section leader," Matthew said, indicating the Color Sergeant's smoking ruin of a body. Matthew would have liked to take *his* uniform. But not with those holes in it.

The Sergeant obediently handed him his uniform. The girl came out, now wearing the uniform with corporal's stripes she had lifted from the female guard she had taken aside. The uniform fit her form very well, almost as if it was self-tailoring—typical of the material of which it was made. But again—something was a little off: the uniform didn't *quite* fit … Although, Matthew had no time to think about that just now.

"Restrain these people," he ordered. The girl, showing remarkable adaptability, turned to. Five minutes later, fourteen black-uniformed people and one half-naked man lay on the floor, bound hand and foot. Matthew waited until the girl was securing the last guard before he stripped off the useless patient gown he wore and donned the Sergeant's uniform. Again, he now wore a self-tailoring uniform that didn't *quite* self-tailor as it should. He also took off the improvised mask—he wouldn't need it anymore—and stuck the bandages into the uniform belt.

"Let's go," he said and led her, not to the hoist, for it was now useless as Matthew had noted a wild EMP had fried its circuits, but to the ladder. Most non-spacers, he knew, would call it a stairwell, but Matthew was a Navy officer and used Navy idiom, especially in Navy installations. The girl followed and shut the ladder door behind them.

As if somehow clairvoyant, she said, "You'll find the electronics storeroom in the hold and the Help Desk next door to it. By the way, you'll want these." She handed him four extra charge packs for his weapons, fully charged and ready to use.

Stowing them in his pockets—he had no time to swap out the charge pack on his EMP gun—he looked up and down the ladder well. Good—this ladder was nearly spiral, with landings halfway between levels, all attached to two pipes that ran from top to bottom. The fastenings left just enough room between them...

He took the two elastic bandages and tested them for tensile strength. It was true, they were not as strong as they should be. But they would hold her weight. With them, he fashioned a harness.

"Climb into this," he said, holding it up before her.

She obeyed, and then he slipped his arms into two remaining straps. This put his back to her, so she gripped him around the shoulders. Then she realized her mistake—he would need the full use of his arms. So she gripped him around his waist, letting the harness straps take the weight.

He swung over the railing at the landing, took hold of the support pipe, and began lowering them. He could just barely stretch one arm before he had to take hold of the pipe with the other arm. The progress was slow—one landing at a time—but far faster than they could have climbed down.

On the way, he said, "Your conduct is exemplary, Sublieutenant Cohen. What's your full name?"

"Ayelet Cohen, at your service, Commander," she said. "And you don't have to ask. I'm with you now. Those pieces of *dreck* rated me expendable, just to get you—and I don't happen to agree with that."

"So I gathered," said Matthew, wondering at her use of a Yiddish curse word.

"Do I take it that you trust me now?"

"Why not?" he asked. "You earned it."

"No, Commander," she said, smiling. "*You* earned it."

"Then you *did* have your own motive for awakening me," Matthew said. "Would that have anything to do with those guards? They wore a uniform I saw before—only during my arrest."

"Are you kid—no, of course not. The powers-that-be would *never* trust the Marines *or* the GPs to do their especially dirty work. Those are SSF."

"SSF?"

"Special Security Forces. Crack troopers." She smiled again as she added, "Or maybe *not* all they're 'cracked up' to be, if you catch my drift."

"Tasked with guarding dangerous, criminally insane patients like me?"

"And the First Secretary, whenever and wherever he goes," she almost spat.

"Revolutionary sentiment, Sublieutenant Cohen?"

At this, she turned sober. "I almost hate to break it to you, Commander, but … yes, sir. For I have never considered our society free at all."

"I don't understand," he said. "Do you mean to say these SSF have always existed?"

"As long as I can remember, Commander," she said. "Sir, may I speak freely?"

"Please do."

"You spent your career in the deep areas. Believe me; it's a lot different here on good, old Sol d. Maybe you never thought about *how* different it is."

"You're right, Sublieutenant," said Matthew. "I never did until at least fifteen years ago. But now I need answers, and badly. Perhaps we can genuinely work for mutual benefit."

They had reached the bottom. He had recognized the main deck level with its two sets of doors. The architects, of course, sought to force people to exit onto the main deck and *not* go below in case of fire. But he had just bypassed that trap.

He hopped onto the last landing and slipped out of the harness. Likewise, she stepped out of it, then rolled it up and stuck it into her belt. Then the two made their way—cautiously—to the hold door. He listened. Not a sound beyond. Finally, he opened it.

The electronics storeroom was the one thing printers couldn't obviate. Printers, especially since the Elves had "improved" them nearly four hundred years ago, could reproduce almost any object, not merely documents. But when printers broke down, they needed spare parts. So one always kept spare parts on hand in case every printer in a building, or aboard ship, went offline.

This shop, Matthew saw now, was larger than he expected. Not only that, but parts storage must have expanded into other rooms.

Half the parts he saw were printer parts; the other half … The Information Technicians should be able to print these other parts whenever they need to. Why store so many in reserve? Something was wrong … very wrong.

"When you talked about reestablishing Central Supply, you weren't joking, were you?" he asked.

"No joke," Ayelet answered. "I started noticing that on my first day here—printers not working half the time."

"And I noticed something a little off about those bandages you requisitioned."

"Like what?"

"They were weaker than they should be."

"Wow! Thank the Name that harness you made actually held my weight!"

"I doubled them up to make sure. And there's more. These uniforms we've stolen? Notice anything odd about them?"

"Yes … come to think of it, they're supposed to stretch or contract to fit, but they're not doing it. In fact, mine just feels sloppy, and it did on that corporal I stripped it off of. And yours?"

"Same thing."

"And look at this!" she said, spreading her arms to indicate the shelves that surrounded them. "I never imagined that the Help Desk needed to stock all these parts! What do you make of it?"

"I'll tell you," said Matthew. "The printers are breaking down. That's why it takes so many spare parts just to keep the printers in this installation functioning. And when they do function, they don't work up to spec.

"It helps me, though. I need parts for wireless and Category Twenty-four Ethernet interfaces. Plus certain kinds of tools: screwdrivers, long-nosed pliers, that sort of thing. And if I don't have to print them, I won't trigger any of your red flags, true?"

"True. And I'm sure I know what those replacement parts look like. Perhaps if we split up…?"

"Good. You search for the parts, and I'll search for the tools." And so they worked. After five minutes of searching, they had what they needed.

"I don't expect you to have received training on how to service a printer," he said when their search was over. "And you certainly wouldn't know how to service me. But I can coach you. If you can handle machine tools, you can help me. Are you 'game'?"

"You bet," she said, then added, "sir."

"Then follow my instructions exactly," he said as he stripped off his borrowed uniform tunic.

Five minutes later, he had working interfaces again. Now he could detect—and break into—the wireless network, which he did. As soon as Ayelet patched him up, Matthew was ready. As he donned his tunic again, he gave rapid, unhesitating orders. "Everything depends on what happens in the next few minutes," he said. "Situations can change in seconds or fractions of a second. So when I say move, move. Got it?"

"Got it."

From the network, he retrieved the layout of the building. "To the Help Desk, then," he said. He wanted one of its hard-wire interfaces. "Follow me," he ordered. And in five minutes, they reached it.

He and Ayelet burst in, long guns drawn. "Hands high!" he barked.

One young man—African, with short-cropped and tightly-curled hair typical of that region of Earth—looked up from the dissected printer he had been working on. He wore a Navy uniform, with the rating insignia of an information technician—and a *chief* IT at that. His eyes widened. Almost on instinct, he raised his hands. Then he struck an attitude of recognition. "Ayelet!" he cried. Such familiarity with an officer! Never mind; that would make things easier.

"What brings you down here?" the specialist continued. "Why are you pointing guns at me? Did you really join the SSF? What…" Then he trailed off. "Wait a minute," he said. "You stole that uniform. What's going on here?" Egad, but that man was quick!

It was time to take control of this conversation. "My name is Matthew Morrow," he said. "And you are my prisoner."

"*Our* prisoner," Ayelet corrected him.

"I don't understand…"

"You don't have to, Chief…"

"Sutton, sir. Chief Information Technician Barry Sutton, at your service."

"Good," said Matthew. "I now ask you to do exactly as … as we say."

"Sure," said the other man. "I mean, aye-aye, sir. I trust Ayelet, Ayelet trusts you, and that's good enough for me. But it would help if I knew what it was all about, wouldn't it? I mean, you wouldn't have to arrest me just to get your hands on a spare printer, would you?"

"That's true enough," said Matthew. "But we haven't time to waste." Then he thought of one more way to persuade this man. "Chief Sutton, that's *Lieutenant Commander* Morrow to you. I'm not asking you anymore. I am giving you a direct order. Obey it. I'll explain later—perhaps."

"Lieutenant Commander … Wait a minute," Sutton said. "You're the 'Mad Android' Ayelet was telling me about, aren't you?"

"Semantics being what they are," said Matthew, "yes."

Now Barry looked at him in wonder—and, was that respect? "You served on *Bonaventure* Sixth and Seventh, right?"

"Yes."

Barry turned to Ayelet, who nodded, then said, "First things first, Barry. We need to get out of this building *now*. The Special Security Forces just tried to kill us both."

"They won't if I can help it," said Barry, grinning. "I know computer tricks the SSF never thought of—and maybe things *you* never thought of, either." He started to describe an example.

"Enough," said Matthew. "You'd never implement that with this console. But *I* could implement it. I have all the wired and wireless interfaces of a Navy-issue personal digital device. You give me your code, and I'll implement it."

"Right," said Barry as he turned to one of his consoles. He spoke rapidly, and the console seemed to take his dictation just as rapidly. Then he said, "Sir, if you'll plug in, you'll have your program."

Matthew did. The program uploaded—fast. Matthew checked it even faster.

"My compliments," he said when the upload had finished. "Now, please gather together that printer you were repairing and any spare parts you might need. Sublieutenant Cohen, help him. Prepare to move, and fast, when and where I tell you."

They both nodded in agreement.

Still plugged in, Matthew accessed the surveillance system. At once, he saw the SSF were closer than he'd thought. It would be a near thing, but they could still succeed. Only, why weren't they coming in greater force? Ah—of course. The SSF had another target. Those now moving in on that target weren't guarding this hospital. Quickly, he accessed the 66-1 file on the target. He adjusted his plan accordingly.

He sent out a few silent commands and felt the harsh thuds as several sets of double doors slammed shut.

"What was that?" Ayelet asked.

"That should hold them for a while—just long enough," said Matthew. "Are you ready to move?"

"Just about," said Barry.

Matthew didn't have time to inquire further, so he simply said, "Follow."

He led them out into the passageway, where, as he expected, a double door at the far end glowed red. "Take that side passageway down ten meters," he ordered, "and then jump into the forced-air vent. *Now.*" They ran. Matthew waited for a hole to appear in the corridor door—and used his shield to reflect the enemy DEW beam back the way it came. He heard a most satisfactory yowl of anguish from beyond the doors. He did not wait for any follow-up; he ran down the side corridor and leaped into the vent.

His two recruits—for that's what they now were—waited for him. Quickly, he relieved them of some of their burdens of parts from the disassembled printer. Then he led them along the ducts to a small room he knew to be vacant.

Barry opened his mouth to ask more questions. Matthew silenced him with a look. Only when they reached the vacant room and could climb out of the vent, he turned to Barry and said, "You had a question, Chief Sutton?"

"May I ask why we're bothering to carry all these parts? Can't we 'print' them later?"

"You know better than that," said Matthew.

Ayelet got the point at once. "He's right, Barry," she said. "We won't have an intact printer unless we cobble it together with all these parts."

Barry struck an attitude Matthew recognized at once. *Why didn't I think of that?*

"Now listen, both of you," said Matthew. "While we've been talking, the SSF have bypassed us without knowing it. Our objective is the short ladder about five meters down the passageway from where we are. We have one chance to make it." He gave them precise directions from where they now stood. "In three. Two. One. *Mark!*" So saying, he opened the door to the small janitor's closet where they had taken refuge. Quickly, he led the way to the ladder.

It was clear. The three took the risers two at a time and emerged near…

"The Admitting Office!?" Ayelet hissed. "But that place is *crawling* with SSF!"

"They are about to get a considerable distraction," said Matthew. He then handed Ayelet a DEW rifle and Barry the EMP gun. "Wait for my signal," he said—almost unnecessarily. *No, wait—Barry looked highly dubious.* Matthew whispered in his ear, "They're bringing in another 'patient.' And I want her. For our team."

Barry nodded. He seemed to have only now realized the high stakes in this game.

Ayelet checked her weapon. Barry asked, "What sort of weapon did you give me?"

"It discharges an electromagnetic pulse," said Matthew. "Non-lethal, but it will destroy any unshielded electronics. The SSF must have developed this with me in mind, but they never thought about its other uses."

"Got it," said Barry, grinning ear to ear.

They waited.

A "rubber wagon" floated down to the driveway/landing pad just beyond the door. Its rearward double doors opened. Out stepped two armed SSF, then two white-clad corpsmen.

The next person to step out made Ayelet's eyes widen. But to her great credit, she narrowed her eyes and flashed

Matthew a quick look of understanding—and grim determination. Matthew, of course, recognized her at once from her file.

Hospital Corpsman Andrea Riley, 168 centimeters tall, weighing about 51 kilograms, with red hair and blue eyes, stepped out of the patient-transport van. She wore a strait-jacket and metal leg hobbles. Her face, and especially her eyes, wore the look of eloquent outrage and puzzlement at her predicament.

Matthew took aim at the hobbles. No sooner had the new patient and her escort of orderlies and men-at-arms stepped in than he fired a burst directly at the center link in the chain.

It parted.

One of the corpsmen suddenly dropped to the floor, writhing and clasping his genitalia in his hands.

"Fire at will," said Matthew. Then, as the second corpsman dropped beside the first, Matthew fired a shot through the heart of the nearest SSF soldier.

Ayelet fired her DEW gun with deadly accuracy and precision. *Had she trained on such weapons? Where? Another mystery for later.* Barry took aim at the triage counter and fired his weapon. *Zap!* Every console and half the lights went dark. Everyone in the AO started bumping into each other in confusion. Everyone, that is, except Miss Riley, who was just downing the last SSF man standing.

"Go," said Matthew and led the way forward. "Barry, with me. Ayelet, pick up Miss Riley."

She didn't waste time acknowledging. She simply slung her DEW long gun, then picked up Andrea, slung her over her shoulder, and carried her outside and into the van. Barry, who seemed to catch on fast, followed Matthew outside. Barry then broke for what humans still called the "shotgun seat" as Matthew raced to the driver's side door. He wrenched it open, reached in, and tossed the driver out like a rag doll. Then he climbed in and slugged the driver's mate—Barry had a lot to learn about hijacking a vehicle!

As Barry tossed the now-unconscious driver's mate aside and his own weapon inside, Matthew heard two good slams. Ayelet must have shut the rear doors. As soon as Barry climbed in, Matthew shut both side doors with a single button press. Then he "jacked in" and put forth his will. The van moved forward about two meters, then lifted off on its maglev drive. Matthew goosed the drive to full speed—and came close to grimacing as he heard the rattling noises and outraged screams aft. Some things a rescue team couldn't help, especially when they had to improvise.

This van was no LCG. Even if he had one of those gravity launches, where could he go? An LCG (which stood for Landing Craft, Gravity) couldn't carry a De Cuellar faster-than-light drive—not yet, anyway. He could go off-planet only if he could board—or hijack—a ship in orbit or an FTL sled. As organics liked to say, *fat chance*.

To top that, he desperately needed information. And he was in just the right place—or planet, anyway—to get it. Logic told him that much. Best, in sum, to fly to a place of relative safety. And *not* in Bethesda or anywhere near it.

As if reading his thoughts, Chief Sutton broke in on them. "We'll be heading for the hills, won't we?" he asked.

"Yes. Up the Potomac River."

Barry unslung his load and extracted a flat-screen laptop. "You'll never crash the barrier with this aluminum can. But maybe I can open it up for you. Just long enough to slip through."

Did this man's talents at "hacking" know no bounds? "Work fast, then," said Matthew. "I'm not wasting any time." He headed west-northwest, away from the hospital. He overflew the sprawling campuses of the Galactic Institutes of Health. Beyond, lay the mid-rise dormitories of the GIH and Bethesda campuses. And beyond *those* lay the Alta Vista, Wyngate, Ashburton, Ashleigh, and many other solar farms. The metal exoskeletons of those photovoltaic arrays looked a little odd at first—but Matthew now remembered the nature of their foundations. Some, not more than half a meter below ground, were the foundations of the single-family residences that had once stood here.

At last, he found the Potomac River. Dropping to a level that skimmed the river, he followed it upstream. At first, this was very difficult since he had to pass a seemingly interminable chain of islands. But he soon realized these islands were uninhabited. They soon gave way to bank-to-bank water, and he went on skimming, well below ground-sensor level.

And finally, he sensed the barrier—an electromagnetic force field—ahead of him. "Chief Sutton, any time you're ready," he said.

Barry looked up with a grin. "When I poke this key," he said, his finger poised over the letter G on the virtual keyboard, "the barrier comes down for *one* second, then goes back up. They'll likely never know it went down."

"Excellent. Stand by," said Matthew. Lightning fast, he calculated the proper moment from the distance, the closing speed… "In three. Two. One. *Mark.*"

The barrier then developed a hole in it only Matthew could "see." Then he was through it—and it closed again. "Excellent performance," he said aloud. "I will recommend you for promotion."

Barry grinned again. He obviously knew irony when he heard it.

Where should Matthew fly next? The United Nations had evacuated this region centuries ago and erected the "barrier" he had just passed through, and many other such barriers. He shouldn't know this terrain at all. Yet somehow, he did.

But, where had he seen it before?

Then it hit him. He had seen it from orbit! And to be more specific, as a high-resolution moving image from a low-orbiting satellite network. He had accessed it aboard *Bonaventure VII.* That act, and the report he had filed, had gotten him arrested. And Galaxy knew what happened to his ship.

Now he knew where to go.

For another hour, Matthew flew roughly northwest. Then he left the river, crossed overland, then returned to the river at the upstream end of a loop. That he could do

this safely was purely due to where he was. No one—
ever—entered Protected Wild Space. And it was far more
vast than was the so-called "civilized footprint" of
humanity on the North American continent of Sol d. Not
even the whole United Systems Marine Corps could find
him on such short notice.

Then he found his target on a high bluff. Nothing but
forest grew there. This was NRD-01-VA-Lucketts. As he
approached, he saw the remnant of a narrow highway
bridge that had once spanned the river. He had seen that
bridge before—from orbit. And something else ...
something at the edge of his memory. The shrinks had
tried to wipe it—but had not completely succeeded. Too
many clues remained, and now he had followed them.

He slowed and carefully started to thread his way into
the forest, looking for a clearing. Then he found it—right
where a town must have once stood, three hundred fifty or
more years ago. Someone had removed it, typical of
Nature Reclamation Districts. The only designator he
recognized in that code was VA for Virginia. Home district
of Marine Base Quantico and a few University of Earth
campuses and historical sites. Nothing like that remained
in this region, except for the foundations of a vanished
town and maybe ... something else. But what?

Chapter 2

When Matthew and Barry opened the rear doors of the rubber wagon, they found Andrea Riley, bruised on her face and arms, but free. Matthew saw her strait-jacket tossed casually in a corner. Ayelet was tending to her as best she could.

"Did you really have to knock us about like that?" Andrea asked. "That hurt."

"My apologies," said Matthew. "I had to improvise. Can you walk?"

The girl checked her limbs. "I think so," she said with a faint Irish accent. Appropriate, considering her name and birthplace of Dublin. "By the way, my name's Andrea Riley. And you are?"

"Matthew Morrow. But you know that already."

"Wait, wait, back up," said Andrea. "How could you know that?"

"I recognized your voice, Corpsman Riley."

"How the Five…!" She trailed off, speechless.

Ayelet said, "Give it up, Andrea. I'm sure he's accessed your entire service record."

"She is correct," said Matthew. "Now, before we go any further: we brought weapons. Let's arm ourselves."

"Good idea," said Ayelet, who started to pass out the DEW guns. Matthew let Barry keep the EMP gun since he had used it so effectively.

"To answer your question," said Matthew as he slung a long gun on his shoulder and took a handgun in his right hand, "I know all about you. I know why the SSF took you into custody—on *my* account. I also remember hearing you speak to this other young lady. You were discussing me—and daring her to bring me out of my coma."

"And why did you rescue me just then?" she asked, obviously wary.

"Why do you think?"

Andrea paused. Then she said, "Before we go any further, yes, I'm grateful to you for not leaving me in the lurch. That is…"

"I know what that expression means," said Matthew. *Thanks to the officers aboard Bonaventure VI and VII for that.* Aloud he went on, "And to continue that thought, you and Ayelet got *me* out of the lurch first."

"Why are you telling me this?"

"So that you will understand, how you say it, 'where I come from.' Did Sublieutenant Cohen tell you how long I had been in that coma? *Fifteen years.* I won't insult your intelligence by telling you I have just returned the favor. In fact, I have traded, on your behalf, one predicament for another: from confinement to exile. I apologize for not asking you first. But I am, frankly, desperate. I also need to know what has happened to me, and the galaxy, for those fifteen years."

As he spoke, he watched Andrea closely. She looked back at him, not with fright, but with appreciation. *Honesty is usually the best policy, as my friends told me more often than I can count.*

"I'll be glad to help if I can," said Andrea. "But first, what's *your* story, Chief…?"

"Barry Sutton," said the Chief. "Ayelet here has been bending my ear for weeks. You might say she prepared me for this little junket well in advance."

Andrea looked at Ayelet, who smiled and nodded.

"All right," said Andrea. "So we can all trust one another. Now, first, I'd like to get out of this van and look 'round."

Matthew made a slight bow and backed away. Andrea slowly got to her feet, walked to the van's rear doors, and jumped down. She walked about three meters away from the van and looked all the way around her. Her face registered wonderment—and then shock.

"Holy leaping creatures!" she said. "Are we in Protected Wild Space!? Now how did you manage…"

"Chief Sutton," said Matthew, "perhaps you should introduce yourself fully."

"Yes, sir," said Barry. "You see, Andrea, I'm a chief information technician, and…"

"'Hacker,'" Andrea asserted. "Does that mean you've hacked all the sensors here?"

Barry looked stricken. So Matthew spoke quickly. "What sensors?" he asked.

"The sensors that surely have to be all over this area to catch anyone who dares intrude!"

"There aren't any," said Matthew. "Believe me; I'd know it if there were."

"Then how ... but of course. If they had powered sensors, they would have to maintain them. And they're too frigging lazy!"

"Precisely. Protected Wild Space must rely purely on the confinement of civilization to its footprint. It assumes no one will ever breach the force fields that ... Wait, don't tell me the phrase ... 'hem you in.' Chief Sutton, here, breached them for us. We have, for all intents and purposes, simply disappeared."

Andrea looked from Matthew to Barry. The look on her face now bespoke profound respect. "Well, sir," she finally said, "let's answer those questions you had. I'm not sure I can help you with the what's-happened-to-you part. I wouldn't know myself. You've been on that psych ward since before I became an adult, after all."

"Of course," said Barry, "I can help you hack your records. But ... well…"

"We don't know how accurate those records would be," Matthew finished for him, "To say nothing of the flags the SSF likely put on them. So let's talk about what's happened to the galaxy. At last report—that is, before my arrest—a lost ship named *Argo* had returned from the Twelve-o'clock Quadrant."

"Would that be USS *Argo* CG-711?" Andrea asked.

"Yes. I remember greeting the return of *Argo* with great anticipation. We all knew by then that *Argo* had tangled repeatedly with the Hive. They had even redeemed a human from her life as a Hive worker—or a Hive warrior, except that the authorities trumped up a warrant for my arrest and commitment before I could get close.

"Two years earlier, the United Systems had finally won their war against the Metamorphs of the Nine-o'clock Quadrant. I can tell you def ... ah, straight: the Metamorphs pressed the Navy sorely."

"That's putting it mildly," said Ayelet.

"And at some time in those two years, my last ship, *Bonaventure VII*, took part in repulsing a raid from the Hive. We, then, returned to Earth, where I accessed some images I shouldn't have—near this very spot, which is why we're here. That is my last memory. Whatever I saw obviously frightened the authorities. Logically, they would never have treated me this way otherwise."

"I always wondered about that," said Andrea. "If you don't mind my saying so, sir ... I'm sorry, sir, but, what service rank did you hold?"

"Lieutenant Commander. I doubt that means anything now, but..."

"It does to me—Commander," said Andrea. "Anyway, I had wondered why the Navy decommissioned *Bonaventure VII* and scattered her officers and crew. Knowing you were once the second officer of that ship, you excited my curiosity. And with a body and enhanced senses like yours, I'm sure you were very valuable to the

Navy. I would have thought you still would be. But Ayelet—that is, Sublieutenant Cohen here—tells me they tried to destroy you back there. Is that true?"

Typical. Organics would find some information too difficult to accept without verifying it first-hand—or close to it. Aloud, Matthew simply said, "Yes."

"What could have made them decide to destroy you after keeping you on ice for fifteen years?" Then Andrea answered her own question. Hanging her head in that odd emotion called shame, she said, "It's my fault, isn't it? If I hadn't teased Ayelet into turning you back on, none of this would have happened."

"Don't blame yourself, Andrea," said Ayelet. "I took my chances. I should have thought of it myself."

"Add this to it," said Matthew. "I would be no closer to finding the answers I seek than I was before. But I have much more than that, for which to thank you. Have you ever tried being in a constant dreaming state for *fifteen* years? With the only constant about your world being change—a change you can never predict?" Rhetorical questions were another organic conversation piece he had learned to use.

His questions were having an effect. The two young women stared with wide eyes and perhaps a fresh appreciation. Chief Sutton wore a look of amazement, then compassion. "I guess it's fair to say you would rather die than live that way for another second," he finally said.

Matthew Morrow would never lie. "Yes," he said.

Silence fell on the group. Matthew saw Ayelet getting another point: why he had dared the SSF to shoot him on the psych floor. Anger—toward specific others—flashed in her eyes for an instant. Then she reached out for his hand. Matthew let her take it. After that, Andrea and Barry each laid a hand on their joined hands. Matthew said nothing. He knew, instinctively, that words were useless. He also felt appreciation—he had not known such friendship since his days on *Bonaventure VII*. Tears—which he, with his organic eyes, still needed—abruptly overflowed. He reached with his left hand to wipe them away—and saw his three companions looking at him with newfound respect.

With some difficulty, he broke the not-quite embrace. "Now then," he said, "we are having a council of war. Let's continue…"

"Hold on," said Andrea. "First, would you mind telling me where you brought us? Beyond the obvious, that this is PWS."

"Not at all," said Matthew. "We're in NRD-Zero-One-Victor-Alpha-Lucketts."

"A Nature Reclamation District?"

"Correct."

"*Incorrect*," someone interjected.

Matthew whirled, and in the same motion, aimed his pistol at the owner of the voice. He sensed his companions responding to the unwanted visitor too. Upon turning, it didn't take long for him also to note the weapon leveled at him—a *projectile* weapon. Like the relatively antique Armalite AR-18, but *very* much improved.

Matthew looked hard at the young man—African, about twenty-five years old. He stood 178 centimeters tall and weighed maybe 80 kilograms without all the gear he carried. Brown eyes stared back at him just beneath a helmet that looked feather-light—but Matthew would guess that helmet could protect its wearer from a killing blow. He wore combat fatigues—Marine green, but … different. His left shoulder bore the single bowed chevron of a lance corporal. The name JAMESON was embroidered on the right side of his shirt, and on the left, the legend USMC.

"Lance Corporal … Jameson," Matthew said evenly, "we are clearly at an impasse. Now, suppose you tell me what kind of exercise you are running in Protected Wild Space—and why you are carrying projectile weapons?"

"This is no exercise," said the young man in a tone both polite and belligerent. "You are standing on the site of the former town of Lucketts in the former—and future—lands of the Commonwealth of Virginia. And you are now prisoners of the United States Marine Corps."

"United *States*, did you say?"

"Correct. Now, I have no idea who you people are or what mission you're on. Nor am I authorized to ask. So, you will come with me and my team."

"I don't think so, young man," said Matthew. "We outnumber and outgun you."

In response, Jameson simply whistled. Then, seemingly out of the ground appeared three more men, all uniformed as young Jameson was, except they wore no rank insignia. And, all carried the same kind of weapons, which they trained on everyone in Matthew's party.

Chapter 3

Congratulations, Lance Corporal Jameson," said Matthew. "I award this round to you. Sublieutenant Cohen, Corpsman Riley, Chief Sutton, stand down."

Ayelet caught his eye. She was obviously about to say something. Then she thought better of it and laid down her weapon. Andrea and Barry did the same.

Jameson held out his hand. "I'll take that sidearm, please," he said.

Matthew carefully safed his DEW handgun, then handed it over. Jameson took it and examined it. Matthew saw the obvious puzzlement in his expression.

Matthew broke the now-awkward silence. "At the risk of sounding trite," he said, "where are you taking us?"

"To see the Lieutenant who leads our platoon," Jameson said—and Matthew, had he been fully organic, would have given an uncontrollable start at that word. For, he pronounced it *loo-tenant*, not *lef-tenant* as Matthew had heard all his life. Jameson went on: "Recon Platoon, Seventh Armored Cavalry Squadron, United States Marine Corps. He'll decide whether you will see the Major and the Ess-Two. Our camp is in the forest, and, in fact, is very close by. That's how we spotted you, coming down almost on top of us the way you did."

"United States of what, may I ask?"

Jameson took just a split second to display wide eyes. Then he drew himself up—just slightly—and grinned at

Matthew. "That would be, the United States of America!" he said.

America! Now there was a name someone—actually several someones—had taught him to fear. A name none dared speak, except to name a reservation for generations of malcontents on Botany Bay. This continent, and another much further south, had carried that name—until the Five Ladies had abolished it. The parts of the Civilized Footprint between Mexico, to the south, and Canada, to the north, now went by the name *Nuevo Aztlán*—except, of course, for the Protected Wild Space on this continent. For that matter, the full continent bore the name *Aztlán*. The southern continent bore the name *Amazonía*, after the great river, largest on this planet, that it featured.

A memory came back to him—a hard-bitten boy's triangular face with curly blond hair, saying he'd like the "American Superspreaders" to come for him and give him a disease that would make it impossible to breathe. A disease named after a crown—yes, the novel coronavirus. Then an upperclassman—Finnegan by name—saying, "S'matter? Afraid the Americans will get you?" But there was something different about those scenes, at least one from the other. *What was it?*

And then he knew. One was definitely a memory, but the other was almost like a dream—but a very richly detailed dream. He made a mental note to himself: *I must investigate this further. Later.*

Out of the corner of his eye, Matthew saw Chief Sutton's eyes bulge out in fear, then display curiosity. Corpsman Riley seemed to receive that name with quizzical indifference. Sublieutenant Cohen received it with shock, then with … excitement?

But why should Americans be here? Why would this non-com invoke *that* name? And something else … but that could wait.

Aloud he said, "Are you serious?"

Lance Corporal Jameson, still wearing that polite smile, said, "As serious as can be."

"The United States of America," said Matthew evenly, "ceased to exist three hundred eighty-two years ago."

"That's the impression we try to give," said the young team leader. "The Lieutenant can tell you we're real enough." *That* pronunciation again.

"I look forward to the enlightenment," said Matthew.

Not one member of Jameson's team, it seemed, knew how to fly a magnetic-levitating van. So the leader gave orders to camouflage it in place. This they did with remarkable effectiveness, as though they were hiding a game animal, not a human construct.

Then Jameson took out what looked almost like a Navy-issue Personal Digital Device. By instinct, Matthew turned on his scanners.

And Jameson barked another order: "Cover him!"

Instantly Matthew found himself staring into three Armalite barrels.

"Stop trying to hack my phone," said Jameson in an icy tone, "or you are dead this instant. Understood?"

"Yes," said Matthew. And he did stop. He didn't want to provoke this young man.

Jameson returned his attention to what he called a "phone." That device was indeed these people's version of a PDD—and remarkably efficient. He moved his fingers in several swiping motions, then pressed his thumb to the tiny screen and held it.

Out of the surrounding woods came what was surely their vehicle. Broad, angular, and perfectly proportioned for humans, it sported a camouflage finish, with the word MARINES in the upper right-hand corner, in unobtrusive black text, on the front, and on each side. The vehicle rolled up to the group. Matthew took in its lines and four rubber wheels. He ran an ordinary radar scan and discovered that this vehicle was all of one piece. The front of the vehicle was one flat plane, running from a lower row of forward lights in an unbroken plane to a sharp edge on the roof and containing a flat windscreen. Matthew looked through the windscreen—and saw no driver.

"Again, you score, Lance Corporal Jameson," said Matthew. "A remarkable vehicle design."

"Save the chatter for the Lieutenant. Now, all of you: walk, slowly, to the rear of the vehicle."

Matthew led the way, and his three companions followed. The side of the vehicle presented an irregular-pentagonal profile, continuing the angular motif. Two doors interrupted it, each with its own window. Matthew scanned the glass and guessed it could take a considerable impact. The rear looked almost like the front, except that the rear plane rose at a gentler angle. It consisted of a small rear-view window and a slatted surface. But those were no ordinary slats—they had photovoltaic surfaces.

Matthew's eyes had always been hyper-alert since he could remember. But he also had supplemental alert systems to point out details even he would otherwise miss. That's how he spotted two unmistakable propellers on the vehicle's underside—counter-rotating, too. Was this vehicle *amphibious?* That was difficult to tell from a casual glance, with the stainless-steel unified body that blocked his radar. But he would guess that it could, indeed, "swim" if it must.

Jameson touched another spot on his screen—and the slatted cover began to roll upward toward the window. The retreating slats revealed an apparent cargo bay. As they retreated, Matthew could see the insides of them as they turned and slid down into their own bay.

Then the bottom plane folded down—and extended itself into a telescoping ramp that soon rested on the ground before them.

"Get in," Jameson ordered.

Matthew stepped forward and climbed the ramp. He guessed how Jameson wanted him and the others to ride. So he walked as far forward as he could, then sat with his back to the forward end of the cargo bay. Ayelet, Andrea, and Barry sat in a row next to him. They said nothing else while the cargo bay cover rolled up and over them, sealing them in.

"Are you crazy?" asked Ayelet. "Letting them take us like this? You could have had him!"

"And get the rest of you killed?" Matthew asked. "Besides, I can still take them by surprise. But I want to know just what sort of operation the SSF have going in Protected Wild Space."

"You think that's what they are?"

"Of course. It's a game—simulate capture by an enemy of the tester's invention to see whether the candidate will break. Just the sort of training exercise the SSF—or, for that matter, Marine Intelligence—would run. Only, why use a vehicle like this? I've never seen this kind of vehicle before. It's built to use gravity, not fight it. Elegant, economical—and proportioned for human beings only. No Elf would fit in here or even in the crew cabin. If the SSF have vehicles like these, I want to know about it."

"Matthew," said Ayelet, "think! That leader's African. An African, leading a team of Caucasians? Totally out-of-character for everything we hear in school about Americans. And a lance corporal leading a fire team? A regular Marine fire team would have a full corporal leading it."

"He *could* be a month shy of promotion," said Matthew.

"Not in a simulation," Ayelet pointed out. "A simulation would pretend to be a textbook organization. Which, this isn't—at least, not any textbook I ever read.

And you're right; a team using a vehicle like this could never include Elves. That's almost a treaty violation."

As they talked, Matthew listened carefully for any sounds from Jameson and his team. He guessed they were confiscating Barry's printer and spare parts. Then, Matthew heard Jameson say sharply, "Careful with that thing! Don't you know a weapon when you see it?"

"What about this one, Pete?" asked another voice.

"Give me that thing!" said the lance corporal. "Bontke, this is worse. One spark from this thing, and our vehicle gets totally paralyzed. Here … let's hope this is safe. Now, everybody pile in."

Doors opened and closed, the vibration carrying through to the cargo bay. Then they "moved out." Matthew could tell the direction easily, and even follow the terrain. Those ground wheels transferred every bump and gradient to a passenger's body. The vehicle was, in fact, moving deeper into the forest, in roughly the direction from which the vehicle had come originally.

Three hundred meters later, the vehicle stopped. Up rolled the cargo bay cover. Jameson stood in the center of his crew. They all carried their guns at the ready, aimed at Matthew and his companions. They also wore the DEW guns, slung on their right shoulders, muzzles up. "Out," barked Jameson, leveling the DEW gun. He had the EMP gun slung over his left shoulder. Matthew got up and helped the others to their feet as the ramp folded down and extended.

Matthew and his friends descended the ramp and found themselves in a camp holding enough tents for nearly fifty men, arranged in six groups of eight each. Most of the groups each surrounded two vehicles like this one—except the vehicles sported wing-like projections made of that same photovoltaic surface material as their cargo bay covers. Matthew realized that this vehicle had its own set of PV wings, neatly folded inside the cargo bay. But two of the groups—squads, he guessed—had pitched their tents around much heavier vehicles—tracked vehicles sporting large rotating gun turrets. Tanks, he realized.

Then Matthew saw the obvious command group in the center of the camp. Like all the others, this group had its own vehicle. He soon realized these structures were not tents at all, but knock-down huts, which, like the vehicle, were of human proportions. The same photovoltaic surface material covered them, and it was of a kind Matthew had never seen before. He wondered how efficient it might be.

Next to this group rose a five-meter-high pole, from which flew a flag new to Matthew: thirteen stripes of alternating colors, seven red and six white, and in the top corner next to the pole, a rich blue field having forty-one white stars on it, in five rows of five stars each, alternating with four rows of four. Dwarfing this rose a fifteen-meter four-sided tower, about five meters on a side at the bottom, made of the same shiny metal as the vehicle that had brought them here. Four men, projectile weapons at the ready, stood guard around it. Four more stood on the platform itself, two carrying binocular field glasses and one carrying two hand-held flags. As nearly as Matthew could make out, each flag was square, divided by a diagonal into two right-triangular regions, one white and the other red. The platform wasn't open; however, it had a roof. Probably using that same new surface material, Matthew did not doubt.

The prominent command hut stood next to the flagpole, on the nearer side of the tower. It was to this hut Lance Corporal Jameson led his charges.

Inside, one slightly older man stood up as the squad removed their helmets, revealing crew cuts—exactly the thing to wear under such tight-fitting headgear. The man wearing the single brass bar on his left shoulder stood slightly taller than the younger man. And he *also* was African! The uniform was the same: camouflage fatigues and dark brown leather boots. True leather, too, not some printed imitation. Matthew looked at once for the man's name: ROBINSON.

Lance Corporal Jameson stood in front of the older man and saluted. "Sir!" he said. "Fire Team Delta reports to the Lieutenant. Four prisoners from UN country, operating some sort of aircraft."

"Incorrect, Lef- ah, *Loo*-tenant Robinson," said Matthew, making an effort to use the local pronunciation. "It is a magnetic-levitating vehicle."

"I'll get to you in a moment," said the Lieutenant. Then to the team leader, he said, "Continue."

Jameson gave further details, including range and bearing on the position where the van still rested. At least, Matthew surmised they were range and bearing. The bearing Matthew recognized easily enough; Jameson gave it in degrees of arc. But the range, if that's what it was, Jameson gave in a unit of measure Matthew had never heard before: the "yard." To Matthew, a *yard* was a facility for receiving Navy ships, or the campus of any ground structure the Navy owned on any planet. Not a unit of measure of range or height or any such! Matthew guessed from the figure Jameson gave that this "yard" was slightly shorter than the meter and about the length of an outstretched arm.

"What are those long guns you're carrying?" the Lieutenant was asking. "Where did you get these?"

"We confiscated them from the prisoners," Jameson said.

The Lieutenant whistled. "Leave these here," he said. "Report in full to the Platoon Sergeant. Give him my compliments and tell him to send Fire Team Charlie to guard that—whatever it is. Tents, bedrolls, the full kit. Then park your vehicle, spread your wings, and hook up."

"Yes, sir," said Lance Corporal Jameson, who saluted. His team unlimbered the DEW guns and left them and the chargers in the corner of the hut. Jameson left the EMP gun among them, and all marched out.

"Now," said the Lieutenant when at last they were quite alone, "suppose you tell me who you are, why you're here, and what mission you're on."

"Morrow, Matthew. Lieutenant Commander, United Systems Navy. Serial number…"

"Stop," Robinson said. "What do you mean, United *Systems?* And what's this…"—here he used an obscenity—"…about you being a Naval officer? Not in that uniform, you aren't—or this lady, either. You're a sergeant, and she a corporal, in the United Nations Climate Force. Are you not?"

Matthew blinked in surprise. *The United Nations Climate Force?* "The United Nations disbanded that Force," he said slowly, "about two hundred years ago. It was their last armed force."

"You've got to be kidding!" cried the Lieutenant. "You show up in that uniform, impersonating an officer and carrying weapons the like of which we've never seen. You are part of a recon party gathering intel for a fresh incursion into our territory. I guess you finally figured out that we're still here, and now you plan to wipe us out. Well, you won't! And, in any event," he said, dropping his voice to a low tone that carried a lot of menace in it, "you're not going to say a word to your superiors. You're going for a little ride to talk to Naval Intelligence."

"I'll be glad to tell them all I know," said Matthew. "But first, I'd like to challenge you with a simple question."

That gave Robinson pause. He took ten seconds before saying, "OK, I'll bite."

"Describe for me, please, the uniform of the United Nations Climate Force."

"Well," said the Lieutenant, "you have me there. That uniform was white with baby-blue trim and baby-blue lettering and accouterments. Jackboots, trousers, tunic, and helmet. And come to think of it, we haven't seen that uniform for well over two hundred years. But a private hunter-forager party spotted the uniform you're wearing at an installation north of here, close to the Potomac River. Fifteen years ago, we first saw it. The Seventh Cav Squadron has been reconning it ever since, through several changes of personnel and command. And then you four came floating almost on top of us."

The first part of that spiel was accurate enough—the United Nations Climate Force *had* worn that white uniform. But the second part gave Matthew yet another clue, as if he needed any more, that this was real. *Why would the SSF reveal an installation they had put Matthew into a coma to hide?* Answer: they wouldn't. Matthew had indeed found friends. The time had come for truth.

Matthew tried again. "This is the uniform of the Special Security Forces."

"I knew it! So there *is* a plan for an incursion!"

"If anyone has made such a plan," said Matthew, "they wouldn't tell me. I have been in a medically induced coma for fifteen years. This young woman freed me from that, and we, four, made our escape from Bethesda Naval Hospital—after we, two, first defeated an SSF section and stole two of their uniforms."

"And just how do you expect me to believe that?"

"By trying a little experiment," said Matthew. This could get awkward, but he could see no other way. "Take your service handgun and shoot me with it."

"What the…!?" A real SSF actor would have sworn by the Five Ladies, or simply "the Five." Instead, this officer had used another expletive, which rolled off his tongue entirely naturally—an Old English curse, one that Matthew knew only from his dealings with a few less than savory characters.

"One shot," said Matthew, "here." He pointed to where an organic heart would be on his body. "But if I may suggest, you might want to stand at an oblique angle."

Robinson stood up slowly and took two steps to his left.

Then he drew his weapon, aimed it at Matthew's chest, and fired.

The bullet bounced off Matthew's chest. His body shield slowed it down but not quite enough. It made a slight dent in his chest, then hit the side of the hut and dropped, spent, to the ground. A verb came to Matthew's mind from the projectile-weapon era: *ricochet.* Robinson goggled.

"Touch my chest," Matthew said after lowering his shield. "Did you do any damage?"

Robinson, gun in hand, reached out and felt Matthew's chest. Then he opened his eyes even wider. "My shot should have dropped you where you stand," he said. What the … are you?"

"You see before you," said Matthew, "a total-body prosthesis. I have nothing organic except my brain, eyes, ears, olfactory lobes, other cranial nerves, and spinal cord. Everything else is metal and plastic, under my direct neural control. As such, my body has certain augmentations. Extra memory banks. And extra coordination circuits for fine work, marksmanship, and even a measure of ambidexterity. I also can receive—and transmit—radio, microwave, and infrared signals. I am physically stronger than you by a factor of at least three. I even carry a personal electromagnetic shield proof against directed-energy and electromagnetic-pulse weapons. And *almost* against the projectile weapons you carry." As he spoke, he closely watched his interrogator, who seemed faintly puzzled at some of the terms he had used.

He continued, "I react by reflex faster than you can, also by a factor of at least three. These two young women obviously must have known at least half of what I am telling you. Perhaps that was enough to convince them they had found a valuable ally. In addition to which, I have held one special command of a skeleton crew of a warship guarding an alien border against external attack. A *spaceship* of war."

The Lieutenant's eyes had widened a little with every word Matthew spoke. Now he simply gasped, "Just what were these 'United Systems' trying to build? Some kind of ultimate warrior?"

"Very possibly," said Matthew. "That is one of many mysteries I now intend to solve."

Robinson whistled. "You could have had me for lunch any time," he said. "I'm not even sure my whole platoon could contain you. Why'd you come so quietly?"

"To satisfy my curiosity," said Matthew.

"What made you decide to trust us?"

Matthew reviewed for Robinson all the clues that led him to accept Americans as real, and not a training simulation. "Our educational system tells us that the Americans were Caucasian, racist, and colonialistic," he said next. "Our memory of you survives as a legend with which to frighten small children—or officer cadets or enlisted recruits. We had thought you eliminated. I am immensely gratified that you are very much alive."

Robinson gaped at him. Then he said, "That still doesn't answer my question."

"Here's your answer, Lieutenant," said Matthew. That pronunciation came more easily now. "If the Special Security Forces had built this camp as a simulation, they would never have used actors of African ancestry or extraction to lead Caucasians."

"Is *that* what you mean by 'racist'?" asked the Lieutenant, who grinned. "They sound like the real racists, meaning no offense to any of you."

"None taken. Besides your ancestry, you gave me the final clue with that last vulgarism you used. In my society, that expression is obsolete. Instead, we use a Swedish expression that the Five Ladies popularized."

"The Five Ladies? Who are they?"

"Ask who they *were*. Francisca Ordoñez Pizarro, first Director-General of Nuevo Aztlán; Ruqayya Tamraz, Jawahir Otayf, and Kanesha Preston, co-Directors; and Gunilla Thorsell, the child climate-change activist who became Secretary-General of the United Nations in the year in which that body became the one-world federation that governs the Earth today."

Robinson uncorked a flood of profanity.

"My apologies," said Matthew. "You must positively hate the Five Ladies."

"'Hate' doesn't half say it!" said the officer. "They began with writing a sick joke of a 'charter' for their new 'North American Polity'—or do they still call it that?"

"Not anymore," said Matthew. "They call it Nuevo Aztlán."

"Figures. Anyway, then they sicced UNCLIFOR on us. UNCLIFOR then laid waste to every part of our country except their favorite cities and suburbs, killed or kidnapped the bulk of our people—why, I could tell you stories that would make your head spin, especially you two women. Tales of children taken and sent to government crèches, forced abortions and sterilizations—and only because we had *very* smart doctors were we able to reverse that last part, after some of the adults so treated escaped, and we rescued others. Those five 'ladies' reduced us to a million strong, and it's taken three hundred eighty years to re-grow our population!"

Andrea gasped. Ayelet growled, and Matthew saw the fire in her eyes.

"And as part of their 'fundamental transformation' … all right, I'll give you an example. We had a monument that had stood for nearly a century to four presidents of the United States. It was on a mountain slope near Keystone, South Dakota. Ever heard of it?"

"South … Dakota," said Matthew. "SD. And Keystone. NRD-01-SD-Keystone. Remarkable for the restoration of a defaced mountain."

"Restoration, my …!" said Robinson. "That mountain—called Rushmore—had the faces of those four presidents carved into it. UNCLIFOR totally wiped those faces off that mountain. The only reason no one carved the faces of those Five—*Termagants*—into the mountain instead is that no one would be around to look at them; I shouldn't wonder!"

Now Matthew understood the naming convention for Nature Reclamation Districts—at least in the middle part of North America. "Tell me this, Lieutenant," he said. "We know of another remarkable NRD called 01-NY-West Point."

"I'll bet you do!" cried Robinson. "The United States Military Academy! Which UNCLIFOR took down brick by brick, stone by stone, after which they erased all the foundations!"

"So *that* was the object of the Great Climate War," said Matthew. "To wipe out your entire civilization—then make it look as if it never existed."

"They certainly tried," said the Marine Lieutenant. "So you can understand why those names aren't exactly pleasing to my ears."

"Indeed, I do understand. And apologize," he finally said. "I hope I can convince you now that I seek you as a friend and ally."

"I'll let you try to convince my superiors. Just a moment." Now he whistled again, but this time as a signal. Another soldier, wearing a single chevron, entered the tent, snapped to attention, and saluted.

"Have the Flag Team flag Squadron HQ," Robinson said. "My respects and I request the squadron CO and Ess-Two to join me in my camp ASAP to hear some intel first-hand."

"Yes, sir." The soldier trotted away, roughly toward that signal tower.

"While we're waiting for my superiors," Robinson said to Matthew, "suppose you tell me, just what *is* the United Systems? Is the United Nations now part of it, and what is that installation out there?"

"Gladly," said Matthew. "But first, may I assume that an 'Ess-Two' is a staff intelligence officer?"

"Sure," said Robinson. "As leader of the Recon Platoon, I report directly to him."

"I look forward to speaking with him. For now, the United Systems is the federation of human- and humanoid-inhabited worlds spanning at least half the Six-o'clock Quadrant of the galaxy. For your information, we divide the galaxy into four Quadrants, centered on the center of the galaxy. By convention, this Sun is in the Six-o'clock Quadrant and defines its centerline. The charter of the United Systems mirrors the charter of the United Nations. The latter charter has changed little in the centuries since it became federal. The five permanent members of the United Systems Security Council are the

United Nations of Sol d—that's our name for this world—the Planetary Union of Tau Ceti f, the Union of GJ357 d, the Star Federation of Epsilon Eridani, and the Alpha Centauri Stellar Concordium.

"Now about that installation. I know now that I must have seen a structure close to it from aloft, fifteen years ago. Specifically, a highway bridge spanning the Potomac River. Or, to be more accurate, its remnants—which, I noted in my flight here, remain today."

"The Point-of-Rocks Bridge," said Robinson.

"In any event," said Matthew, "I reported this and some other anomaly to my captain. I assume he passed the report on. That was our mistake. To my complete surprise, the Naval Criminal Investigative Service signed a warrant for my arrest, a warrant the SSF executed. And, I now learn, the Navy decommissioned my assigned ship and scattered her officers and crew. Those officers were my only friends in the Naval service until I met these three. I went into a coma, and fifteen years later, this woman awakened me from it."

"And you are?" the Lieutenant asked Matthew's three companions.

Matthew nodded to his companions, who introduced themselves.

"And why have two United Systems Naval officers and two petty officers entered our territory and passed a force field to do it?"

"If you mean, how did we technically accomplish that feat, credit Chief Sutton here," said Matthew, who started to explain.

"I didn't ask *how*. I asked *why*."

"I led them here," said Matthew, "to investigate more closely that installation I saw that prompted the authorities to confine me. And to make double sure of my escape from Bethesda Naval Hospital by escaping the entire Civilized Footprint."

"'Civilized Footprint.' Is that what they call UN country?"

Matthew nodded, saying evenly, "It is."

"And why are these three people following you?"

"Each for their own reasons," said Matthew. That would be the simplest thing to say.

Lieutenant Robinson advanced toward Ayelet. "Sublieutenant Cohen," he said in an almost formal tone, "would you care to tell me your reasons?"

She looked at Matthew, who nodded. Then she said, "For a very long time, I have thought of starting a revolution against the United Nations and United Systems."

And not only thought about it, Matthew now realized. She had trained for it—including weapons training far beyond the minimum weapons training of a nursing officer. And it would seem she had recruited these two others. So *that's* why you activated me. All you needed was some convincing from Andrea here that you, at last, had the perfect opportunity.

Lieutenant Robinson had seemingly turned curious. "And what is your motive for revolting against the UN?"

"Sir," she answered, "I am Jewish. Four hundred sixty-nine years ago, my people won recognition as an independent country."

Jewish. Of course! That explained her Middle Eastern accent—and knowing Yiddish.

"Would that be the State of Israel?" Robinson asked.

"Yes!" she cried. "And the federalization of the United Nations *also* saw the UN renege on its promise to our people. They scattered my ancestors all over again in what we call the Second Diaspora."

"Actually," said the Lieutenant, "the great bulk of Israeli residents, then living, found their way to the United States during the Re-Wilding War—what I think Commander Morrow here called the 'Great Climate War.'"

"Excuse me, but…'re-wilding'?"

"That's what you call it when you literally scour all trace of civilization and revert the land to the wild—meaning, the condition it was in before any human being ever trod on it. Anyway, nearly all Israelis came to the United States to join up with us. Their descendants live with us today, though as citizens of a government-in-exile, complete with its own army."

"You mean the State of Israel exists?" Her eyes shone with obvious admiration—and wonder.

"Yes, it does," Robinson said. "They live in a large cavern complex that connects to the New York Caverns— long story there."

Ayelet gasped. "By the Name," she whispered, "that is the most wonderful news I have ever heard in my life."

Lieutenant Robinson smiled. "I'm glad to be the bearer of such good news," he said. "But for now, please tell me how you imagined Commander Morrow would be willing and able to help you."

Ayelet explained about breaking Matthew out of his fifteen-year coma and her hopes to have him as an ally. Matthew, listening to this, smiled.

"And why would he be valuable to you in that way?"

"Because he is…" She turned to Matthew again. Seeking *his* permission to speak?

"Got it," said Robinson. "You knew he was a Frankensteinian experiment and thought you could recruit him."

She blushed crimson and said, "Yes, though … What's 'Frankensteinian'?"

"What the … Haven't you ever read *Frankenstein*, by Mary Shelley?"

"I have," said Matthew. "The story of a scientist who assembles a lifeless human body from multiple cadavers and animates it."

Ayelet gasped, covered her mouth with both hands, and looked at him with a mixture of awe and … pity? "Matthew," she said, "I'm so sorry…"

Matthew turned to her with a smile. "Quite all right, Sublieutenant," he said. "In any event," he said to their host, "one of my friends and fellow officers aboard *Bonaventure VII*—my last ship—recommended that work to me. She suggested it might reflect my own origins."

"You mean no one's told you where you came from?" asked Steve Robinson. "Now, with all due respect, I find that hard to believe."

"I come from Berks World," said Matthew. "What I don't know is *why* I came to be what I am."

"Berks World?" the Lieutenant repeated. "Where's that?"

"Planet Proxima Centauri b."

"Proxima … Centauri," the Lieutenant repeated. "Part of that 'Alpha Centauri Stellar Concordium' you mentioned?"

"Not quite," said Matthew. "Proxima technically orbits the stars known individually as Rigil Kentaurus and Toliman, but at 13,000 astronomical units' distance. Proxima is a red dwarf star. Its inner planet has no air, so the Berks World colony was entirely underground."

"*Was?*"

"The colony failed utterly when someone—no one ever learned who—opened the airlocks." *Now, where had that piece of information come from?* To be sure, no one had told him. Then it must have come to him in his dreams— or memories. Disconnected memories—*and maybe the organic portion of them?* His *in*organic memories, consisting as they did of Erasable Electronically Programmable

Read-Only Memories, were highly organized. *Libraries* should have such organization. But his organic memories were confused—and even the two sets together were … incomplete.

"And how did you become a Naval officer? How did you even *survive?*"

"The Captain and crew of USS *Bonaventure* Five, CC-61, rescued me from the now-evacuated tunnel complex on Berks World. Or, so I have been permitted to know. The landing party found me unconscious—which is to say, shut down—in a partially sealed compartment, where I at least had time to close my eyes. My eyes might be organic, but the lids are not, so I can make a gas-tight seal. My ears have similar protection—if they didn't, I'd be deaf. But my memories go back only to my awakening in Bethesda Naval Hospital, the almost sub-adult education I received there, and my subsequent enrollment at the United Systems Naval Academy."

"Wow," said Robinson. "This is already a lot more than I should be authorized even to listen to, much less ask. Well, the Major and the Ess-Two are on their way. You can tell them about it. Me, I just lead the Recon Platoon. Anything I see or hear as sensitive as that, I report.

"But they're not here yet. So I'm going to go right on interrogating you and *hope* that will save time. So, what can you tell me about that Special Security Force you mentioned?"

"It is tasked with guarding prisoners like myself or the First Secretary of the United Systems. And much else, I gather, though I don't know what."

"Do you expect them to come after you?"

"As a matter of fact, I do," said Matthew. "I apologize for placing you at additional hazard."

"Forget it. My people will have to face that 'hazard' to get our lives and lands back. But, what I really need to know—would you expect that installation we are reconning to be an advanced base for an armed re-entry into United States territory? Or would it serve some other purpose?"

"Like you, I suspect it has existed for at least fifteen years, possibly longer. Whether it serves for reconnaissance or a staging area for incursion, I do not know. But whatever purpose it serves, the SSF have kept it secret, not only from the general public but also from other United Systems military units. In fact, the United Nations calls this region Protected Wild Space, and allows no one inside it."

"So—bottom line—*none* of you know what United Systems troops are doing going in, and out of a space they were supposed to have closed off at least two hundred years ago after they got tired of looking for us and the population we guard."

"No," said Matthew, "we do not. But I am just as curious as you. If you and I can come to a temporary treaty, I would be pleased to scout that installation for you."

"Whoa," said the Lieutenant. "You're getting ahead of yourself. If you're going to treat with anyone, it will be the Major. And how do I know he or I can trust you?"

"I have committed myself to finding certain answers I know neither the United Systems nor the United Nations will tell me," Matthew replied. "Yours is a rebel population. *I* am a fugitive. Now, Lieutenant, how do *I* know *I* can trust *you?*"

The Lieutenant paused—obviously to consider the question. Then he grinned ear-to-ear. "That makes us even," he said. "You can trust me because you know, and I know, we now *have* to trust each other." He offered his right hand. "Shake?"

Matthew had never understood the significance of that common gesture by organics. But suddenly, he made the connection. Two persons, clasping hands in friendship or mutual salute, could not raise weapons against one another. Without a word, he offered his own hand—and gave the Lieutenant's hand just enough of a squeeze. But the Lieutenant was a little dubious. "Say," he said, "you're holding back on me."

"No, Lieutenant," said Matthew. "I merely wish to avoid crushing your hand."

The Lieutenant's eyes widened again. "Holy…!" he swore. "I completely forgot about that. Thanks for remembering!"

"That's nothing, Lieutenant Robinson."

"And now I'd like you and all your companions to join the Major, the Ess-Two, and me for dinner as soon as they get here. That is—if you can eat food?"

"Actually, I can," said Matthew. "It's an efficient way for me to recharge. I also found that ability extremely useful for preserving working relationships in the wardroom of a capital ship."

"Son of a…"—another expletive— "your doctors … builders … whatever, thought of everything."

Not quite everything. He didn't get a chance to speak, though, for just then, the mosquito-winged soldier—which Matthew assumed was a private-first-class with that insignia—who had earlier taken a message to the signal tower, knocked at the hut door. "Come in!" said the Lieutenant.

The soldier came in and saluted. "Sir," he said, "Flag Team reports an AFV approaching from the direction of SHQ."

"Good! Pass the word to the cook tent that I will be dining here with six guests."

Chapter 4

After about ten minutes, two officers entered. The older one, sandy-haired, square-jawed and barrel-chested, wearing gold starburst emblems on his upper arms, spoke first. "Lieutenant," he said, "this had better be good. Would you mind introducing me to your guests?"

Robinson began by introducing Matthew and his friends to "Major Campbell." Then he said, "Commander, I present my squadron commander, Major Joe Campbell, United States Marine Corps."

"Thank you, Lieutenant," said the Major. "Ladies and gentlemen, with me is Captain Ian Vincent, my Intelligence Officer." The other officer, a slightly-built, brown-haired man with two sets of silver bars on his shoulders, nodded slightly.

"Commander Morrow," said the Major, "I must say, that's a very strong handshake you've got. Prosthetic?"

"Actually, Major Campbell, it's more than that," said Matthew. "It's part of a total-body prosthesis." He went on to explain that, and his background, just as he had to Lieutenant Robinson. Who, listening to this explanation for the second time, smiled knowingly.

"Holy…!" cried the Major. "Just how many of you exist?"

"Only myself, as far as I know," said Matthew.

"I should hope so!" said the Major, still just as excited as before. "I'd hate to face a whole army of you. And I devoutly hope you're friendly."

"I am a fugitive, Major Campbell," said Matthew. "Surely that makes me friendly enough."

"Your *creators* are copycats," said Captain Vincent. "The technology you carry was not in the public domain. *None* of it. It belonged to Leon Vincent, or more particularly, to one of his companies. Leon Vincent, by the way, happens to be my direct ancestor—and was the most prolific and visionary inventor of his day. The United Nations seized all his patents before the Re-Wilding War. That makes them stolen intellectual property, even if they are nearly four hundred years old.

"Fortunately for you, the Vincent Neurological Company still exists, and they've improved on the basic product. If you'd like, I can introduce you to their scientists. Maybe they can enhance you."

"I look forward to meeting anyone who can give me such enhancement," said Matthew. "But first, Lieutenant Robinson summoned you because I have a story to tell. And, as I gather, so do you."

"That's right, Commander," said Major Campbell. "Lieutenant, yes, this *is* good. And totally unexpected. We should get right on it."

"And we will, sir," said Steve Robinson. "But first, this is about the dinner hour, and I've already informed the cook tent. And I see the KPs are already here."

Indeed, a team of kitchen police asked permission to enter, which Robinson granted. They brought a fold-up table and folding chairs and set them up. Someone somehow produced six mess kits and laid them out on the table as Lieutenant Robinson unpacked his own to use. Matthew noted that each mess kit consisted of a skillet with a folding handle, a bowl that fastened over it, and a metal knife, fork, and spoon inside. *A remarkably compact kit,* Matthew thought. And one that let its user eat better than protein bars in the field.

The KP team left, and then two of them came back, carrying a large stew pot between them. One other man, carrying a ladle, accompanied them. At a nod from Robinson, they started to ladle out a sweet-smelling stew into the mess kit bowls. With that done, Robinson dismissed them, then left do-not-disturb orders and closed the door to the hut securely.

"Ladies and gentlemen," said the Major, "I suggest we sit down." And he did, taking one end of the table while Robinson took the other. Captain Vincent sat to the Major's left. Matthew took the seat to Robinson's left. Ayelet sat across from Captain Vincent, and the two petty officers sat across from Matthew.

The Major picked up the fork before him. Everyone took that as a signal to start eating. And about half a minute into the meal, Barry Sutton spoke. "Sirs," he said, "this is the best meal I have ever tasted. What is this meat, first of all?"

"Venison stew," said Lieutenant Robinson. "Elk venison, the most common game we can find in this region. Roosevelt elk, in fact—one of the best variants."

"Well, whatever it is," said Barry, "it's good. And the chance to smell it in advance—we just don't get that privilege. And this is real meat, isn't it? Not an imitation?"

"What's the matter?" asked their host. "Do they keep your people on a vegan diet?"

"No, but the meat we get is artificial."

The Lieutenant wrinkled his nose at that. Captain Vincent decided to take it up: "And how does your society make this 'artificial' meat? I recall that the infamous Wilfred Torrance—well, maybe you don't know that name…"

"We do," said Barry. "Popularizer of his own brands of workstations, servers, and their software. His brand became very popular until the Five Ladies decided that proprietary *anything* shouldn't exist. But he also suggested growing meat from fungus. Like the portabella mushroom, only on a grand scale."

"Yes, that's the man and the idea," said Captain Vincent. "Do you still use his solution?"

"We do, but not the way you think," said Barry. "This is going to sound a little strange."

"'Strange' is my business, Chief Sutton," said the S-2. "Tell."

"Well, you see, Captain, we print everything we eat."

"'Print'?" Vincent's eyes widened. "You mean, from a three-D printer?"

"Yes, Captain," said Ayelet. "A 'printer,' to us, is a self-contained device that can reproduce any object after scanning it once. It can use any of a wide variety of substrates—that is, raw materials—and shape them at will."

"And *that* includes *foodstuffs?*" asked the Major, incredulous.

"Just what does this 'printer' use?" asked Captain Vincent. "Some kind of goop made of protein, sugar, and fat? Or the primordial soup from which the UN insists we 'evolved'?"

"It's a lot more sophisticated than that, sir," said Barry. "But yes, that's about the size of it. A printer uses a stock amino acid solution, starch slurry, monosaccharide syrups, oils, even a cellulose stock. It can also convert minerals to metal. In fact, I was carrying such a device when Lance Corporal Jameson and his team picked us up."

"Cluster … Sorry, sir," said Robinson.

"That's all right, Lieutenant," said the S-2. "I well understand your shock. This goes beyond the original Agenda Twenty-one and the Convention on Biological Diversity that led to the Re-Wilding.

"You, Commander Morrow, are telling us, in effect, that the UN actually put an end to animal husbandry and even to farming. Correct?"

"In a word," said Matthew, "yes. And to most industries. But not without outside help."

"Now, hold on," said Vincent. "This is just the sort of thing Wilfred Torrance *would* invent. And you're telling me he didn't?"

"No, sir, he did not. The printer came to us from the first extraterrestrials to contact us."

"I want to see this printer of yours in action," said the Captain.

"And so do I," said Major Campbell.

The arrangements took fifteen minutes. Lieutenant Robinson sent for another table, and Barry set up his printer on it, connected the lattice-confined fusion apparatus that provided its power, and charged it with food substrate. What took the longest was writing a unique program to hide the printer from any network device that could be scanning Protected Wild Space. "Probably they aren't," said Matthew, "but we shouldn't take chances." Barry agreed with his point.

"Now," said Matthew when all was ready, "let's try a very simple snack—a portion of elk venison jerky."

Barry spoke, and the printer hummed, strained a little, and produced the snack. Barry reached for it.

Matthew held out his hand. "Hand that to me," he ordered.

Barry nodded and handed the jerky over. Matthew chewed it, injected artificial saliva into it, and ran a full chemical analysis on the sample.

The results shocked him. *Why hadn't anyone seen to this repair twenty-two years ago?*

But then he realized why. Aloud, he said, "Ladies and gentlemen, I would not recommend eating printed food. Not for any of you."

Ayelet gasped. Andrea asked, "What … what did you find?"

"For one thing," said Matthew, "this venison is genetically defective."

"Are you sure?" Ayelet asked.

"Absolutely, now that I've sampled actual venison. The printed sample tastes as if it comes from a genetically modified bull elk. Ayelet, I mentioned to you earlier that the printers were breaking down. This is yet another example.

"But I found worse. The printed product contains a sample of a promazine derivative."

"*WHAT!?*" asked Ayelet.

"Proma-what?" asked Andrea.

"Whoa-whoa-whoa," said Steve. "What are you saying?"

"Are you telling us, Commander Morrow," said Captain Vincent, "that your authorities have been—*drugging*—their own people all this time?"

"Just a mo'." said Barry. He used his PDD's near-field communication capability to query the printer for information.

While he was doing that, Matthew turned to the S-2. "Yes," he said, "that's exactly what I'm saying. I first noticed this adulteration twenty-two years ago when I reported aboard USS *Bonaventure* CC-81. I reported it to my commanding officer, who took it for a programming defect and ordered a correction. I had no idea that the problem was more widespread. Now I conclude that, as far as the authorities were concerned, it wasn't a problem. It was their intention."

Just then, Matthew noticed Barry's face. It was ashen. Matthew held out his hand. "Place your PDD into the palm of my hand," he said. "I can send and receive via NFC also."

Barry complied. Matthew read the code output—and nodded in understanding.

"What?" asked Ayelet. "What's going on?"

"The printer," said Matthew, "carries deliberate code to introduce the promazine derivative. In fact, it's identical to what I thought was errant code aboard *Bonaventure*. I cannot tell, just now, whether the genetic defects represent another deliberate substitution. That could result simply from coding errors from multiple iterations of imperfect copying."

"Like a genetic mutation," Barry offered. "Disgusting, either way."

"Mutations are one thing," said the Major drily. "Drugging people against their will is quite another. And that means this printer is positively dangerous to use."

"Yes—though, maybe we can mitigate that." He turned to the Chief. "Chief Sutton," he said, "I want to know: can you rewrite that code?"

"Yes, I can," said Barry. "I can cut out the drug routine, and any routines for other weird chemicals. But are you sure we need to? I mean, now that we can eat *real* meat…"

"Chief," said Matthew, patiently, "I could never in good conscience allow this program to remain on any printer now in use. Not if I can do anything about it."

"You mean," said Barry, face lighting up, "that you want to introduce a virus on the network to remove this code from everybody's printers?"

"Yes," said Matthew. "That is an absolute moral imperative—and reason enough for revolution."

"I agree," said Ayelet. "I'll never eat printer food again, even if it's either that or starve. Nor should anyone else. Do you all know what promazine and its derivatives are?"

"I know," said Matthew. "But Andrea and Barry might not. Major, Captain, Lieutenant, do any of you know?"

"Our squadron surgeon likely knows," said Major Campbell. "But tell us anyway."

"They're what we call major tranquilizers," said Ayelet. "The psych attendings give those to psychotic people, usually those suffering from paranoid schizophrenia or some such. But, give that kind of thing to a normal person, and you can turn them into who knows what— but I'd guess they're aiming for a population of sheep."

"A 'population of sheep,'" Major Campbell repeated. "A famous phrase from the Re-Wilding War. The great General Terence Crawford used it often. A fascinating individual—and time."

"What I'd like to know now," said Barry, "is how long this has been going on."

"At least twenty years, as I said," said Matthew. "But it will go on no longer."

"So that," said Major Campbell, "is what you mean by revolution."

"Yes," said Matthew. "I already knew I carried a death mark. Now I see that others do, too. You cannot imagine that I would ignore that. Not if I can wake people up."

"I must ask you, ladies," the Major broke in. "How much do *you* know about any of this?"

"Not about the drugging, specifically, Major Campbell," said Ayelet. "But I've long suspected many other things." She explained about that, too. That led to an explanation of her Jewish background.

"I can confirm," said Major Campbell, "that the State of Israel still exists, though not in its rightful place or even its rightful geographical location. Their military will definitely want to talk to you, Sublieutenant Cohen.

"As for you, Commander, your people, and mine will definitely benefit from a military alliance. I don't know how things work in your service, but in ours, commissioned officers have the power to negotiate temporary treaties. The Senate would have to ratify them, of course, but I'm confident that I could win ratification."

"Why, if I may ask?"

"Because the United States has its own reasons to go to war," said the Major. "This land we're camped on once belonged to us. We want it back. Three thousand miles east-to-west, fifteen hundred miles north-to-south—and that's not even including the lost states of Alaska and Hawaii…"

"Excuse me, Major," said Matthew. "'Miles'?"

The Major opened his mouth to reply—and shut it almost as quickly, for Lance Corporal Jameson had just entered. "Sir!" he said, raising his hand in salute. "Your pardon—ah, sirs—but the lookouts report that a squad of what looked like armed scouts, uniformed like our guests, have landed in a definite VTOL flying machine next to the vehicle our guests used. My apologies—I must not have camouflaged it as well as I thought."

Instantly, Matthew ran a diagnostic on his systems, then a quick scan. No sign of radio emissions that he could account for, but it wouldn't hurt to be sure. "Captain Vincent," he asked, "can you scan me for stray radio or infrared emissions? I wonder whether I am carrying a homing device."

The S-2 cursed, then whipped out an enhanced PDD and waved it up and down in front of Matthew. Then he shook his head. "No such sign," he said. "But I see your point. I take it you know who those scouts are?"

"Special Security Forces," said Matthew. "They must have followed my trail. And maybe *I* don't carry the homing device, but that rubber wagon does." He didn't have to take long to explain what that was.

Lieutenant Robinson spoke next. "Find your squad leader, Jameson," he ordered. "Pass the word: recon, engage, and capture if possible. And tell the Platoon Sergeant to go on full alert."

"Lieutenant, if I may," said Matthew, now standing, "I should accompany that squad."

"And I," said Ayelet, also standing.

"You heard, Jameson," said the platoon leader. "Give these two back their weapons and introduce them to your squad leader. Then get out after those intruders. *On the double!*"

Clearly, "on the double" meant the same to Marines everywhere. Everything happened fast and efficiently. Matthew, Ayelet, Corporal Jack Swigert, Lance Corporal Jameson, and a full squad were moving out, in two of those wheeled AFVs in less than a minute. Corporal Swigert drove one, with Matthew and Ayelet riding with him and his Fire Team. Lance Corporal Jameson drove the other.

Swigert watched the large viewscreen that seemed to handle not only the usual vehicular functions but also reconnaissance—with both radar and IR. Very quickly, he spotted the enemy, who were still inspecting the maglev rubber wagon. He stopped. "Lock, load, and move out," he ordered.

They did. Matthew had his EMP gun, while Ayelet carried a DEW gun. The Americans carried those modified Armalites that seemed to be government-issue.

One look at the SSF told Matthew all he needed to know. The squad leader and half his squad carried EMP guns; the rest carried DEWs. So they were after Matthew.

Their ship was a more typical military ship—saucer-shaped. Too small for an LCG, but big enough to carry a squad.

Swigert had his team approach slowly. Out of the corner of his eye, Matthew saw Jameson's vehicle move off to the side. *Where was he going? Oh, of course. An encircling maneuver.* These Marines must have practiced that many times.

Matthew raised his body shield as the team closed to within five meters—or slightly closer.

Now Swigert raised his voice. "Freeze, or you're dead!" he barked. "Drop your weapons!"

This encounter did not go as well as it had for Jameson and Fire Team Delta. In an instant, the SSF were in combat stance, weapons unlimbered—and firing. One of the first shots dropped Swigert to the ground. Matthew didn't have time to look. Without hesitation, he aimed his EMP weapon at the maglev scout craft and fired. The result was as if lightning had struck the craft. As he half expected, two more SSF came pounding down the craft's aft boarding ladder. So his shot had disabled that craft, at least temporarily.

Ayelet was already firing her DEW gun. Two SSF went down before it, and two others went down when the American Marines riddled them with bullets. But they were losing the battle; the SSF were too many.

That is, until Fire Team Delta, with Jameson in the lead, hit the enemy from behind.

The battle ended with all ten SSF dead—plus Corporal Jack Swigert, USMC. The first DEW shot had pierced his heart.

* * *

Matthew stood to one side, feeling grim, as Lance Corporal Jameson made his report to the three officers back at the camp. Lieutenant Robinson listened, then said, "Well done, Corporal Jameson. As of this moment, you are acting leader of Squad Two. I'll put you up right now for a second stripe."

"And I will confirm that," said Major Campbell, looking as grim as Matthew felt. "In fact, I'll want to decorate you as soon as the excitement winds down. For now, you've got a squad to lead. And we have a council of war to convene. That's all."

The new corporal saluted and left.

"Corporal Jameson's report shows that you certainly handled yourself well, for a 'nursing officer.' I might like to inquire into how you got the weapons training you clearly have, but we don't have time for that. Instead, I'll accept you as friendly—and very effective. How'd you like to be a Marine?"

"Honored, sir," she said.

"Good," said the Major. "As of now, you're the assistant platoon leader of the Recon Platoon. And you, Chief Sutton—I'll assign you to this platoon as an electronics specialist. Your first task will be to repair that magnetic levitating fighting vehicle and bring it in."

"Yes, sir," said Barry.

"I think you'd better get to it, Chief," said Robinson. "Find Corporal Jameson and have him escort you out there right away. Ask for Squad Two."

Barry saluted and left.

That left Matthew, Ayelet, the three Marine officers, and Andrea Riley.

"If you don't mind," said Ayelet, "suddenly, I'm famished. If there's more of that elk venison stew left…"

"Help yourself," said Major Campbell. "In the meantime, where were we?"

Ayelet took a mess kit and a full helping of stew, then withdrew slightly to eat.

"You were about to explain what a mile was," said Matthew.

"Oh, yes," said Campbell, who went on to introduce Matthew to a whole new system of measurement. Campbell called it the United States of America Patriotic System. At first, Matthew found it dizzyingly complex, especially compared to the decimal *Système Interstellaire d'Unités* to which he was accustomed. But as the Major described it, Matthew found it eminently logical. Why shouldn't any system of units have different units of length for different applications—and units which, furthermore, came closer to the human, or humanoid, experience? A *mile* was a thousand standard *paces* on the march, whereas a *foot* was literally the length of an average human foot. Or, an average Neo-Inuit or Porcoid or any other foot, for that matter—except for an Elfin foot, which would be one-third longer. And why not? Even SI yielded to a non-decimal convention when describing intervals of time or astronomical distances. Why shouldn't that hold for distances in everyday usage?

Major Campbell explained that the distances he quoted earlier amounted to forty-eight hundred kilometers east-to-west, and twenty-four hundred kilometers north-to-south—to two significant figures. "Our system goes a lot further than length or mass," he said. "But that can come later.

"For now, we are now living underground, underneath land that was ours. We send out hunter-forager parties all the time—at great risk—to get healthier foodstuffs than we can produce underground. And we constantly reconnoiter—looking for any clue to how the UN beat us the first time, and how we can beat *them*."

"Which means," said Matthew, "that you are at war. And you have already taken a casualty."

"Right," said the Major, frowning again. "Ian, why don't you begin? This is your bailiwick anyway."

"Thank you, sir," said the Captain. "Now then, you mentioned extraterrestrial helpers before."

"Yes, we did," said Matthew. "First to contact humanity were the race we call the 'Elves.'"

"Did you say *Elves?* But Elves figure in children's stories."

"Not these Elves," said Matthew. "These are real."

"What do they look like?" asked Major Campbell. "Point-eared albino nightcrawlers? That's one version I've seen, though only in pictures."

"They do have pointed ears," said Matthew. "But their skin has as much variation in tone as I see in this platoon, maybe more. They also stand about one-third taller than you do but are much more slender. They come from Tau Ceti e. In fact, when Juan de Cuellar first showed off his faster-than-light ship, an Elfin ship was in that part of the sky at the same time. They saw de Cuellar's ship, followed it back to Earth, and made contact. Sometimes, I suspect the Elves had always been reconnoitering Earth."

"Sir," said the S-2 to his superior, "this suddenly reminds me of Area Fifty-one."

"'Area Fifty-one?' What's that?" asked Matthew.

"Area Fifty-one," said Vincent, "also known as Groom Lake, Nevada, was a secret base of what was then known as the United States Air Force. Rumors always said they kept crashed spacecraft there, including one that crashed in Roswell, New Mexico, on, or about, 8 July 1947. That is…"

Sensing the slight hesitation in the Captain's manner, Matthew said, "That would be modified Julian day number three-two-three-seven-four. Furthermore, that an Elfin ship might have crashed on Earth so long ago explains many things."

"So that's your dating system? Modified Julian day numbers?"

"Yes. They apply universally throughout the galaxy."

"Just how can you calculate an MJDN that fast?" Vincent asked. "Or did you know the date already?"

"Since regular Julian day numbers begin at noon on 1 January 4713 BCE Julian, and modified Julian day numbers are offset from these by the number 2400000.5, they're easy to calculate."

Vincent shook his head. "For you, maybe," he said. "*I* could not. Do you have auxiliary processing systems and arithmetic logic units to help you?"

"I have," said Matthew. "Plus the *Encyclopedia Galactica*, in chip form. Which includes a full set of the Seven Constants of the Universe."

"Seven Constants?"

"The basis for the seven basic measured quantities— time, displacement, mass…"

"I get it," said Vincent. "But we digress. Now that story is 470 years old, and we still don't know what really crashed in that farmer's field. But some crude pictures made it onto the Global Internet of what purported to be that ship's crew. Now you tell us that ET civilization is real, and has been known for … How long?"

"Three hundred eighty-five years. But you say you have pictures? May I see them?"

For answer, the S-2 pushed his meal aside, then brought a leather case with mechanical snaps and a lock holding it shut onto the table. Taking a key he had strapped to his wrist, he opened the case. From it, he extracted a single sheet of paper and handed it to Matthew.

He unfolded and examined it carefully. It was a crude drawing, almost like a child's drawing, of an Elfin two-person space coracle, which Matthew told them about.

"And just what *is* a 'space coracle'?"

"A small vessel, typically with a crew of two, or at the most, three," said Matthew. "The Elves use them for reconnaissance and also to aid in large ship repair. This design is typical of the class."

"Then the rumors are true," said the other officer, dropping his voice low. "And these?" He pulled out two more sheets of paper and handed them over.

The heads of the subjects of these drawings were a little on the bulbous side. But the ear points and the slender physiques left no room for doubt. "These," he said, "are Elves."

"Wait until Naval Intelligence hears about this," said the S-2, almost whispering.

"Just a minute," said Lieutenant Robinson. "Did you say Tau Ceti e? But that's one of the permanent United Systems Security Council member systems, isn't it?"

The Major cleared his throat. "Do I take it," he said, "that the United *Systems* copied the charter of the United *Nations?*"

"Yes, sir," said Matthew. "They certainly did."

The Major looked at Matthew—hard. "I think you'd better tell us more," he said. "All of it."

Matthew first explained about the United Systems. "And to repeat, yes, the Elves are the intelligent race of the Tau Ceti system. As I said before, when Juan de Cuellar first demonstrated faster-than-light travel, he attracted Elfin attention. As a result, the Elves made contact and offered the United Nations their printer technology and other forms of technological assistance. This came at a critical moment for the United Nations, which was on the verge of economic collapse at the time."

"How convenient," said Captain Vincent.

"Yes, I suppose it was. This is the version of history every UN schoolchild learns. But I, myself, have long suspected a thing I never shared with any Elf. Namely: the Elves reconnoitered Earth long before the De Cuellar demonstration mission. They were waiting for our ancestors to show themselves worthy of contact. Or, perhaps for another kind of opportunity."

"With that," said the Captain, now becoming increasingly agitated, "I would certainly agree. We have all the reports, going clear back to Spencer's Sighting in July 1864."

"I'm not familiar," said Matthew. "Could you enlighten me?"

"In July 1864," said the S-2, "First Lieutenant Elbridge Gerry Spencer, United States Army, reported finding a crashed spacecraft very like this coracle you describe. That happened in the northern reaches of the State of New York. He pulled a single crewmember from it; one apparently injured so badly he needed to have both arms taken off below the elbow. His superiors murdered Lieutenant Spencer to cover up the story.

"And I could point to other stories, including Colonel Shaw, who fought off two of these 'Elves' who tried to abduct him and his companion in Stockton, California. I could talk about the Caerphilly Incident of 1909, when a larger ship landed near Caerphilly, Wales, and its crew actually *spoke to one another* before witnesses."

"Then my suspicions," said Matthew a second after the Captain had finished speaking, "were correct. The Elves *did* surveil the Earth before the De Cuellar demonstration."

"But why?" asked the Major. "Why not just come right out and talk to us?"

"I'll tell you why! Sir," said the Captain, now getting angrier with every word he spoke. "They were *really* waiting for us to become a threat to them. And when we did, they made an oh-so-subtle change in our history."

"Now wait a minute, Ian," said the Major. "I heard that theory at New Quantico. God knows we all heard it. But you also know no one ever presented proof. Are you now seriously suggesting that these—Elves, as Commander Morrow calls them—intervened in the Re-Wilding War?"

"How else do you explain it, Joe? We had those UNCLIFOR pukes beaten and on the run. Then all of a sudden, lightning, and even meteors, began to strike— more specifically, striking *us*, preferentially. To strike military units and our whole industrial base, *including* the Vincent Automotive Factories in California, Nevada, New York, and Texas. *Not to mention that massive meteor shower that took out the Hoover Dam!* Meteors struck that dead on target, too accurately to be totally natural. Dad burn it; you *know* that, Major! And you also know—when you *really, really think* about it—that the UN could never have developed techniques to weaponize lightning and meteors. No—these Elves did that to us."

"Your intelligence officer is correct, Major Campbell," said Matthew. It was hard to say, with his entire world seeming to collapse on top of him. "I had never thought of that before. But now, the gaps in my education make sense. The Elves are the oldest partners of humanity in the United Systems. They were the first to join the United Nations in creating it. And they have always presented every appearance of being ethically and technologically ages ahead of humanity.

"But now," said Matthew, taking a pause, "I have reason to believe that is not the case. Not, that is, regarding their ethics."

When Vincent turned to look at him again, his face conveyed a fresh respect. Major Campbell simply said, "Do you want to tell us more?"

"I must, whether I desire it or not," said Matthew. "First, I am not native to this world. After I was born, I lived the first eleven years of my life on the planet Proxima Centauri b, which I called Berks World.

"But that isn't important. What *is* important is the incompleteness, and inaccuracy, of my education." *Inaccuracy? Lies.* "Captain Vincent, the evidence you have presented has been a profound revelation to me. Let me begin with an observation about the country you serve. In point of fact, I know only this much about the United

States of America, other than its defeat in the Great Climate War, which you call the Re-Wilding War. Legends, Captain. Legends of a racist and colonialistic power that bade fair to subjugate the entire world—and to stifle it with an excess of carbon dioxide from manufacturing and transport and other operations, using the so-called fossil fuels of petroleum, its derivatives, and buried methane."

"Lies," said Vincent. "Especially the racist and colonialistic part."

"Well," said Major Campbell. "that *was* part of American history once."

"But by the time of The Re-Wilding War, that was over and done with! Except the UN wouldn't have wanted to admit that. The United States government should never have agreed to establish it."

"And here," said Matthew, breaking in, "you have helped me identify a prime example of indoctrination and propaganda. Nowhere does any officially approved textbook even mention that the United States of America established the United Nations."

"Somehow," said Campbell, "I don't think it would surprise Naval Intelligence. Nor the Fleet Admiral. The President, though—I often wonder about him."

"So you *do* have a navy, in addition to a Marine Corps?"

"Yes," said Campbell. "We have a Navy—though I'll admit, not much of one. Two ships of the era, decades ahead of their time, are the real muscle. But we also have five genuine antiques. Wind-powered—and wooden. One frigate and four replicas of the first colony wagons to land on our shores. They vanished during the Re-Wilding War, then came back with the two modern ships—two hundred years later. We keep them for a simple reason: if it can move or fight, it's an asset, and considering what else our country lost, we can't afford to discount any assets, no matter how antique."

"I noticed the tall tower in this camp," said Matthew. "I had thought it only a watchtower. Is it also a signal tower?"

"It is. Above ground, we communicate by flag semaphore. We have ever since we first started to reconnoiter the surface."

"Did you stay underground because you knew you have enemies in space?"

"Yes, though we didn't know exactly who they are," said Campbell. "We always knew that the UN defeated us when lightning and meteors took their toll. Many of us have long suspected these were weaponized, as Captain Vincent said a moment ago. So we always knew to stay out of sight from space."

"And how extensive is your above-ground communication?"

"We can reach everywhere in the Re-Wilded lands. It's how we communicate with our ships, and the adits—oh, excuse me; I ought to explain that. Here and there, we've built above-ground entrances. Each one opens into a cave and has several elevator shafts connecting it to our undergrounds. *Deep* underground."

"Excuse me, Major—'elevator?'" Matthew asked. Then the answer came to him. "Ah, yes. We call such a thing a 'lift.' Or in the Navy, a 'hoist.'"

"Yes, I can see how that definition would work. And the word 'adit' is the same word for the entrance to a drift mine. Many of our adits are actual entrances to abandoned drift-ways. That's how our society began—we fled into our mines and literally dug down from there.

"As I said, we use flag semaphore to communicate above ground and with a ship close to shore. For really urgent messages, we light periodically spaced bonfires or send an autonomous vehicle loaded with dispatches. Same methods the Continental Army used, but slightly updated."

"The Continental Army?"

Major Campbell took a deep breath. "Yes," he finally said, "the Continental Army. The very first army of what became the United States. An army that fought its first battles more than six hundred forty years ago."

"Major, I must confess my total ignorance of this."

"Then prepare yourself for an education, Commander."

* * *

About an hour later, Matthew was marveling—he had no other word for it. Campbell, Vincent, and Robinson didn't have the kind of instant library access to which Matthew was long accustomed. But they had memories that more than made up for that lack. "And I promise you," Major Campbell had said, "that somehow, I will get you to the Capitol complex in Cumberland Caverns and get you a chit to visit the New Library of Congress. I think you'll find that very valuable."

"I look forward to it," said Matthew.

The United States of America had an incredibly rich history. It had begun in the aftermath of a war that had drained the treasury of its mother country, the United Kingdom of Great Britain and Ireland. The Townshend Acts—the Tea Act—the Boston Massacre—the Boston Tea Party—all set the stage for the First and Second Continental Congresses and the Declaration of Independence. War, in fact, broke out over a year earlier; the Declaration cited this. War continued for seven years—and Matthew definitely looked forward to studying George Washington's campaigns and battles.

Eleven years after the Declaration came the Constitution of the United States. A document that remained in force and effect for 236 years. It had been a treasured document at one time, one that respected the right of ordinary citizens and lawful residents to arm themselves! To arm themselves at least as well as, if not better than, an infantry, if not necessarily artillery. And it protected true property—things one *owned*—by saying what the government took, it must buy at a just price.

For more than a century, the United States of America stayed out of the affairs of continental Europe, as violent as they had been. They had to—for a "War Between the States" convulsed this federation of polities. *That* formed the basis for the accusations of racism—and human slavery—that attached to the Americans.

And the Elves started surveilling these United States during that War. That, Matthew deduced from the stories Captain Vincent had already told and other stories that he revealed in addition. "We have film footage on file of sightings of what the US Navy called 'unidentified flying objects,' since Roswell," Vincent explained. "Ordinary civilians saw those objects, too. But the Navy and Air Force covered it up. They even encouraged people to believe they had seen stray prototype test aircraft."

Then a change came. It came gradually at first, beginning with a war called the "Spanish-American War." For the first time in its history, the United States acquired non-adjacent territory through direct armed conquest in a war that might not even have been totally defensive.

With the end of that war came another bad habit: laying and collecting permanent taxes to repay war debt and replenish a depleted war chest. And beginning in 1913 came another change that Ian Vincent blamed for everything that followed: the creation of something called the "Federal Reserve System," that would issue *bills of debt* in lieu of precious-metal coin and bullion.

Five years later, America went to war with European powers, this time in Europe itself. It was now America's turn to suffer the same economic stress that once had plagued the United Kingdom. America had no colonies to lose but did lose her economy—not immediately, but eleven years later. Twelve years after *that*, America went to war again—in *two distinct theaters at once!*

This Second World War had seen the establishment of the United Nations. Alger Hiss—the Dumbarton Oaks

Conference—names Matthew had heard, but in a totally false context, he now placed in their proper context.

"And about three years after the founding of the UN," Matthew observed, "came the Roswell Incident. What sort of development were your armed forces attempting at the time?"

"Faster-than-sound flight, for one thing," said Joe Campbell. "The first demonstration of that took place in that very year. The Roswell crash happened earlier, though."

"That would have made no difference to the Elves," said Matthew. "They would have redoubled their effort to surveil the Earth after a war of that magnitude, especially using atomic weapons." Matthew reviewed for his hosts the rest of the history of the twentieth century and the early twenty-first. As he expected, these Americans had versions of events different from Matthew's old lessons.

In 2008, so Captain Vincent told him, came the election of a candidate for president who was "not even a natural-born citizen," who ran on a platform quite similar to that of the Five Ladies. Within a year of his assuming office, the reaction set in. The year 2016 saw the election of a president determined to reverse the changes his predecessor had made. The last year of his first term was stormy, with a pandemic, "very likely planned, and in any event far less dangerous than supposed," and an outbreak of civil unrest in major cities.

"Excuse me, Captain," said Matthew at this point. "Pandemic? Would that be the novel coronavirus?"

"Then you know."

"Not much, beyond legend—another legend with which to frighten small children."

"Well, it was da … that is, frightening enough," said Vincent. "I might as well tell you what our ancestors figured out after all the wars were over. We had a sort of … well, he wasn't exactly the surgeon general of the United States, but he somehow got an authority superior to his. His name was Ottavio Fausto, and he directed the civilian infectious disease institute. For years he directed policy on the novel coronavirus until facts came out that he could no longer deny. Namely: that he *created* it by *weaponizing* one of many viruses that cause coryza."

"The 'common cold?'"

"You got it. He then gave his prototype, and his notes, to the Wuhan Institute of Virology in Wuhan, People's Republic of China. An Institute which, for my money, ought to have been named *People's Liberation Army Biological Warfare Corps, Viral Division*. It was in Wuhan that the disease broke out—broke out, nothing. *Was deployed,* I say, though that's not official. People suddenly were falling ill with a new disease they called 'Coronavirus: Disease of 2019,' or 'COVID-Nineteen,' or just plain 'COVID.' And it came out just in time to muck things up in American Presidential politics."

"How so?"

Vincent began to tick off points on his fingers. "The President was unable to convene the massive crowd-drawing rallies to which he alone could draw people in sufficient numbers. Then, election officials all over the country let people vote *by mail* and drop their ballots off in drop boxes. *Unattended* drop boxes. It turned the election into a total joke, especially since most precinct-level election officers were members of the President's opposition party anyway. Add to it that the ballots were fed to scanner-tabulators, *which turned out to be network-connective, and that should never have been allowed.* And, at least one sympathetic researcher demonstrated—and left records of his research—that all those scanner-tabulators received instructions from a foreign country."

"The People's Republic of China again?"

"The same. And the result? The President's opponents literally cheated him of a second term and—if you can believe this—elected in his stead an old, befuddled politician as president and a maniacal 'intersectional feminist' as vice president.

"Well, after that joke of an election, the State of Texas began considering a referendum on secession. That referendum didn't pass in the first year—and a lot of other things happened in that year," Vincent said. "Among them: the introduction of what the government said were immunizations against novel coronavirus. Only they weren't immunizations at all. Not only were those who took them more likely to get the disease itself, but also—and this was something that took a long time to sink in—those preparations were fatal about a third of the time. Not necessarily immediately—though some people died within forty-eight hours—but definitely over a ten-year period."

"Once again, I confess, I knew none of these details," said Matthew, not knowing what else to say.

"I knew them," said Ayelet grimly. "It also affected my people. The State of Israel was affected to the very degree you mentioned. One-third fatalities within ten years, one-third severe debilitation and sterility, and one-third no apparent effect."

"Same in our country," said Vincent. "Some of us suspected that the preparations came out in designated lots—one-third deliberate killers, one-third debilitators, and one-third saline placebos. But we never found out. In the wars that followed, the companies that made the preparations were all on the opposite side. Not ours. But I digress.

"Over time, people started to rebel against the quarantine and 'forced-immunization' regime. And against other things besides. Beginning late in 2021, people— including my own ancestor—started moving out of the States that went along with these tyrannies and into States that refused. It got so that the great one-way truck rental companies were sending deadhead caravans back to States like California and Oregon, from States like Texas and Florida, just to service people who wanted to move out. Only, this happened after the Census of 2020. So the tyrannical States ended up with a representation in the House of Representatives they didn't really deserve, and no one was willing to run another Census.

"And here's the important part: in 2022, a real warrior—a former Army officer whose willingness to stand by his men actually led to their mustering him out of the Army—got elected Governor of Texas. The next year, of course, he took over with a new legislature. They took up that independence referendum, and this time, it passed. And when it did, civil war inevitably broke out. That war ended with those Five Ladies of yours—well, four of them, anyway—on one side, and patriotic Americans, now calling themselves Texans, on the other."

"And for that reason," said Matthew, "there was never any conquest of one side by the other. Just a split, like what was left after 1783."

"Correct. Well, those Five—Termagants—created the North American Charter. This charter respected none of the rights of the original Constitution and, instead, mirrored the United Nations Universal Declaration of Human Rights. No, not rights. More like allowances. Ten States ratified the new charter, to begin with. California, Hawaii, Oregon, Washington, Minnesota, Michigan, New York, New Jersey, Connecticut, and Massachusetts. They called themselves the North American Polity."

"Today, they call themselves Nuevo Aztlán—the New Aztec Polity," said Matthew. "And what happened to Texas and its allies?"

"Oh, well, the Greater Republic of Texas renamed itself 'The United States of America,' Why not? Those other people didn't want the name, so we took it back. And the same politics that split the old United States split Canada in two. Two of their provinces, Alberta and Saskatchewan, petitioned to join us.

"But we totally—totally—underestimated those Nuevo Aztlán people. You want to know the real reason they lost? Because they took the 'Covid Jabs' and we didn't. Those who stayed behind in the States that ratified the North American Charter—well, a third of them died, as I told you, and another third had their brains wiped out from thousands of 'micro-strokes' from that infernal Jab. So Nuevo Aztlán was a country with a much smaller population, especially considering the soldiers and sailors they lost trying to keep us from seceding. Not only smaller, but half the population they had left to them were literally moronic. They had to rebuild their army, and fast. So what do you think they did?"

"Recruited from the other member states of the United Nations."

"Yes! How did you know?"

"The United Systems formed their Navy and Marines in much the same way."

"Yes, well, when Nuevo Aztlán did that, they gave themselves over to the United Nations and turned it into a real governing body, with tax authority, world police—and army. Including the United Nations Climate Force." Vincent paused, sighed. "It's almost as if they sold their souls to the devil just to spite us. And spite us they did. The Re-Wilding War—excuse me, the Great Climate War—broke out shortly thereafter."

That war ended with the United States totally forgotten by civilized … Here, Matthew caught himself. The United States still existed and was just as civilized, if not more. But—incredible as Matthew still found it—it literally existed underground. The adits with their lift shafts, chiefly in mountains or high hills, were the only evidence of their society above ground. And the Americans had cleverly hidden every one.

And *now,* Matthew understood Captain Vincent's attitude. For his ancestor, Leon Vincent, almost singlehandedly reinvented electric vehicles and space transport. He even set up an operation for digging vast tunnels for long-distance ground transport. But the ungrateful Nuevo Aztlán arrested him and prepared to try him—for *treason.* Because, not only did he invent the forerunner of the AFVs and tanks Matthew had seen, but he also was the prime "defense contractor" of the Republic of Texas during the Second War Between the States, also known as the Texit War.

"Another thing I don't understand," said Matthew. "How did Leon Vincent get into a position where the Nuevo Aztlán police could arrest him?"

"Well, he still had factory installations in California and New York, as well as in Nevada and Texas. He was visiting his factory in Buffalo when they nabbed him. Anyway, the…" (here Captain Vincent uttered a parentage slur) … told my ancestor they would make him Minister of Industry if he would just issue a command for all his vehicles to override their drivers' inputs and report to UNCLIFOR assembly points," Captain Vincent said. "But he fooled them. He actually sent a firewall, the first he'd ever installed. It made all his vehicles impervious to any such command. When his captors found out what he'd done, they threw him down the hole at Sing Sing, the New York State prison in Ossining. They were going to ship him out to Dartmoor in England. But we didn't let that happen."

He went on to explain that General Terence Crawford, leading the Unauthorized Virginia Militia, sent a team to rescue Leon Vincent. They used armored cavalry units like this one—with Leon Vincent's new electric trucks, modified with inboard, counter-rotating electric motors— a design element the United States Marines had seemingly retained. And while this team crossed the Hudson River, breached Sing Sing, got Leon Vincent out, and recrossed the river, the regular Army invaded rural New York. "Trying to secure Buffalo, actually," said Vincent. "That factory installation was very valuable."

But then came the meteor strikes, which allowed UNCLIFOR to prevail. Those Americans who did not fall prisoner to UNCLIFOR, or dead in combat, fled into various drift mines. Vincent then used his low-earth-orbital communications network, while it still remained, to order some of his tunneling teams to drive their tunnels to connect all those mines. Thereafter, he devoted all his energies to expanding his transcontinental tunnels into a network of underground cities. *And he succeeded.* Or at least his sons, grandsons, and great-grandsons did.

"And a good thing, too," Steve Robinson said. "We always thought cameras were constantly looking down on us from space. Now you confirm this. It's a wonder no one has seen us."

"*I* saw what was left of that bridge," said Matthew. "That's why…"

Captain Vincent broke in, "Yes, you said you'd been in a medically induced coma. So they know how dangerous you are to them—in more ways than one. Right?"

"Yes," said Matthew. "So I have only two alternatives. Fight or die."

"I suspected most of this," Andrea added. "Except for learning that the destruction of the dam at the base of NRD-01-CO-Mead was a deliberate act. You know that as Lake Mead—or at least its bed, which is all that's left of that lake, except for a totally unfettered Colorado River.

"Still, I never accepted the notion that civilization began with our walling ourselves off from ninety percent or more of the land areas of all continents."

"And, being Jewish," said Ayelet, "I am a student of even more ancient history—and wider-ranging history. History in which the United States played its part, too."

"The State of Israel," said Major Campbell. "I repeat: they'll want to talk to you. But first things first. Do I correctly assume that, in your society, the authorities hold all the weapons?"

"Correct," said Matthew, "No one but a law enforcement officer, a member of the Navy or Marines or SSF, a VIP, or that person's bodyguard, *ever* carries a weapon. The printing of weapons is strictly forbidden, and all printer codes interdict any such orders."

"Does that include common eating utensils?" said the Major. "Those could become pretty nasty weapons."

"Not the ones the printers turn out. They're made of plastic, or sometimes wood. Never metal."

Major Campbell sighed. "Doesn't anybody cook his own meals in your society?"

"You can run a restaurant, purely for recreation," said Andrea. "But you need a special license for that. The licensure requirements are even stricter if you're running an Oriental restaurant, with all the sharp knives they use. Anyone who handles those must re-up every year. And one red flag, and you're done. If they don't send you to Botany Bay."

Robinson suddenly fell absolutely silent.

"Lieutenant?" asked Matthew. "Do you actually know that name?"

When the Lieutenant spoke, he was more sober than ever. "Botany Bay," he said, "is where, according to rumor, the old UNCLIFOR units used to send people they arrested out of our territory. We never learned where that was…"

"That, I can tell you," said Matthew. "The UN evacuated the Commonwealth of Australia to form the Rigil Kentaurus and Toliman colonies. They then turned that entire continent into a complex of rehabilitation centers—meaning prisons—and mental health facilities for the criminally insane. And reformatories. 'Botany Bay' was the original name of what is now the New South Wales District. Today it applies to the entire continent."

"You mean it still exists?" asked Vincent.

"Yes. It is *the* place of confinement for all adult, juvenile, and criminally insane offenders."

"And probably descendants of our people," said Campbell.

"Correct," said Matthew. "The American Reservation covers the entire western third."

"Naval Intelligence will definitely want to talk to you about that. Now back to UNCLIFOR. They appeared shortly after Ratification. The Steele Corps deployed here—under the command of Field Marshal Christopher, First Earl Steele of Brenchley. I'd guess they wanted to avoid having troops go native. Lord Steele commanded the Great Re-Wilding. His troops literally repossessed all the motor vehicles our ancestors used to own and drive, and even the heavy-duty trucks. After that, they swept through and tore down every village, town, and city of less than a million people…"

"And, I assume, every single-family residence," said Matthew.

"Well, of course," said Vincent. "I don't suppose your people have single-family residences?"

"In the Civilized Footprint, all cities have a population of a million or more, except for academic, scientific, and government centers. And people live in high-rise dormitory complexes, never single-family residences—except for the First Secretarial and other high commissioners' and other palaces."

"Yeah, that fits," said the S-2. "But two hundred years ago, they just pulled out, and then up went the force fields. We never saw UNCLIFOR units again or that uniform they wore. Not a sight of them in all this time, and we still don't know why."

"Because," said Matthew. "you obviously withdrew so deeply into, and *under*, Protected Wild Space that they literally couldn't find you. Then they decided that you couldn't survive and wouldn't be worth the effort to hunt down. The last Commandant of UNCLIFOR, Field Marshal Bernardo Ordoñez-Pizzaro, insisted you still existed but had no proof. So the Security Council disbanded his force. They didn't found the Special Security Forces until far more recently—I would estimate fifteen years ago, but I might be wrong about that.

"Still, I don't quite understand why they never detected your Navy. They would never have disbanded the United Nations Navy if they had."

"Well, perhaps our wooden ships don't rate any threat assessment," said Vincent. "And the two modern vessels each have the radar signature of a fishing boat and even less of a signature from orbit."

"But what about their power plants?" asked Matthew. "Aren't they nuclear?"

Vincent laughed and swore. "…no," he said. "Originally, they ran on natural gas, a fossil fuel. But when they finally rejoined us, generations of machinists' mates had somehow converted the engines to burn hydrogen. They also built fuel cells, photovoltaic panels, and electrolyzers. It was a lot simpler than trying to drill for natural gas in the wild. And it worked—so we left those systems in place."

"All this suggests," said Matthew, "that they still don't know you're here."

"But that doesn't make sense," said Robinson. "What about this installation we're here to recon? What's it there for, if not for recon?"

"We don't know," said Matthew. "And that makes it priority one that I scout it, also. That is the reason for my confinement; I know that now."

"But if you confirm it," said Robinson, "what are you going to do with the information?"

"I won't try to reinstate myself with the UN, certainly," said Matthew. "None of us will. Is that correct?" He scanned the faces of Ayelet and Andrea. They nodded, Ayelet more emphatically.

"Then what?"

"We will use it as a recruiting tool," said Ayelet. "We don't have to return to the Civilized Footprint; we can hack into the discussion networks from here, with Matthew's help. Right, Barry?"

"Right."

"And I will use it to contact my fellow Jews, to rouse them to action."

"I will use this information to re-form the Irish Republican Army," said Andrea.

"Does your friend, Chief Sutton, have contacts of his own?" asked Vincent.

"I'm sure he does," said Ayelet.

"Wow," said Vincent. "We seem to have quite a gathering of revolutionaries, don't we? And you, Commander—what do you get out of this?"

"My own survival. I am at war with the United Nations and United Systems. They started that war when they confined me. After this, the war can only escalate. So I will escalate it, too. Revolution is the only way."

"Commander Morrow," said the Major, "you wanted a treaty of alliance. You've got it. As senior officer present, I am authorized to grant it. When Captain Vincent finishes drafting the complete report of everything we've heard, it *and* the draft treaty will be on their way to Cumberland where the United States Senate will surely take that treaty up."

"If I may suggest," said Matthew, "when your Fire Team took us into custody, my companions were about to share with me some history of other happenings throughout the galaxy. The Senate, and your intelligence agencies, might wish to take all this into account. We can have that discussion now, and I have no objection to having you, Captain Vincent, and Lieutenant Robinson attend."

"Let's do it, then," said the Major. "But first, Steve, how about having this table cleared?"

Chapter 5

The KP team had cleared the table, and now they would have complete privacy. Matthew didn't doubt that. Better still, Barry had returned with the armored flying vehicle, which now rested in the middle of the camp.

"I had a spot of bother repairing it at first," Barry said. "I needed a multimeter, so our hosts lent me one. But at first, I thought the batteries were weak on that AFV. That's what the multimeter seemed to say. Which was crazy—the SSF would *never* attack in a vehicle that wasn't up to full fighting trim."

"Let me guess," said Captain Vincent drily. "You're still used to your SI units—and the volt, in those units, is considerably weaker than the volt we use."

"That's what Corporal Jameson set me straight on," said Barry. "What's more, the unit of current was named differently—something called a *franklin*. But how?"

"Besides breaking away from the SI units of time, length, mass, and temperature," Vincent replied, "we *also* broke away from the SI unit of electric current. And amount-of-substance and luminous intensity, but you wouldn't have found those relevant. What's relevant is that our society made a *complete* break from any system the UN would use.

"But enough of that. Suppose you all tell us everything about the history of the Earth, beginning, let's say, on MJDN 60863," Captain Vincent said. "That was the date of the New Charter. On our side, everything went to pieces. Now I want to hear about your side."

The telling took another hour. It began with the decision of the truncated United States Armed Forces (that is, the part that followed the New Charter) to recruit from all member States of the United Nations. It continued with the inauguration of the United Nations as a true government, which eventually moved its headquarters from New York City to London. Ayelet told the story of the Second Diaspora, a thing new even to Matthew. Andrea continued with the De Cuellar demonstration and the meeting with the Elves, who had introduced printers and other technologies.

"Your total gravity manipulation is amazing," said Ian Vincent. "But after all, that space coracle that crashed near Roswell must have had that."

But when did the United Nations Climate Force withdraw at last from Protected Wild Space and disband? None of them knew for sure. Captain Vincent's estimate for the withdrawal date was the best guess any of them could come up with.

The American officers listened raptly as Matthew narrated in detail the history he had witnessed. Not about his early life—he still couldn't remember anything about that—but about his training and his experience—in three separate ships named *Bonaventure*, specifically, the fifth, sixth, and seventh ships that bore that name. He also revealed as much as he could—with a disclaimer about its trustworthiness—about the history of the United Systems before his birth and "rebirth." Captain Vincent shook his head. "And to think," he said, "that we missed it all—hidden underground as we are."

At last, Matthew asked Ayelet, Andrea, and Barry to bring him up to date on galactic events following his confinement. He learned two salient things. First, the SSF began as a "special intelligence section" during the Metamorphic War. Second, the Nine-o'clock Quadrant, where the United Systems had settled after that war, abruptly ceased communications two years ago.

"My God!" cried Captain Vincent. "Your United Systems just fought the French-Indian War all over again! And after that—why, it's amazing how patterns of history repeat themselves. Two societies, one debt-ridden, and one—the colonies of the first—free and clear. And one tries to tax the other…"

"That's right!" said Barry. "The United Systems *did* try to lay some taxes on Terra Nova and New Midgard and several other worlds!"

"And they protested," said Vincent. "And now they're fighting for their independence, just as we did. Joe, we *must* get this before the Senate—and the House! We should be part of this, even by being a thorn in the UN's side."

"We will," said Major Campbell. "That much, I promise you. A chance to retake our territory—above ground and below—and also help another society sharing our ideals. I know those politicos have their differences, but when they hear about this, they'll put them all aside."

"Begging your pardon, Major," said Matthew, "but, can we really assume that? From the history you gave me, politicians, and their electorates, can be notoriously fickle."

"Oh, we've taken another step to prevent *that*," said the Major. "During the Re-Wilding War, absolutely everyone was under arms, part of regular forces or irregular militia. So when we first held our own elections, everyone was a veteran and even had combat experience. So we put a new rule into our Constitution that one would need to serve in some capacity, other than law enforcement, that involved laying his life on the line in order to vote. We took that lesson from a little incident that happened a year after the Second World War, in a little town in Tennessee called Athens. Have no fear. The kind of fickle behavior you describe, can't happen anymore. We make sure those who vote understand that voting is serious business."

"Interesting," said Matthew. "For what services other than military might a resident of your society win a vote?"

"Anything that enhances the health of our civilization," said the Major. "The sandhogs who constantly dig and drill to expand our habitation, the hunter-foragers that go out and get real fruits, vegetables, and livestock, that sort of person. Early in our history, we granted the franchise to the obstetrician-gynecologist and the urologist who perfected a way to reverse surgical sterilization, to the first practitioners who learned their techniques, and to their first patients."

"Yes, I heard about the forced sterilizations," said Matthew.

Just then, a familiar face burst in, and his demeanor showed he was angry. "Lieutenant," he said breathlessly, "you will simply not believe what just came in."

"Well," said the Major, "please share. That is, unless Lieutenant Robinson is getting eyes only messages."

"Oh, no, sir," said Corporal Jameson. "This is for the Major and the Captain, too."

"Save the third-person talk, Corporal. Let's hear it."

"Sir, we're ordered to withdraw!"

"Withdraw!" exclaimed all three officers in chorus.

"Sir … if the Major pleases … I just don't know what to make of it, so…" And he handed the Major a stiff wooden pad. This pad held a piece of flimsy paper that apparently held the message.

Major Campbell scanned it. Then he said, "Corporal Jameson is correct. I haven't the vaguest notion of what is happening in the United States Congress. But we have rather sudden orders to disengage and withdraw from the surface at once. And they give *no* explanation. Corporal, you're sure this is a complete transcript?"

"Yes, sir, it is."

The Major cursed. And then the Captain cursed even more loudly and longer.

"Commander Morrow," the Major asked, "what were you saying about fickle electorates?"

"Again, Major Campbell," said Matthew, "I rely on your own history."

"Fear," said the Major. "That's all this is."

Was it? Suddenly, Matthew wasn't so sure. His extra analytical chips kicked in—wouldn't Captain Vincent love to know about *those*. So good were they, that he was the one officer who could beat the ship's mainframe at chess aboard *Bonaventure VI*. Now he used them to process that withdrawal order. And it took him no more than a millisecond to realize that fear was *not* the driver. In fact, that order changed everything these officers thought they knew, and everything *he* thought *he* knew. About the SSF, the installation they had seen, and even his own construction. If he were right…!

Aloud he said, "Major, I think something else is at work."

"What could that be?"

Matthew started to lay it out slowly. "Consider, this" he began. "The SSF sent a squad to apprehend me. We destroyed it but, it was with your help, and you took a casualty. Maybe I didn't disable their craft soon enough. Suppose they sent a warning to that installation we're talking about?"

"But you just said your authorities don't know about us!"

"I had thought they didn't. It would seem, with some certainty, that I was gravely mistaken."

"You mean they've known about us for … How long?"

"A few decades, perhaps," said Matthew. "For longer than I have been alive, certainly."

"Why longer than you've been alive?"

"Because that's why they built me," said Matthew. "To attack you. At a time when at least a company-sized infantry strike force, consisting of officers and soldiers in total-body prostheses like mine, could invade your adits and root you out without having to perform orbital bombardment."

"But how could that matter to our own authorities, unless…" Major Campbell trailed off.

"My God," said Vincent, very slowly. *God?* An odd concept—but one Vincent clearly took seriously. Major Campbell had mentioned it, too.

"You're not suggesting … treason, are you?" Vincent turned pale as he asked that.

"Yes," said Matthew.

For half a minute, everyone fell silent. Then Major Campbell said, "All right. On my own authority as squadron commander, I am setting those orders aside. Now we must act. Suggestions?"

"I have three," said Matthew. "First, make *some* move at least to *appear* to comply with the withdrawal order. Except that you withdraw to strategic places. If treason really is operative here, your forces should move into position to combat it."

"Good catch, Commander," said the Major. He leaned toward his S-2, saying, "Ian, I'll need the Recon Platoon to flag a dispatch to Captain Jellicoe with A Troop. Have him send B, C, and D Troops back to their home adits—but keep A Troop topside and split it three ways. Send one platoon each to Harper's Ferry, Millville, and Charles Town. They're to camp over those adits and stand by for further orders."

Those orders, Matthew decided, made sense. This Captain Jellicoe would likely be the senior troop commander—an ideal choice for a staff-level operations chief. The place names were not familiar to Matthew, but that could wait.

"Steve?" Vincent asked the platoon leader.

"Yes, sir!" said Lieutenant Robinson, looking up from a tablet device.

"You mentioned three suggestions," said Campbell to Matthew. "What are the other two?"

"Second, that you have this platoon remain where it is. I may need it."

"You got it," said Vincent.

"Third?" asked the Major.

"That I scout that installation," said Matthew.

"*Alone?*" asked Vincent.

"Yes."

"Are you crazy?"

"No, Captain Vincent. I told you before, I must fight or die. Furthermore, that installation is the key."

"Right," said Robinson. "With your permission, Major?"

"You've got it."

"Commander," said the platoon leader, "I can outfit you any time—that is, if you don't mind using a dead soldier's kit."

"I suggest," said Matthew solemnly, "that Corporal Swigert would have wanted it that way."

"First," said Vincent, "send that dispatch to Captain Jellicoe. Then attend to the Commander here. If you need the Major or me, we'll be at Squadron Headquarters."

Chapter 6

It felt good to run. It felt good to move under one's own power and actually *get somewhere*. It felt good to be alive, awake, and *free*. *This is how freedom feels,* Matthew thought as he made his way alone. Easily he covered the ground in long, loping strides that no organic would have dared take in this rough country. Deftly, he stepped around rocks and fallen branches without ever breaking stride.

His tactile sensors told him of the breeze he set up with his passage. He didn't waste processing power analyzing the breeze for wind direction, temperature, humidity, or any such. He just let himself enjoy running through the woods. And, for the millionth time, he sent a silent "thank you" to his friend, Lieutenant Commander Eric Shaka, chief engineer aboard *Bonaventure VI* and *VII*.

Where was Eric now? As likely as not, languishing in some dead-end assignment. That would change. *Somehow.* Later.

Matthew still wore his stolen SSF sergeant's uniform. It had the advantage of darkness, now that night had fallen over northwestern Virginia. In a container slung over his right shoulder (it was actually a shoulder quiver for a longbowman), he carried two semaphore flags. They had once belonged to Corporal Swigert, like all his kit. Lieutenant Robinson had given him some quick lessons in flag semaphore before he started out. With that and his many interfaces, Matthew could communicate by any means.

Just now, he was following a signal the like of which he hadn't heard in a long time. He'd picked it up about five minutes earlier as he moved northwest. He found it ridiculously easy to track—because its designer had *intended* for others to track it.

What kind of amusement was this? An RFID signal. *In Protected Wild Space?* And it was moving slowly—for a game animal. Any bird flew far faster than that—some faster than 120 miles per hour, in fact. Ian Vincent had given him new values for the Seven Constants. With those, Matthew could compute American Patriotic equivalents of any distance measure—or any weight measure. This signal moved on the ground—at no faster than five miles per hour, too. About the best speed of a human being.

An escaped convict? But that was ridiculous. Earth had no rehabilitation centers nearby. This was a Nature Reclamation District in Virginia, not a detention district in Botany Bay!

Yet, the bearer of that homing signal was definitely human. And a slow-moving human, too.

Matthew had locked onto that signal and was now following it hard. An escapee, or whoever this was, would have information. The type of information the Seventh Cavalry Squadron had come here to find. Information Matthew now needed more than ever.

As Matthew tracked the signal, he saw at once where the bearer was trying to reach. Obviously, this fugitive didn't know very much about how to evade. Tracking him (her?) was easy. So Matthew used his spare processing power to listen for other signals.

He quickly realized he had strayed into an area with many transceivers—enough to build a fair-sized network, like a game preserve. But every legal memory bank told him that was flatly unlawful. Yet, he was now traversing one.

So this was why the SSF put me into a coma, he told himself. An illegal game preserve—and the SSF were running it. This, as Lieutenant Robinson would no doubt say, was "dynamite."

Now he was close enough to read the fugitive's heat signature. And what he felt next almost paralyzed him. This was worse than cybernetic block—he knew what that felt like.

It was outrage. Searing, blinding outrage.

Someone had somehow equipped a *child* with a homing device—strap-on or implant; it made no difference yet. The fact was, someone had then released that child into this semi-wild environment for the original captor, or others, to chase. Now that child needed help. And Matthew remembered: he *had* been a child, once. Wanting adult help and not getting it. Well, *this* child would not lack help!

Ever so slightly, he turned to maneuver where the child was headed, shortly before the child would get there. If he tried to follow the child directly, he (or she) might hear. And then run into worse trouble because now, Matthew detected other heat signatures. Human signatures. Adult signatures.

And one of them was getting nearer to the child.

Matthew didn't need a decision-analytical unit to tell him what to do. He turned at once to intercept the adult.

A burly man was running hard after the child, pausing now and then to look at a wrist strap-on PDD, and stood 178 centimeters tall. He didn't even see Matthew coming. Not even when Matthew tensed both his legs and launched himself into the air, using just enough force and in just the right direction …

He hit the man squarely in the left side of his chest, wrapped both arms around him, and bowled him over.

"What the Five…!" cried the man. "You're supposed to chase the kid, not me!" Then he took another look at Matthew and said, "Wait a minute. Wait a frigging minute! I never saw you before! You're not on the guest list! And what's with the gold paint job?"

Matthew said nothing; he just stared.

The man reached for that strap-on PDD on his wrist…

… And Matthew shifted his grip, and in an instant, had unstrapped the device and now held it in his hand. He ran a quick scan. It was a PDD, all right … the kind of device his Marine friends called a smartwatch. Matthew sent it a software command to shut down.

"Now," said Matthew, "start talking. What 'guest list'? What kind of hunt are you on?"

"You're frigging crazy!" cried the man. "I'm telling you nothing!"

Then he started to fill his lungs.

"HEL...!"

Matthew hit him in what Dr. Girard once called the "solar plexus"—and felt the man's spine snap from the blow. He then whirled, caught the net that was about to drop over his head, and recast it over the man who had thrown it. In less than a second, that man was cursing and thrashing, trying to get free.

"Let him go," said another voice. Matthew turned—and found himself looking into the business end of a DEW long gun. He turned, ever so casually, to face the gunman, who repeated, "I said, *let him go!*"

Matthew did not obey. He simply stood where he was, taking in what he saw. The gunman wore the uniform of the SSF, with corporal's stripes. So this was how the SSF rewarded their personnel—with guard duty at an installation like this.

"You'd better open that net on the count of three."

Matthew stared at the Corporal—an ice-cold stare.

"One."

You're going to die, Corporal. I have just sentenced you.

"Two."

Matthew checked his shield. No problem...

"Three."

The beam lanced out—then bounced off Matthew's shield and back through the Corporal's heart. The non-com dropped to the ground in a heap.

Five more beams connected with his shield. All five bounced back on their sources. So now Matthew counted one man thrashing in a net and seven men—one corporal and six privates—dead. And six long-barreled DEW guns ready to pick up.

Lightning-fast, he broke the net wrangler's neck. Then he took a deep breath. He must get back into *some* semblance of control.

He slung one DEW gun on his right shoulder, next to his flag quiver. Quickly he tied the rest in a bundle, using some clinging vines. He hoisted this bundle to his left shoulder. Then he leaped toward the last direction in which the child had been running. He picked up more than the RFID and heat signature—he had the scent, too. A boy's scent. Sixteen years old, or more nearly seventeen. He swallowed his gorge. Off he went. Nearing the boy, he bounded high in the air and landed in his path.

Remarkably, this boy did not cower from him. Instead, he gritted his teeth. "Mister," he snarled, "if you take one step toward me, you're going to get it right in the balls."

Matthew held both hands out, palms up. He hoped the boy would take that as non-threatening.

"I mean it," the boy went on. "You frigging jerks have left me nothing to lose now. I'm not taking that treatment again. Not even if I have to die."

"I know you'll find this difficult to believe," said Matthew. "But I am here to help you."

The boy uttered an obscenity, then said, "It's just a game with you. Nobody gets in here without a special pass. Not unless they're *brought* here, like me."

"Do you think I killed one hunter and seven guards, and took their weapons, just to 'have you all to myself' or some such thing? Do you really think I'd have a 'pass' if I could kill so easily?"

That gave the boy pause. It took him ten seconds to get the point. "I see what you're saying," he finally said. "It wouldn't be fair to the other hunters." Then he got angry all over again. "*Frig* that! How'm I supposed to trust you?"

"Let me prove it to you," said Matthew. Who, all the while, had been sweeping the area with his sensors. And at once, he detected the RFID chip implanted in the boy's neck. "You want to talk about *fair?*" he went on. "Fair to one another, maybe. Never to you. Those hunters cheated. They put a little DF bug into the base of your neck. Right about here," he said and put his own hand on the equivalent spot on his neck to demonstrate. The boy reached toward the spot on his neck. His eyes widened a little more, then narrowed. He had found it—but still wasn't ready to trust Matthew.

"I can take that capsule out of your body, and then they'll never find you again," Matthew went on. "But you're going to have to trust me. After that, if you want to run, you can go wherever you like."

"I want your oath on that."

"Naturally. I swear it on my own life. Will that satisfy?"

The boy considered awhile, then said, "Yeah, … I guess so. So how do we do this?"

"You just sit where you are, as I'm doing." He sat before the boy, Lotus-fashion. The boy assumed the same posture.

"Now hold perfectly still," he said, with dead calm. He reached for the spot, put both hands on it, one on each side. "You won't even feel it, though it might be a little sore afterward. Take a deep breath." The boy did so. "Now hold it…"

He applied just the right amount of pressure. The little capsule, small enough to swallow, popped out. He held it up. Blood dripped from it.

At last, Matthew felt the incredible tension bleed out of his body. He gathered a few leaves, the best he could manage, to dress the wound. He handed them to the boy. "Hold these against the spot; it's bleeding. Do you understand?"

"Sure, I do," said the boy. "I was just in my first year of Scouting when they snatched me." He got angry yet again—he obviously had a lot of anger to work off. "*Frigging* …!" he said, swearing. "My own Scoutmaster! *He* put the snatch on me. I swore every day I'd kill him." At least the boy did more than just talk. He was working to improve on that improvised bandage even as he ranted on about the disgusting thing that had happened to him. Obviously, he knew more woodcraft than most boys his age. Maybe that was one thing, if the only thing, in which he could take any pride.

Matthew, for his part, carefully placed the RFID chip inside a wild rose. If he could get himself, and this boy, away from here fast enough, a bull elk or a white-tail buck would happen along, eat the rose, and be on its way—with the RFID chip in its belly. The Seventh Cav were making their strategic retreat, so no one would kill or capture such a beast for a long, long time.

The boy looked up. "Say, Mister," he said, "we have to get away from here, and I mean *now*. I was making for the free spot…"

"Oh, is *that* what they told you?" he said, hearing the sarcasm in his voice. "They not only cheated; they lied. *I* know the blind spot. Will you trust me again?"

He nodded.

"You can't run fast enough to get out of here," said Matthew. "But I can run fast enough for both of us. Did you ever learn the one-man carry?"

"Yeah!" he said with an excited smile.

"Then climb onto my back and hold tight."

"I won't weigh you down?"

Matthew laughed—and rejoiced that he *could* laugh. Still smiling, he said, "You're a featherweight. I'll barely notice you. Now come. You said yourself—we must hurry."

The boy hesitated no longer. Maybe he didn't trust Matthew completely, but already he had made an "adult" decision. A man's decision. Without another word, he hopped on in the classic pose.

Matthew stood and took off at the longest lope he could manage—twelve miles per hour. Just let any hunter, or even any guard, try to catch him now.

He'd told "a little white lie." He didn't positively *know* the blind spot. But he could *see* it readily enough with his wireless-carrier sensors. He would explain that to the boy—later.

The boy hung on. And Matthew felt, rather than saw, how the boy must feel. Still scared—but now giddy with what must be relief.

He took the boy to the one-man camp he had prepared—again, using authentic American Marine gear. But he took a roundabout way, crossing several streams—leaping them if they were narrow enough, fording them if not. At least he, unlike the boy, wouldn't leave a scent.

He bent over enough to let the boy jump down. Then he uncovered his supply of venison and prepared another meal. Halfway through his preparations, he caught his charge looking at him longingly, even suspiciously, because he was preparing only *one* meal.

He smiled again. "This meal's for you," he said.

"Really?" the boy asked, still uncertainly.

"Yes," he said. "All yours. You see, I don't have to eat unless I have another reason to. I can get my energy in other ways." He worked even as he spoke, using his new Marine-issue knives to cut the venison steak into bite-sized pieces. After that, he served the meal to the boy—in Corporal Swigert's old mess kit.

As the boy sat down to eat, he smiled. *At last.* Halfway through his meal, he asked, "Where did you get this?"

"I killed it," said Matthew. "Just before I reconnoitered the preserve. See?" And he pointed to the quarters of the white-tailed buck he had killed, along with the trophy and the hide.

The boy looked suspicious. "That's not allowed," he said.

"A lot of things aren't allowed," said Matthew. "That doesn't make them wrong. Likewise, a lot of things *are* allowed. That doesn't make them right. And I've seen enough 'allowed' things to keep me angry for … for an ordinary lifetime."

"Like what?"

"Like what happened to you," said Matthew.

He knew he was taking a fearful chance as he said it. This boy had a lot of anger in him, ready to explode like a demolition charge. But another *Bonaventure* shipmate once almost begged Matthew to talk to her about what might be troubling *him*. On that occasion, he'd needed to talk. Badly.

Now *he* would play the counselor. For this boy, for whom *he*, Matthew, was now responsible.

"Don't worry," he said. "Just talk. I know you want to talk, even if you're afraid to."

"Who said I want to talk?" The anger was back, full force. "All right! You want to hear about it? You want to hear all about what they did to me? Not to mention hunting me like an animal?" And the boy did talk about that. Once he started, he couldn't stop. Just listening to it made Matthew involuntarily clench his metal teeth and narrow his eyes.

Then the boy said, "And don't expect me to ask for my mother, either! Or my father, for that matter! Where are they? Why didn't they get me out of that scrape?" *That* almost brought tears to Matthew's eyes. The hint of a memory—of adults he trusted who didn't help him—came back.

Finally, the boy paused, and a bit longer than merely catching his breath. In a different tone, he said, "Look, Mister. I'll take my chances with you. *You* got me out of that scrape. No one else did. And, sure, I'd like to know about all the cool stuff you can do. I mean, you're like somebody who stepped out of a twentieth-century comic book! And if you think I'll just slow you down, just say so, and I'll go my own way. But I am *never* going back home. Somebody else will put the snatch to me if I do."

"Are you sure you're not protecting them?" Matthew asked. It sounded abrupt even to him, but he had to try.

The boy looked as if Matthew had punched him in the gut. "From what?" he asked.

Recalling a passage from a textbook he'd accessed for some reason, he said, "Pedophiles often threaten the parents of their victims."

"Pedophiles—wait. I get it. Like those people who were holding me." Suddenly the boy wasn't snarling anymore. He started to look a little scared—and then a *lot* scared. "Yes!" he said. "That's exactly what they did! But … after awhile … I got so I just … didn't care."

"And *that's* what you're afraid to face," said Matthew. "Don't worry about it. Nothing that's happened to you, nothing you're feeling, can possibly be your fault.

"But you said you would 'take your chances with me.' Well, if you do, you will do exactly as I say, when I say it. Once upon a time, I was an officer in the US Navy. I've been in battle. I've commanded a ship in battle. And, since my escape, I have made a very interesting discovery." He told the boy about the Americans.

"Are you serious?"

"Absolutely. Haven't you noticed? I served you a dinner using field-issue cooking and eating kits. They didn't come out of a printer. Someone made those—the old-fashioned way."

"Wow…!" Clearly, the time for cursing had passed.

"I'll tell you all about them and take you to their camp. They'll likely teach you many things.

"In return," said Matthew, more sternly, "you are going to work, and think, twice as hard as you ever did in your life. Twice as hard, indeed, as you ever thought of working. These men are soldiers; they're at war—and war is very serious business. I also am at war. Either they or I will turn you into a warrior. You'll probably never fight like me; my body is artificial. But you'll fight well enough."

He knew he had to wait to let the boy drink *that* in. The boy grinned. "So *that's* how you could make twenty klicks per hour in the forest!" he said. "And your body *felt* like a machine. But you can't be a machine. No machine can think!"

"And that's truer than you know," said Matthew. "I am a disembodied brain using a total body prosthesis. But I am *not* a robot. A robot is a slave. I am a free man. And a rebel."

"Cool," said the boy, obviously warming to him. "But how'd you get into that body? I mean, somebody had to build it for you, and all."

Matthew explained briefly about his artificial body and Dr. Frankel.

"Wowww," breathed the boy. "But you mean you were once an ordinary human being, like me? What right had your doctor to snatch your brain like that?"

"From the records my former commanding officer found," said Matthew, "I don't think Dr. Frankel could have helped me any better by doing anything else. I must have been..." He trailed off. *What* must he have been? Paralyzed? *Dead?* It seemed incredible ...

"And just what ... *can* you do, that ordinary humans can't?"

"Many things," said Matthew. "You will learn what at least some of these things are when I must do them to achieve an objective."

"After all that effort they made," the boy asked, "why are you at war with them?"

"That war began more than fifteen years ago," said Matthew, who explained that, too.

"How'd you get out?"

"A very striking young woman literally pushed my 'on' button. You'll meet her someday. Anyway, as I said, this is war, and war is not a game. Now I will *never* ask any sexual favor of you, and I'll make sure my friends never ask that of you, either. *Never at any time.* But in anything else—what I, or one of them, says, goes. Will you accept that?"

"Yes, *sir!*" And the boy actually stood up and raised his arm in salute.

Matthew raised his own arm to return the salute. "Congratulations," he said. "You have just joined the ranks of the United States Marine Corps."

"United *States?*"

"Correct," said Matthew. "The United States of America. And from now on, I am building another fighting force, which I'll likely call the Free Earth Revolutionary Forces. Until I have any credible fighting force organized, you may call me Commander since that was close to my rank in the Navy. Or use my full name, Matthew Morrow. That might—or might not—be the name I gained at birth. But it's the name I now bear. What is your name?"

The boy took a breath—then let it out. Had he thought at first to give him a fictitious name? Then he drew breath again and stood up straighter. "Zachary Radner, sir," he said. And Matthew, reading his vital signs, knew he was giving his true name.

"Zachary," he repeated. "An ancient Hebrew name, meaning 'God remembers.' At least someone named you well. For you will remember this day."

"I hope so. Sir."

"I'm sure of it. For now, you have another title: recruit private. Your training begins now. Finish your dinner. In an hour, your real work begins."

* * *

Night fell again on NRD-01-VA-Lucketts. Zach Radner had taken easily to the physical training. He seemed more in love with what his own body could do than with anything Matthew could do, which was as it should be. And now Zach prepared to take his first night watch.

The historical databases told of mass armies that had enlisted children. They typically did so when making revolution—or in the last desperate stages before their ultimate defeat. Lines came to him from *La Marseillaise*, the national anthem of Captain De Grasse's home country of France: "We, too, shall enlist, when our elders are no longer there!" The Captain of *Bonaventure VI* and *VII* had taught Matthew that stirring fighting song shortly after his emotional breakthrough had occurred.

Matthew would wait to tell Zach about this—much later. For now, Zach was content. He craved adulthood and the power that went with it. Power to hurt his enemies as they had hurt him. Matthew would, of course, give him a bigger objective than that.

Was Zach's attitude tragic, in one so young? Well-meaning psychiatric theorists might say so. But Matthew understood what they did not: you can't give back a stolen childhood. He also knew something else was wrong with what they said, something … buried. Deep.

Matthew gave up trying to uncover the memory just out of his reach—for now. Zach was on watch, with instructions to wake him at 0200. He really did need sleep, same as any organic. His brain was organic, after all, and would suffer without it. So he settled down and composed himself for sleep.

He dreamed. This dream differed greatly from the enforced fifteen-year dream out of which Ayelet had awakened him. In fact, *that* had been no dream. He should have realized it long ago. This was his first free dream, free of the electrical stimulation to which the psychiatrists had subjected him.

He was running again, as before. But he was not running *after* someone. He was running *from* someone. Someone bent upon killing him. Someone who *could* have killed him easily, for he did not have a body of metal and plastic. His body was flesh and blood. *Vulnerable* flesh and blood, as his pursuer had proved, viciously, more than once.

He noticed something else. Everything was larger than he had ever seen. *Have I shrunk?* That made little sense, for his adversary wasn't much taller than he. No, not smaller. *Younger.*

Then it came to him … He knew this dream, a memory, from when he was just a boy of eleven!

Voices. Jeering voices. He made out the words. *"Get him! Get him!"* And his enemy came on.

He broke for the one open place he could see: the town street. Out of the corner of his eye, he saw the bus moving toward him. If he could just get past it, he might escape.

His enemy took a flying leap and bowled him down—right in front of the bus, which came on, its driver not seeing either boy in time.

He cried out in terror—

And then he felt feather-like blows to his cheeks. A voice cried out, "Sir! Commander! Wake up!"

He jerked up and opened his eyes—and stared directly into the eyes of Zach Radner. His newest recruit looked worried. How much time had passed since that boy had genuinely worried about someone other than himself?

"I'm sorry, sir," said Zach. "But you were making so much noise, and your orders had been for quiet in camp. What happened to you? Sir? That is—if you don't mind my asking."

Matthew shook his head—a motion that now seemed normal and natural. He hadn't ever done that, not since … not since his surgery. Yes, that must have been it. Erich Frankel's neurosurgical team had allowed him no memory of what had brought him into their care. But now …

"That question is entirely within your orders, Private Radner," he said. "A sentry is responsible not only for watching but for investigating, at least until his superior can take over. Well done."

"Thank you, sir."

"Now, to answer your question, I will tell you only this much. The rest you must consider classified. I just had a memory come back to conscious recollection. A nasty one, but one I had been seeking. That might happen again. If it does, you now know what to do. I will explain further when, and if, it becomes relevant." *And when I can explain fully,* he didn't add.

"I understand, sir," said the boy. "Can you get back to sleep, sir?"

Matthew swept the stars with his eyes. Then he said, "I won't bother. It's almost watch-changing time anyway. You go to sleep. I'll keep watch until morning."

"Thank you, sir." Zach saluted. Again Matthew returned it.

Chapter 7

Matthew did more than keep watch. Painstakingly, and with much effort, he dug rocks out of the ground and built the tallest cairn he could build and not have it fall over or collapse from its own weight. Somehow he managed to build one ten feet high. It would make a good signal tower.

The eastern sky was just lightening up, and the planet Venus, as the morning star, was just appearing when at last, he climbed the cairn. Nothing but his quiver with the semaphore flags, one DEW long gun, and his US Marine-issue binoculars encumbered him.

He scanned the southern sky and found what he was looking for: the signal tower of Robinson's camp, only just clearing the trees. Lowering the field glasses, he reached backward and took out the two flags. These he used quickly, sending the attention call.

He used the glasses again only long enough to verify that the signal watch had returned his call. Then he sent a quick message: CROW TO RACCOON FND REAL RATS NEST #1 JUVIE WILL U JOIN PLS SEND GAZELLE.

He guessed—hoped—that Ayelet would pick up on the Standard translation of her first name. He stowed the flags and climbed down with his equipment. Once on the ground, he walked over to the sleeping boy. "Wake up," he said, giving the boy a gentle but firm nudge.

"Yes, sir ... Oh, yeah, it's morning," said Zach. Then after he'd levered himself up by one elbow, the boy took in the cairn. "You built *that?*" he said in awe.

"Yes," said Matthew. "My newfound friends should be on their way. I'll feed you a meal, and then I need to take another look south."

"Let me, sir," said Zach, now getting to his feet.

Matthew took a split second to think about that. Then he handed Zach the binoculars. "Go to it," he said.

Zach climbed the cairn more easily than Matthew would have expected. Once on top, he turned south and raised the binoculars. Matthew watched him focus, then caught Zach's surprised expression.

"I've never seen anything like that before," Zach said. "Two vehicles, riding on ground wheels. Very angular. But why don't they float?"

"They are Armored Fighting Vehicles," Matthew explained. "American civilization has had to hide for three hundred seventy years or more. They never developed geomagnetic levitation. Where they lived, they never needed it."

"Oh," said Zach, a broad smile forming on his face, "I just got an idea."

"About what?"

"We can take that game preserve."

Matthew looked up at the boy directly. "Say that again?" he asked.

"I'm serious," said Zach. "With your capabilities, help from those friends of yours, and my knowledge of that place, we can take it. In a little more than a week will be the perfect time."

"Why?"

"Because they're planning a big ceremony of some kind, something to do with the full moon. When they do, they'll be admitting people they don't necessarily know. You could walk right into the front door—and I can slip across the perimeter at any of a number of spots they don't even bother to patrol. Once inside, we raise a ruckus that will draw all the perimeter guards. That's when your friends move in. Those two vehicles, riding low to the ground—a cinch."

"Well, you've done one excellent thing," said Matthew. "You gave me a valuable piece of intelligence far enough in advance. As you know, the moon is well into the waxing crescent phase and will be at first quarter in two days. The moon will be full about seven days later. That gives us nine days to make a *real* plan, a plan more likely to succeed, and maybe one with a greater gain. But you might as well know: I summoned that squad just now.

"And get this: your part of the plan—and I can already start sketching it out—won't need any technology higher than a bow and arrow. But it *will* require you to become a warrior. We talked about that before. Are you willing?"

"Yes, sir!"

"Then hurry down. I can recharge electrically, but you cannot. And you must be hungry."

"Yes, I am!" said Zach with a broad smile. He clambered down a few levels, then jumped the rest of the way.

* * *

"What did you mean by 'a real rats' nest'?" Ayelet asked.

"A most unpleasant discovery, and one relevant to your primary training, Sub—ah, Lieutenant," said Matthew, for Ayelet no longer wore her stolen SSF uniform. Instead, she wore Marine greens and sported the silver bar of a first lieutenant.

"By the way, Corporal Jameson," said Matthew, "thank you again for issuing me Corporal Swigert's kit."

Jameson smiled a self-deprecatory smile. "Happy to oblige, sir."

Ayelet spoke again. "Lieutenant Robinson detached Squad Two to 'render us any and all assistance.'"

"A full squad. Excellent. And Andrea and Barry?"

"Still back at camp, already making contacts, as I have done, too. Barry and Andrea started their own cells. And I already have my contacts." Ayelet took on an angry expression. "Finding that promazine derivative was all our contacts needed to hear," she said.

"The SSF installation is of far greater—and worse— import," said Matthew. "May I introduce my latest recruit, Zachary Radner. I'll let him tell you what that installation is."

Zach told his story. Corporal Jameson's jaw dropped. Ayelet swallowed hard.

Finally, Jameson spoke. "Commander," he said, "please tell me you intend to attack that 'installation,' as you called it."

"Yes, indeed," said Matthew. "But first, let me inspect your squad."

"With pleasure, sir. I like that semaphore platform, by the way."

Squad Two, consisting of Fire Teams Charlie and Delta, was expanding Matthew's original camp to accommodate themselves. Their vehicles were "sunning," as Jameson called it—taking as much charge as they could from the sun.

"Yes," said Matthew when his inspection was done, "this can work. My stolen SSF uniform will get me inside *if* I can somehow obtain a forged identification card. But in the meantime, what I need most is reconnaissance. Private Radner here knows the inside. I need to know the outside."

"Leave that to us," said Corporal Jameson. "We'll manage. Though, frankly, I find this whole setup monumentally difficult to believe. A game preserve? With *children* as the game?"

"Yes," said Matthew. "It explains my arrest. This is not an open secret but a very strict one. Obviously, the SSF is a very secretive community."

"I can see," said Ayelet, "why you asked for me. Young man," she said to Zach, "tell me honestly. How do you feel about all this?"

"Angry. Wanting revenge. I admit that. I've got no home, and I've taken just about the worst thing an adult can do."

"We understand. Fully," said Matthew. "That's why we're laying on this operation."

"The United States will offer you political—that is, a home when this is over," said Jameson.

"Just a minute, Corporal Jameson," said Zachary. "You look familiar."

"Why?" asked the Corporal. "I've never seen you before in my life."

"But *I* have seen a boy who looks a lot like you."

The revelation hit Jameson like a thunderclap. "You … you have?"

"Yes."

"Can you describe him?"

"Sure thing," said Zach. "He's—oh, I would say—135 centimeters tall…"

"He means four feet five."

"And black, like me? Regular size, with short-cropped hair like mine, and brown eyes?" Jameson was getting more agitated with every word.

"Yes."

"And did he tell you his name?"

"Yes. Tom Jameson. That's another thing—I recognized his last name from your name tag. Do you know him?"

"He's my brother!!"

Ayelet gasped.

For Matthew, it felt like finding a piece of a jigsaw puzzle.

"You're telling me my brother is in that place!?" Jameson was rapidly getting beside himself.

"Corporal Jameson," said Ayelet abruptly, "come with me."

Jameson stared at her, wild-eyed. Then in a lower tone, almost a defeated one, he said, "Aye-aye, ma'am."

The two of them walked away together.

"What?" asked Zachary. "Did I say something wrong?"

"No, not wrong," said Matthew. "But think about it. How would you feel if you had a brother in a place like that? Don't worry—he's with my fellow officer. But we have a more important thing to consider. Did Thomas Jameson ever tell you how he came to be snatched?"

"No, not really," said Zach. "In fact, he didn't want to say anything about where he came from."

"He's probably protecting his society," said Matthew.

Zach stared at Matthew for several seconds. Then he said, "Wait a minute. Now I get it. Tom Jameson is an American!"

"Yes."

"Holy…" said Zach. "But how could they have snatched him? Even *I* didn't know about America. But he didn't say whether he was caught on the surface, or whether … but that's impossible."

"Maybe not," said Matthew. "Not if somebody's committed treason."

"But what do we do about it?"

"What do you think?" asked Matthew. "We attack, just as we planned."

"Well, you can count on me, sir! Anything I can do to help."

"I'll hold you to that," said Peter Jameson, who had suddenly rejoined the group. "May I take that as a commitment to some hard training? Because I'm going to train you myself—as hard as you've ever trained. Are you with us?"

"Yes, sir."

"Save the 'sir' for Commander Morrow and Lieutenant Cohen here. You will call me 'Corporal.' But I'll make you hate that word as much as you've ever hated anything."

"With all due respect, Corporal," said Zach, now drawing himself straight up, "after what I've been through, I can take anything you throw at me."

"Yeah?" said Jameson. "We'll see about that!"

"Yes, Corporal."

"All right, give me ten right now."

Zach now vindicated Matthew's early physical training. He knew what the non-com expected of him and executed ten push-ups, if not quite flawlessly, at least competently.

"Now, give me ten laps around the camp. *On the double!*"

As Zach started to trot away, Matthew said, "I see you don't waste time."

"We haven't time to waste, sir," said the new squad-leader-cum-drill-instructor. "There's a lot more to this than my brother being in that place. We just confirmed that … *treason.*"

"Agreed. But are you sure you're all right? That must have come as quite a shock."

"Don't worry about me, sir. The quickest way to get my brother out of the lurch is to make this operation succeed. Lieutenant Cohen set me straight. First: how many people will be infiltrating?"

"Two," said Matthew. "Myself, as a 'clean' infiltrator, and Zach as a 'dirty' infiltrator."

"Make that three," said Ayelet. "I'm going in, too. Clean or dirty."

"Just how much training have you given yourself?"

Ayelet smiled. "I could always use some polish—from a superb athlete like you."

Matthew considered that. Well, she *had* acquitted herself well in that last night action. In the end, instinct decided for him. "Agreed," he said, "so long as *you* agree to accept my judgment of your fitness for the operation."

Ayelet let three seconds go by. Then she nodded.

"By the way, sir," the new corporal went on, "your young recruit impresses me. Of course, that's not a real Marine-style push-up, where you clap your hands when you push up. But I can teach him that. Next question. Commander, we've never been able to figure out these guns. You called them 'dew' guns. What does that mean?"

"Directed-energy weapons," said Matthew. "And I see you brought the electromagnetic-pulse weapon as well."

"That's the funny-looking long gun ending in the antenna array?"

"The same. All these weapons run on a very powerful and energy-dense battery. Charging these new weapons will be a problem."

"No, they won't," said Ayelet. "We captured that AFV from the SSF last night, remember?"

Matthew smiled broadly. "Yes, Ayelet," he said, "we certainly did. In fact, Barry flew it in."

"Shall we flag him to join us?" Jameson asked.

"Yes!" said Matthew. "And more: send the full particulars of what we've found, including what Zach said about your brother. Lieutenant Robinson will know what to do with that intel." *I hope.*

* * *

"When you gather evidence," Barry said, "you don't fool around!"

"No, I don't," said Matthew. "And what's more—I'm not finished."

It was hours later, and the MLAFV now rested just outside the camp of Squad Two. Barry, who had flown in aboard it, asked, "I understand you have some weapons to charge up?"

"We have," said Matthew. "Corporal!"

"Yes, sir!" said Corporal Jameson.

"Have your men give their DEW and EMP guns to Chief Sutton for charging."

"Yes, sir," said the new non-com and trotted off to obey.

"Now then," said Matthew, "as long as you're here, Barry, I need a report. How did Lieutenant Robinson receive my intelligence about Corporal Jameson's brother?"

"Well, first, he nearly hit the overhead," said Barry. "Then he flagged Squadron HQ. Major Campbell answered almost immediately. He told the Lieutenant that this installation is a prime objective and that he would 'secure other objectives.' I gather that's doubletalk."

"Not quite," said Matthew. "By now, he has assets underground as well as above. I imagine he's issuing further orders. Things are bound to get ugly."

"Got it. Anyway, the Lieutenant detached Fire Team Echo from Squad Three to fly this baby—after I showed them how. They've brought their own weapons and have room to transport prisoners."

"Good. Now, how good are your contacts?"

"Some of them are real hackers, like me," the Chief said.

"Good," said Matthew. "I need someone to forge an ID—preferably of an SSF sergeant."

"Got it," said Barry. "I'll need to collect a retinal image from you for that."

"You shall have it," said Matthew.

"Just one ID?"

"Only one," said Matthew. "I don't want the enemy to know—yet—just how alert our allies are. This objective is not that big a target."

"Will you need any other recon?"

"Yes," said Matthew. "Remember: we suspect the Americans' cover is already blown. But I need to know how many command levels have been briefed on them and how high. Don't bother reconning the preserve; these Americans can handle that."

Ayelet broke in: "Matthew, are you sure you want to slip in with just the three of us? And with Zach, a former inmate?"

"A former inmate knows the inside of that camp better than any other source I have," said Matthew, ticking the point off on his left index finger. "Second, our action is largely a distraction for when this augmented squad attacks in force." Middle finger. And now the ring finger point: "Third, Zach is now every inch a soldier—and so are you." And now on the little finger: "And last, and possibly most important: every day we wait, another child suffers rape—or murder."

Ayelet nodded grimly.

"The revolution is beginning in earnest," Matthew went on. "This one action will help solve a problem the Americans didn't even know they had. And it will start to convince our people that revolution is not only possible but a moral imperative."

"It could work the other way, though," said Barry. "Once the revolution moves beyond idle talk, people start thinking seriously about how much they want to change the government."

"A chance we'll have to take," said Matthew. "A chance any revolutionist takes."

"Sir," said Barry, "do you need me in this camp for anything else?"

"Just make that ID for me, and then you can return to the platoon camp. When you do, share everything with Andrea. We need more recruits, and now."

Barry worked immediately to produce one false identification—a staff ID for Matthew. While he did, Matthew signaled to Ayelet. "Walk with me," he said and led the way partly into the trees away from the clearing. Ayelet followed.

"First," said Matthew, "thank you again for re-awakening me and for all the help you've been since. Having said that, I know that you've prepared for a moment like this for a long time. You've proved that—twice—in action. You were right; all you needed was a little polish. But that takes motivation—and that kind of motivation is never random. You also said you already had a network of like-minded contacts. So let's have it. Just how long *have* you been planning revolution?"

Ayelet drew herself up and faced Matthew squarely. "Ever since," she said, "I discovered that the United Nations lied to my people. Or at least that part of them who *hadn't* joined the State of Israel, three hundred eighty-five years ago."

"Would you care to explain?" Matthew asked in a lower voice.

"Gladly," she said. "I'm going to start with some very ancient history so that you'll have some context. You see, Matthew, for as long as we, Jews, have existed, we've divided ourselves into different sects. We've always had a sect that didn't believe in the Eternal One or anything spiritual. Twenty-five hundred years ago, it was the Sadducees, during the time of the ancient Roman Empire, and earlier than that, during the Seleucid Empire before the Romans conquered Syria.

"And in the nineteenth century of the Common Era, another Jew arose who thought a lot like a Sadducee. His name was Karl Marx."

"*The* Karl Marx?" said Matthew. "I had not known he was Jewish."

"Jewish, but by birth only," said Ayelet, drawing her lips tight. "He taught that it was immoral to earn money from the labor of another. To him, that was another form of slavery. Instead, the state should run all projects higher than simple handicrafts. And…" Ayelet sighed. "All too many Jews believed him. You'd think my people would have broken away from Marx when the first nation-state to embrace his theories started to persecute our people."

"The Union of Soviet Socialist Republics?"

Ayelet nodded firmly. "How much do you know about that polity?"

"The settlers of Novy Mir tried to copy their political and economic system, and without printers to help them," said Matthew. "With tragic—even abominable—results. I … once knew a witness." But he was *not* ready to talk about that witness. At least … not yet. "And now that you remind me about Novy Mir, the whole United Systems is headed for a fall even harder than the one on Novy Mir. I just told you to imagine a command economy without printers. Now imagine one with printers, only they stop working."

Ayelet gasped. "You're right!" she said. "Oh, I can almost imagine it now. But where was I?"

"Telling me about the USSR."

"Well, as you know, that polity failed in its day," said Ayelet. "But still, the foolish ones among my people felt the ideals of Marx hadn't gotten a fair experimental trial. So they kept trying, and cooperated with the UN. As if those 'immunizations' weren't enough, they took an active part in the Great Climate War."

"But you descend from some of those same people, do you not?"

"To my shame," said Ayelet, "yes. But Sadducees and Pharisees—the ones who tried to keep to tradition, though they were far from perfect themselves—weren't the only sects among the Jews. You had the Essenes, who were fanatical record keepers. They copied out and buried our sacred texts in caves where two Arab boys, of all people, found some of them in 1946. Gregorian, that is."

"The Dead Sea Scrolls," said Matthew. "But I thought they were lost?"

"No," said Ayelet, looking triumphant. "They simply disappeared from the Israel Museum in Jerusalem. I think we both know that the State of Israel beneath one or more NRDs in New York has them. But even before that, the Essenes had their modern imitators, too. Sometime during the Great Climate War, they created their own secret repository."

Now it was Matthew's turn to gasp for the first time in his life. "You cannot mean that *you* found this other repository!"

"*I* didn't," said Ayelet, almost impishly. "But my grandfather on my mother's side did. It consisted of an old network-attached storage server. After he died, my grandmother shared its contents with me."

"Incredible!" cried Matthew. "That's priceless! And *your family* found it, after all these centuries! Is that repository secure?"

"Absolutely," said Ayelet. "After I read those scrolls, I knew our people were believing a lie. I started organizing a rebel movement right away. We call ourselves the Zealots, after yet a fourth ancient Jewish sect."

"Whence 'zeal' and 'overzealous' in Standard," said Matthew. "Just what did you discover?"

"That Marx had left so much out! The Eternal *never* forbade someone to direct another's labor to realize an income. He said only that a worker deserves a just wage. And He laid down a law that … Well, the best way to explain it is that one man's waste could be another's sustenance and that one ought not deny that. That law provided that poor people surrounding a farm could gather what seeds fell during harvest and provide for themselves that way. But to go from there to collectivizing everything, and then abandoning farming and industry completely—our original writings support *nothing* like that!"

"And once your Zealots learn that the State of Israel still exists," said Matthew, "they'll be even more ripe for revolution. Thank you, Ayelet. May I assume I still have your trust?"

Ayelet's face lit up—so this was what "beaming" looked like. "Implicitly, Matthew," she said. "You've earned it, as I said. Do you trust me?"

"Yes," he said without hesitation. "*You* earned *that.*"

At that moment, Barry waved at them. So they returned to camp, Matthew leading.

Barry had indeed finished forging an identity card for Matthew. It made him a security guard—a stroke of boldness Matthew appreciated greatly.

The three conversed for another fifteen minutes. Then Matthew sent another semaphore message, asking that Andrea bring the rubber wagon out to ferry Barry back. He would need to brief Lieutenant Robinson on the operation to come.

Then on MJDN 204115, they scored another intelligence coup.

* * *

Corporal Jameson sounded an alert that woke all the small squad camp. Matthew stepped out of his small tent and met Jameson at the camp's edge. Ayelet and Zach Radner joined them, too.

"Look," said Jameson, handing a pair of binoculars to Matthew. He pointed to a part of the sky where Matthew could already see a few star occlusions. Matthew raised the binoculars to his eyes, focused them, and locked onto an object. He recognized it at once.

In the sky, coming in for an apparent landing, was a saucer-like vessel with a prominent ventral bulge. An LCG.

As she came closer, he read the ship's name, a registry number, and some other markings—in Elfin script.

Silently he engaged the recording routine that stored his sensory impressions in his secondary memory. This was evidence of criminal behavior in the highest echelons of the United Systems—and possibly of treason against his new allies, the Americans.

As he watched, the LCG dropped into what must be a landing field, hidden in the forest in or near the preserve. And it didn't take off. He stopped recording.

"Perfect," Matthew said aloud. "If we work out our rescue correctly, we'll liberate not only several children but another vehicle as well."

"An Elfin LCG," hissed Ayelet. "What indeed does that say about the Elves?"

"Nothing good," said Matthew. "We move tomorrow. *Early* tomorrow. H-Hour will be zero two hundred. That vessel will take off with a *different* passenger manifest. And *we* will be its pilots."

"Roger that," Zach said, with feeling.

"Once again," said Jameson, "you're sure you don't need my men as a spearhead?"

"We three can handle that," said Matthew with a smile. "But I want you and your men to prepare to mop up. You'll take station with one ground vehicle at the main gate—call that the six-o'clock. Have your other ground vehicle come in at ten o'clock and the flying vehicle at two o'clock. I'll make sure nobody takes off from that camp— don't worry; their craft is vulnerable that way. Your orders are to take prisoner as many VIP guests as you can identify and round up—but let *no adult escape alive*. At my signal, you move in."

"Aye-aye, sir."

* * *

Early the next morning, Matthew, Ayelet, and Zach were at the border of the preserve. Matthew had no weapons other than his hands and feet—and his body shield. He could never do a clean infiltration with a long-barreled DEW. But if those fools followed their usual procedure, they'd issue him one. Again, perfect.

Zach carried a longbow and a full quiver, hanging by a leather strap from his left shoulder. Ayelet carried a slightly different sort of weapon—a crossbow.

Matthew swept the stars with his eyes. Of course, that was a little more difficult, with the waxing Gibbous moon overhead. But though the moon washed out some of the stars, those at the horizon told him the time. 0115.

The only *real* problem that big moon presented, was lighting up what would soon be a battlefield. With a little help from Corporal Jameson, Matthew had taught Zach and Ayelet how to see in the dark. Even without infrared goggles, the three would *own* the night. True, that moon would cancel out part of their advantage. But they couldn't help that.

He whispered, "Remember how I taught you to tell time from the moon and stars?"

"Yes," Zach whispered back. "Though I still can't tell it to the exact minute, the way you do."

"You don't have to. See that star, not far from that treetop?"

"Yeah."

"The star is going to draw dead even with the treetop. When that happens, move in."

"Right."

Ayelet didn't say a word. She just lightly clapped Zach on the shoulder.

Matthew left Zach where he was and signaled Ayelet to move to the spot she had picked out for her separate infiltration. This she did with one last smile and wave to Zach. Matthew moved to the main gate as fast as he could get there. He made it in ten minutes, again, according to plan.

Matthew, wearing his stolen SSF sergeant's uniform, inserted his false ID into the wallet he had also taken that day. Then he walked to the trail—more like a road—to the main gate.

With the complete confidence of a man knowing where he was going and with perfect authority to be there, he strode up to the main gate, not breaking stride until the guard said, "Halt."

He halted.

"Identification, please."

He produced it.

The guard, who wore the stripes of a first sergeant, inserted the card into a chip reader, waited five seconds, then nodded in apparent satisfaction—with a touch of irritation. "Step forward for retinal scan," he ordered next.

Matthew did so. The retinal scan took another three seconds.

"You're late, Sergeant," said the guard, handing back the card. "Report to Captain Coleman for assignment—and I wish you the joy of explaining to *him* why you showed up at the last instant."

Matthew simply nodded, took back his card, and walked inside the gate. He wondered at the slight discourtesy he had encountered. Did two more chevrons mean *that* much in the Special Security Forces? Or were all those personnel on edge after the failed raid a few days ago? No matter. Very shortly, everything would change. Profoundly.

He took a little extra time in reporting to this Captain Coleman. If he was already late, what difference would an extra five minutes make? Besides, he wanted to find that vehicle.

And there it stood, in all its sixty-five-foot breadth and thirty-three-foot height. Matthew had flown vehicles like this several times; *Bonaventure VI* and *VII* both carried them in his day. Of course, he'd flown the much-smaller rocket whaleboat, which also had a gravity drive. The Elves had designed this craft to carry a platoon-sized fighting force, land them on a hostile planet, and take off again—fast. Like much else, they had given—or more likely, sold—the design to the United Systems Navy. Sold it for what, Matthew couldn't begin to guess.

But what was this? Only *one* guard? Matthew harbored no illusions; until he learned otherwise, that craft had a skeleton crew aboard. But perhaps ...

Two minutes later, he was at the obvious guard force headquarters. Again, like one who had every reason to be present, he strode up to the single guard seated at a simple desk and held out his identity card. Like the gate guard, this one took the card and scanned it. But he didn't hand it back. Instead, he said, "Wait here, Sergeant." Then he picked up a PDD, dialed a frequency, and spoke in low tones.

A minute later, Matthew found himself face-to-face with a man wearing captain's bars. Almost by instinct, he raised his hand in salute as he read the name tag on the officer's uniform: COLEMAN. The Captain paused ever so slightly before returning the salute.

"Are you ill?" he asked.

"No, sir."

"The ... you're not. You're jaundiced. Extra printing privileges do not license you to abuse alcoholic beverages. Anyway, you had orders to report here at least forty-five minutes ago. Well?"

"I apologize, sir," said Matthew. "The higher alert status in Cornwallis occasioned my delay."

The Captain nodded and seemed to think that over. "Yes," he said, "I can see how it might—we had an incident a week ago, and our service also had a squad go missing the day before. But, of course, showing up late has its consequences. So instead of a position nearest the festivities, you will guard the landing craft for your pains. Tell the guard at that post that you are his relief."

Matthew pulled his best "crestfallen face" as he said, "Yes, sir," and saluted. The officer returned the salute and handed Matthew another card. Matthew's senses told him that this card's chip held a requisition for a DEW long gun and his immediate orders.

Matthew had to put himself on automatic to get to the armory without betraying his elation. That officer had reacted to the delay—which Matthew had deliberately planned—exactly as Matthew had expected. Affecting just the right amount of chagrin, Matthew reported to the armory Sergeant, who handed him a DEW that held a full charge and was at least in passable working order. On his way to the landing craft, Matthew took time to inspect it a little more closely. Then he stepped into some bushes and took about fifteen seconds to open an access plate, perform a simple repair someone had neglected, and pop the plate back into place. So he reached the landing craft at 0150, in plenty of time.

Handing out his order card, he said, "Ready to relieve you, Sergeant."

"You mean it?" the other said, actually smiling.

"Yes," said Matthew without further explanation. "My orders, in case you have any question," he went on, handing over the extra card.

The guard, wearing an air of hardly daring believe his luck, took the card and scanned it. When he did, his face lit up with an elation he didn't try to hide. "Thank *you*,

Sergeant!" he said, handing back the card. "All's well—and has been well since I came on duty here. The orders are simple: nobody approaches the LCG for any reason. She stays where she is, unless, and until Captain Coleman gives any other word."

"Understood," said Matthew. "Does she have a crew aboard?"

"One each, apprentice pilot and copilot; that's all."

A manageable obstacle. "Then, if you have no further instructions for me, I relieve you."

"Just one question," said the other guard. "Why the last-minute relief?"

"Because *I* am a last-minute addition to the guard force," said Matthew.

The other Sergeant grinned. "I get it," he said. "Tell you what: I'll take some pictures for you."

"I would appreciate that," said Matthew—and that was no lie. With his senses, he could tap into the photography/video upload channel the other's PDD would no doubt use. So he would have another mobile camera on the scene.

The other Sergeant shook hands with Matthew, who managed not to crush the offered hand. Then the other Sergeant gave a jaunty wave and loped off on a northwesterly bearing.

Instantly, Matthew extended his wireless sensors. The service set identifier and password were easy to crack.

Thanks to Barry's spoofing technique, he could sign in and leave no packet trail.

Oh, what arrogant fools these SSFs were. So supremely confident in their own protocols, never having any serious opposition, they had forgotten the very meaning of *security*. It meant more than bullying the civilian population and members of other services. Mainly it meant, to quote another common organic idiom, "having eyes in the back of one's head," which the SSF obviously did not.

The "festivities" were now beginning. Through the camp cameras and the camera his counterpart had carried to the camp amphitheater, he could see a clear gathering. VIPs had arrived on the LCG, all right. He spotted the small knot of Elves, easy to recognize with their tall stature as well as their pointed ears. And he almost started in surprise—the lead Elf was wearing the ceremonial gold jewel-encrusted collar of the Elfin Ambassador!

That explained the transport. And much else. And raised more questions for later.

Matthew now wondered what sort of officers would draw this kind of assignment. He hacked into the camp adjutant's file—remarkable that this camp had one—and found the 66-1 files on the officers. Most of the officers' files were unremarkable—but Coleman's stood out. His last assignment had been at—well, well—the Botany Bay Psychiatric Institute, Captain Brianna Belle Folsom, officer-in-charge. Specific duties: redacted.

Instinct again. *He must take that officer prisoner.* And find out whether this Captain Folsom had been briefed on the Americans.

Matthew used the camp cameras to scan the ranks of other VIP visitors. Humans, mostly. But he saw representatives of two other species: Neo-Inuit from GJ357 d and Porcoids from Epsilon Eridani d. And other humans wearing a costume that vaguely suggested that of Rigil Kentaurus f. So all the permanent members of the Security Council had "representatives" here.

No Morgens, though. Was their homeworld too distant? Or was this due to nearly a century of war between the United Systems and the Morgenetic Empire? Or a deeper reason? Did Matthew dare hope that at least *one* race, human or not, with a reputation for honor, deserved that reputation?

He suddenly wanted to look *anywhere* else. So he accessed the perimeter cameras, especially where Zach and Ayelet, respectively, were supposed to come in. No sign of either, not even any sign of recent passage—no, wait a minute. A little dimple here, a little grass smudge there. The SSF Sergeant guarding the monitors couldn't have noticed, or the whole camp would be ringing with lockdown alarms. His two teammates were good. Ayelet, especially, was proving her worth.

As he switched on his built-in recorder again, he crept up the boarding ladder and into the LCG. With catlike steps, he arrived on the main deck.

He found himself in a large room with reclining upholstered seats, all oversized. Each had a set of seatbelts. Seatbelts—on a ship with total gravity manipulation. And a VIP transport, at that.

Obviously, this wide-open passenger country served to transport a press corps. The apical podium near the flight-deck ladder confirmed it. He crept to that ladder and started to mount it.

All the while, he was watching the main camera feed to the monitor watch desk. That feed was now coming from a camera and a four-channel stereophonic microphone group in the amphitheater. He could imagine the Sergeant at that desk keeping eyes glued to that monitor—for the obvious Camp Commandant (*not* Captain Coleman after all; that worthy had a front-row seat) had mounted the stage.

"Gentlebeings," he said in a tone half-serious, half-salesmanlike, almost like a carnival barker or circus ringmaster, "the ceremony of the Autumnal Equinox is about to begin. Give your attention to the performers."

What assailed Matthew Morrow's appalled senses was something resembling an ancient Bacchanalia, or perhaps the Saturnalia of ancient Rome. Except this included not a single female performer. The performers were all human males, ages varying from twenty to twenty-five, wearing blatant women's abbreviated costumes and apparently clean-shaven, not only on the face but over the entire body. How odd that he had never before beheld such a spectacle. Then again, he had never seen anything like this game preserve, either.

But this spectacle gave Matthew an immediate advantage. As he expected, the pilot- and copilot-under-instruction were watching that same feed. They paid Matthew absolutely no attention while he reached forward toward the right temple of each one. He knocked them both out with simultaneous blows.

As he hauled each Elf out of his seat, he still noted what was happening on the amphitheater stage. From stage right, the children started to walk on. Or rather, a few adults were *pushing* them on. They half-walked, half-stumbled, partly because they didn't want to be there, but also because their hands were tied behind their backs. The wide eyes in most of their faces told a tale of almost primal fear. That is, *only* their eyes could tell that—because their mouths were full of cloth held in place with bandanas knotted at the backs of their necks.

That foolish guard was capturing all this on video—and Matthew easily intercepted the feed from the guard's PDD and also followed the upload stream to where he was storing a copy of the file. The file had no encryption. The directory did, but of course, Matthew had already broken that code. He made sure to download a copy into his own secondary memory. Now he had two kinds of recordings and two kinds of evidence.

Quickly he warmed up the LCG's drive. Just in time, too—for the amphitheater scene just gained a new "prop." A large stone slab, riding on gravity glides, was sliding onto the stage. The children stared at it in fresh horror—a horror that redoubled when the Camp Commandant produced a dagger having a jeweled hilt and a very nasty-looking curved blade.

"Let the sacrifice begin," he said.

Matthew called up the helm control routines. He would need time to make a stealthy approach. Those Elves would have to lie where he dumped them; he hoped they wouldn't come to anytime soon. No one else was watching the lander, of course. He took off and moved in, just above treetop level—Matthew didn't want to risk rustling any branches.

The transvestite performers singled out one of the children, a little girl. As she kicked and tried to scream through her gag, they hoisted her high and carried her to the stone slab—the *altar*. But slowly. Unbidden, a phrase came to the foreground of Matthew's organic brain: *milking the crowd.* These were performers; they were enjoying themselves—and were prolonging the moment.

And then time skipped backward for Matthew Morrow—for he suddenly found himself, or a much younger version of himself, looking up at a set of leering faces. Faces like those the celebrants now wore, except they were boys' faces. And none of them would think of dressing up like a girl! No, sir. But they were holding him down, and someone was approaching with a knife …

A *thwang* brought him back to the present. He saw the girl, now in four-point restraint and lying on the altar. The Commandant was still holding the knife. But now, the fingers of the Commandant's right hand loosened. The knife fell from his grip and clattered harmlessly to the stone slab next to the girl. The Commandant staggered— and fell forward. And everyone present—plus Matthew— could now see the arrow sticking out of his back, buried within him.

All this time, Matthew had put the LCG on autopilot. With his wireless interfaces, he hacked its controls so he could pilot it remotely. Now, he dragged the two apprentices off the flight deck and dumped them into two press-corps seats. Then, with a quick check of his DEW gun, he sent a command to the LCG to drop to six feet off the ground. He ran down the boarding ladder, jumped, and made for the amphitheater at a dead run. The LCG, at his order, retracted its landing legs, returned to treetop level, and followed.

That other guard hadn't taken the shot capturing the killing of the Commandant. But the surveillance cameras had. They showed everyone in the amphitheater too stunned to move for a critical second. During that second, the rope holding the girl's right wrist to the altar abruptly parted. Matthew barely registered the crossbow bolt that had cut that rope. Almost immediately, the girl, hand now free, snatched up the fallen knife. *Snap!* She had cut her left wrist free. Then she shoved the Commandant's dead body off her, and, *snap! Snap!* The cords holding her ankles fell—for the blade was razor-sharp.

A performer moved in, trying to restrain her again. Suddenly his eyes went wide, he cried out half in pain, half in surprise—and then he fell to the stage, another long arrow sticking out of *his* body. By now, the other performers had arrows sticking out of their backs or chests.

But now, the guard Matthew had relieved, having long since turned off his PDD, took aim. He must have seen Zach! But before he could squeeze the trigger, he dropped his weapon—and collapsed, with a crossbow bolt in the side of his neck.

Matthew kept running on full automatic, and the LCG kept up with him. As he ran, he cycled through all those cameras to see what they were picking up. He made his plan accordingly.

Regaining conscious control of his body, Matthew sent quick autopilot commands to the LCG, which then began to fly autonomously. Now he raised his DEW long gun. Just in time, for now, *two* guards had acquired Zach— and a third had acquired Ayelet.

None got the chance to fire. Ayelet killed her guard just as Zach killed one of his. The other took a critical fraction of a second to react—and Matthew shot him.

Matthew swept the stage with his eyes. *Good!* That little girl—actually twelve years old, not so little after all—had torn or cut off her gag long since. She was just cutting loose the last of her fellow captives when the Elfin Ambassador moved in—and drew a knife of his own. She didn't assume any combat stance or waste any other time. She simply waded into him and filleted him like a fish. The eleven-year-old boy she had just cut free rushed to relieve the fallen VIP of his knife. The other VIPs never came near. They just started running pell-mell back to the landing field.

Matthew had to catch this through a combination of "out of the corner of his eye" and sampling the surveillance feed. It was time. He sounded a loud whistle. He hoped Corporal Jameson and his team would hear it and move in.

In the meantime, what seemed like the entire SSF guard force occupied his full attention. But he took time to send a command to the LCG to fly out of sight of the amphitheater and come in for its landing backstage. Those VIPs would never find it and would have no escape.

He would have to kill every SSF in this place. So every time a guard stood in his way, he killed him without hesitation or mercy. To his relief, Zach dropped out of the tree in which he had been hiding and continued shooting at the other guards. Ayelet occasionally dropped a guard with her crossbow but couldn't reload nearly as quickly. Ayelet had chosen her weapon for accuracy, not reload speed.

When Zach had shot his last arrow, he threw off the strap of his quiver, dropped to the ground, rolled, and came to rest—clutching a fallen DEW gun. Some bushes hid him from the view of the guards—but not the stage.

Matthew gave his next signal, then strode onto the stage, cradling his gun at tactical carry and staring icily at the assembled onlookers. Ayelet stood six feet to his left, holding her crossbow in an alert posture, bolt aimed forward and down. Zach stood six feet to Matthew's right, holding his gun at the ready—straight at Captain Coleman but ready to aim at any other target if needed.

Captain Coleman opened his mouth to speak, but another man—Caucasian and dressed in the oddest civilian clothes Matthew had ever seen a man wear—stepped forward. He stood about five foot nine and must have weighed 200 pounds. A black beard covered most of his face.

The portly civilian affected a tone of outrage. "What is the meaning of this?" he said, nose turned up. "Do you know who I am?"

"No," said Matthew. "Do tell."

"I," said the man, drawing himself up to his full height, "am Averell Harriman Morton. I happen to do a lot of business with your superiors. You will pay dearly for this bit of mutiny."

"Don't presume to tell me what I will pay, nor what for, Mr. Morton," said Matthew. "You are our prisoner. And so, Captain Coleman, are you."

Captain Coleman stepped forward, holding a DEW handgun leveled at Matthew. "How dare you say that, soldier?" he said in what must be his best ice-cold disciplinarian's voice. "You will be charged with mutiny and multiple counts of murder—and that includes the murder of the Elfin Ambassador. I hold you personally responsible for that, the same as though your hand wielded the knife. What do you have to say for yourself?"

"I will say it just once more," Matthew said, returning ice for ice, still holding his long gun at tactical carry. "You are our prisoners." He caught Zach grinning ear-to-ear. Ayelet wore a more solemn and determined expression. Captain Coleman's jaw went slack. What must he be thinking at a time like this?

Matthew didn't care. "Your ambassadorial guest tried to kill a child," he said. "You and your superior aided and abetted that. I *also* charge you with kidnapping, intentional endangerment of children, attempted murder of another of same, and too many crimes against nature to count. These children are my witnesses. You both will face justice. *Revolutionary* justice."

"Oh, we *will?*" said Coleman, his voice now dripping with contempt. "May I remind you that my forces, however much you have thinned them out, still outnumber yours. Put down your weapons, all of you."

"No," said Matthew. "I give you fair warning: *you* put down *yours.*"

Captain Coleman opened his mouth to speak again—then abruptly shut it. When he did speak again, he used a different tone. "Wait a minute," he said. "*Wait a minute!* You're not jaundiced at all. That 'skin' of yours is gold leaf. You're Matthew Morrow, aren't you?"

"And what took you so long to realize *that?*" As Matthew spoke, he glanced around him. The children made no sign of recognition. But the eyes of the SSF all widened. Maybe he could scare them a little more. "Actually, that's *Lieutenant Commander* Morrow to you, which means I outrank you."

"The *Five* you do, you renegade!" shouted Coleman. He raised his weapon to fire ... then cried out in pain, gripping his right upper arm with his left hand. "*Fire at will!*" he cried.

Several beams of directed energy struck Matthew, bounced off his body shield ... and killed the men who had launched them. The dead fell to the ground where they had stood. Those who did not fall dropped their weapons and ran away toward the landing field, some of them stepping over one another to escape. "Averell Harriman Morton" tried to run, but Matthew tackled him, bore him down, and held him.

That's when every light in camp went dark.

Matthew heard more DEW fire and even louder projectile fire from three separate locations. Good for Corporal Jameson! He must have taken out the generator with the EMP gun Matthew gave him. His augmented squad were now intercepting—and dispatching—the SSF.

Matthew summoned the LCG. It was time to evacuate.

Zach stood up, his shiny new DEW gun now slung over his right shoulder, muzzle up, and retrieved his bow and quiver. "Sandy, Tom, get everybody up," he said. "An LCG will touch down here, very shortly—see? Here it comes. We're getting out of here, *now.*"

Ayelet flashed Matthew a jaunty smile. Then she rushed over to the same guard Matthew had relieved earlier. From a uniform pocket, she retrieved his PDD and held it up.

Down came the LCG to a hover. All three landing legs deployed, their feet about a foot off the ground. The craft snapped off several treetops and bent some trees almost double. Though this wasn't obvious, Matthew had ordered the craft to face *up*-stage—so that the boarding-ladder leg, in the spacecraft's stern, would be foremost.

"Zach," said Matthew, "secure the prisoners." He handed Zach his long gun, then picked up a large rock and set it just beyond the landing leg. That was as much signal as the children needed. Tom nodded to Sandy as she formed the girls into a column and ordered them to climb aboard, one at a time. Sandy came last while Zach finished binding the two prisoners.

Then, Tom had the boys climb aboard. And when they did, they each carried a DEW long gun and had another one slung over the right shoulder—obviously imitating Zach. Some of them even had handguns tucked in their belts. Now where had they ... but, of course. Young Tom must have ordered his boys to pick up those guns while Sandy was leading her girls aboard. Matthew liked that. Underage, his irregular platoon might be, but it included at least three good leaders.

Matthew faintly heard sounds of a struggle coming down the gangway and then shrill sounds of triumph. Another good move: Sandy and her girls, with some of Tom's boys to help, must have subdued the two Elves.

While this was happening, the two ground AFVs appeared. Before Matthew could speak, Zach shouted, "Don't worry! They're friends! Just get aboard!"

The boys showed every intention of just leaping aboard on their own—all but young Tom. Instead, he joined Matthew to greet the newcomers. Corporal Jameson dismounted one of the vehicles—and instantly jumped for joy. "Tom!" he cried. "Remember me?"

"Pete!" yelled Tom—and then boy and man met in a brotherly embrace.

Then the Corporal came up to Matthew and saluted. Matthew, returning it, said, "Well done, Corporal. I take it this is your brother?"

"He sure is," said the Marine, grinning broadly. "And we've rounded up those VIPs. Having three vehicles is mighty convenient."

"Here are two more prisoners for you," said Matthew, indicating Coleman, still nursing his wound, and Morton.

"Wait! I know you!" said Jameson. "You're Averell Morton!"

"Yes, and if you know what's good for you, young man, you'll unbind me."

"No such joy," snarled the Corporal. "You're going to stand trial for crimes against nature. You, and that crooked Senator and two Representatives who were part of your 'party.'"

"How dare you? You had orders to withdraw! You will face court-martial for disobeying!"

"Oh-ho!" said the squad leader. "So *you're* the one who ratted us out. Do you actually tell a Secretary of the Navy what to do?"

"I'll have you know I tell the President and Vice President what to do!"

"Not anymore, you don't! Besides everything else, now you'll stand trial for treason!"

Matthew had to interrupt. "*Treason*, Corporal?" he asked.

"You betcha! This piece-of-… is a high muckety-muck businessman," said Jameson. "I had wondered how Morton Enterprises could suddenly bring out technology to rival anything the Vincent companies came out with.

Well, now we know. And when we get back to the adit, there will be hell to pay."

"Do you mean to tell me," said Matthew, slowly, "that this man, and some of your VIP prisoners, are Americans, like yourself?"

"Americans, yes, but not like me. These are traitors."

"Obviously, I need to get a report to Major Campbell. In the meantime: reinforcements will likely arrive very shortly. So give yourself, maybe, five minutes to pick up anything of value." He told Jameson where to find the armory. "Then load your prisoners and start back to camp. On second thought: bring that Senator and the two Representatives here, and put them, Mr. Morton and Captain Coleman, aboard the LCG. You will find two Elfin prisoners on board; take them off and bring them back with you. I wouldn't advise putting them into your maglev; they are a qualified pilot and his apprentice. I'll most likely get back to camp long before you do, so I'll make the report and deliver the high-profile prisoners. Don't worry about us; we'll take care of ourselves."

"Yes, *sir!*" said Jameson and barked out orders.

"Ayelet," he said, "that was good shooting. But don't forget; any PDD is a homing device."

Ayelet smiled derisively—almost. "Don't worry, Matthew; I can defeat that kind of homing," she said. Then she took a few seconds to pry the device open and remove the battery. Matthew ran a quick scan of the airwaves.

"Good job," he said. "Now, let's get aboard."

She smiled and fell in behind him.

Tom stepped aboard the LCG. Zach brought up the rear, a long gun over one shoulder, bow and quiver over the other, and another long gun in each hand. He handed one gun each to Matthew and Ayelet. Matthew slung his weapon and boosted Zach aboard, then helped Ayelet aboard. Then he bounded aboard the LCG with one step.

Inside, he slapped the button to close the door. He swept the main deck with his eyes and noted the five high-profile prisoners, each lashed into a press seat. "Ayelet," he said, "take charge of these prisoners. Guard them well. The rest of you, take seats and strap in. Zach, with me."

Tom and Sandy, Matthew noticed, still had everything in hand. Zach followed Matthew up the flight ladder to the cockpit—where, for the first time, Matthew noted the dome covering the entire flight deck, filled with micro-monitors. Just now, they displayed the view outside, their images blending seamlessly into a view that was like looking through glass.

Matthew turned to Zach, saying, "You're going to have to learn to fly this craft, and quickly. Take the left-hand seat; its controls are complete. Here," he said, and quickly accessed the new-pilot authentication page on the flat touch screen. "Place your palm in the outline," he said when the reverse outline of a palm appeared. Zach did so. Matthew took three seconds to forge an authentication for Zach, wirelessly.

"Take off and head east for five seconds," he said. "Then try to thread your way back to the platoon camp as best you can, at just under treetop level."

"What about the squad camp?"

"Corporal Jameson struck that camp already. He attacked in full force, remember?"

"Aye-aye, sir!" said Zach, grinning. He then proceeded to vindicate a judgment Matthew had made long ago. Show a teenager how to work the controls of any small craft, and he will learn to pilot it very quickly as if it were a game. While Zach was having fun "playing the game," Matthew was busy installing a full spoofing package into the craft's cybernetic systems. He was also watching through those ground-level cameras, which were still active. Sure enough, as he had ordered, every SSF guard and VIP lay dead—except for the various prisoners, of course.

"Having a little trouble, sir," Zach said. "The trees are just too thick here."

"That's all right," said Matthew. "The enemy is dead or captured anyway. Go around to east or west, and try for five minutes to find a wide trail. If you can't, just take us up to clear the trees." He then gave Zach a compass heading to follow.

"Aye, sir ... Wait. The forest is clear here—opens onto a meadow. Shall I use it?"

"Hover where we are while I check the sensors," he said. He was already seated in the right-hand seat. Now he called up a full tactical display that filled the viewing dome. A full 360 by 180-degree sweep of the area showed no sign of pursuit—nor indeed, of any intelligent life.

"No one around to see us," he said, setting the viewing dome back to a simple outside view. "You are clear. This is your flight. Make it quick."

"Yes, *sir!*" said Zach, raising one arm in a quick salute.

Matthew returned it and headed below.

The children, he saw, were all seated and strapped in. Ayelet sat next to the five prisoners. A quick glance told Matthew they were secure. Matthew walked to the podium, stood behind it, and tested its microphone. It was live.

"Boys and girls," he said, "may I have your attention?"

Every child aboard fell silent. Sandy and Tom looked at him as any two Marine sergeants might. The other children wore expressions that varied from open suspicion to slight skepticism to grudging acceptance to gratitude—and even, in some cases, to some kind of worship. This could get awkward—or maybe not.

"My name," he began, "is Matthew Morrow. May I introduce you to Lieutenant Ayelet Cohen." He nodded to Ayelet, who gave a brief wave. "She's…" Did he really want to explain what a psychiatric nurse was? No. "She's here because she knows something of what you went through. You can trust her. Talk to her. Believe me; she's heard it all." As if to confirm that, Ayelet gave a firm nod.

"Our friend on the flight deck," Matthew went on, "is Zach Radner—but I believe at least some of you remember him." Both Sandy and Tom nodded. "A little more than a week ago, I discovered that 'game preserve' we just left, and rescued Zach from it. Then I sent word to some good friends. We all agreed to come back for you—and I want to commend you boys, but especially your leader, for thinking to pick up those guns and bring them along." At that, Tom nodded, looking a bit shy.

"Thomas Jameson, I presume?" he asked.

"Yes, sir." He even managed a proper, if awkward, salute.

Matthew returned it with a smile. "And you," he said, turning to Sandy, "what's your name?"

Sandy got up with alacrity. "Alessandra Rossini, sir," she said.

Ah-ha. Italian. Matthew smiled again. "Let me guess: the Commandant picked you out to die first because you were a troublemaker."

She smiled an impish smile. "Yes, sir," she said. "Would you believe me if I promised not to make trouble for you?"

Matthew laughed. Then he said, "I'll take that as a high compliment—though, of course, I'll hold you to that. Because I'm going to ask you to continue leading these girls for the time being—and I want you to understand what that means. You, too, Tom. My comrades and I wanted those guns for a reason. To put it simply, we are at war."

A chorus of "Wows" greeted that statement—though Matthew could tell instantly that one or two each of the boys and the girls were upset. Sandy and Tom looked back at him with the most solemn expressions he had ever seen on a child.

"Yes," he went on, "I said, 'war.'" He explained all the clues: the ambassador, the SSF, everything. "That means the society into which most of you were born has some *very bad people* running it—and all the way at the top of the government."

"Actually, sir," said Tom, "you know I'm an American. I never felt safe explaining to these others what that means. But I'm not the only American here."

"Oh?" Matthew asked. "All right, raise your hand if you're an American."

One-fourth of the children raised their hands, including Tom.

"All right," said Matthew. "Suppose you, Americans, and you, from the United Systems, introduce yourselves. You, Americans, will have quite a story to tell. I promise you; it's going to shake up your government, too, and at the highest levels. We have an entire squadron of Marine cavalry to help us. They know something about the problem, and we're going to tell them a lot more.

"The rest of you," he went on, "listen up. The best way you have of at least trying to stay alive is to join up with Zach and me. I realize that's a lot to think about—but maybe it's time to stop thinking and start acting."

Sandy stood up again. "Mr. Morrow?"

"Yes?"

"Maybe Tom and I should talk to everybody," she said. "It's just that … that is … Well, it's been a long time since we could trust any adult—or thought we could. Now you're telling us to trust you, and Miss Cohen, and maybe a handful of other adults. Some of us have figured that out, but for others, it's going to be a lot harder."

"I understand," said Matthew. "Perfectly. Shall I leave you all to yourselves, or shall I send Zach back to talk to you?"

"If you can spare Zach," said Tom, "we'd appreciate it. He can fill us in."

"I'll send him down right away," said Matthew. "Of course, I'm going to ask you to take charge of these prisoners. I need not tell you how dangerous they can be. Ayelet, with me."

Ayelet got up and joined Matthew. The two young leaders saluted him again, and again he returned the salute. Detailed protocol about saluting could wait.

He found a set of controls in the podium and touched one. He felt, rather than saw, a large flat viewscreen light up above his head. He turned to look. As he expected, it was showing the view forward. His passengers wordlessly conveyed their pleasure at the sight.

He nodded to Ayelet, and both went back topside.

"How's it going, Zach?" he said as he and Ayelet entered.

"We'll easily be back at camp by daybreak, sir," Zach replied. "And—well, I hope you don't mind, but I've been trying to figure out some of the other controls. And I ran across something I wasn't sure about."

"Oh?" said Matthew. "Show me."

Zach did.

Matthew broke into a broad smile. "Zach," he said, "you just earned the grand prize. Hasn't he, Ayelet?"

That was her signal to check out what Zach had found. She gasped. "This vessel's cloaked!" she burst out.

"'Cloaked'?" Zach asked. "What's that?"

"It means we're totally stealthy against visible light," said Ayelet in wonderment. "It has an extra system for total adaptive camouflage—we call it 'cloaking.' And you just found the 'on' switch."

"No … no fooling?"

"No fooling," said Ayelet with a grin. "Go ahead—throw it."

Zach did. Instantly the view outside darkened slightly, then brightened again. "What happened?" the boy asked.

"Everything outside just got a little harder to see, that's all," said Matthew. "The viewing dome had to readjust. But from outside, no one—and I mean *no one*—can see us."

Zach grinned from ear to ear. Then he turned serious. "May I ask a favor, sir?"

"You may ask," said Matthew, "and I'll judge whether I can grant it."

"Would you let me talk to those kids down below?" he asked. "At least some of them still remember me, and we've got some catching up to do, and … well…"

"As a matter of fact," said Matthew, "they just asked to see you. So if you have no threats to report, we relieve you. And *mind those prisoners*. They'll be desperate—and devious."

"Not to worry, sir," said Zach, who put the LCG on autopilot. Then he rose from his pilot's seat and saluted. Matthew returned it and watched Zach go below, shutting the small hatch as he went.

As Matthew took the left seat, he waved to Ayelet to sit in the right seat. As she did, she said, "You know, Matthew, those kids are about this close to a mental breakdown." She held up thumb and forefinger about an inch apart to illustrate.

"I expected that," said Matthew. "Which makes me doubly glad you joined the team. Those children will have an even better reason to trust you—when they're ready. In the meantime, do you think you could learn to fly an LCG?"

Ayelet smiled again. "I managed to wangle some unofficial pilot training."

"In addition to weapons training," said Matthew. "Very good."

"Only, why *is* this vessel cloaked?"

"You wouldn't expect the Elfin Ambassador to flit about to an entertainment like the one we just interrupted, in a space launch everyone could spot with a casual glance, would you?"

"But I thought the Far-elves invented this kind of…" Then she looked Matthew in the eye—and must have caught his smile. "Another lie from the Admiralty?"

"Likely from the Elves themselves," said Matthew. "After what we saw down there, and learning the true history of NRD-01-CO-Mead, I wouldn't put anything past the Elves. Would you?"

"No."

"And that goes double today. The Elves must be under the rule of a particularly vicious faction among them. That's the only explanation for that Ambassador's behavior. His predecessor tried to make peace with the Far-elves after an illustrious career with no other than Captain Nelson of *Bonaventure II* and *III*. Then he died, rather abruptly. I always wondered about that."

"And what about the Americans? Our job just got several times trickier, didn't it?"

"Yes, it did," said Matthew. "We just have to trust Major Campbell. I'm sure of him."

Ayelet fell silent for a minute while Matthew flew on. Then she turned to Matthew—and he could tell she had something serious to ask. He made a quick sweep of his monitors, then turned to face her. "You have a question?" he asked.

"Yes," she said, took a deep breath, and let it out. "This vehicle could take you into space, and I know you wanted to get off this planet, and..." she stopped.

"And become a fugitive, subject to summary execution by the first Navy ship, or *Elfin* ship, to intercept me?" Matthew shook his head. "Besides, I like to finish what I start."

"You could evade detection for a long time, you know."

"But ships under cloak can't recharge; or shoot, either. Missiles, maybe, but not a DEW cannon. But all that aside, I have two imperatives: to help out the new friends I have made; and to find out what has happened to my old friends."

"Your old captain and his officers?"

"Yes, among others," said Matthew. "The answers are right here on Earth. Some of those old friends might be, too. I must find them."

"And the new friends?"

"The Americans, if I can persuade them. These children. Your Zealots. And you."

Ayelet didn't say anything. And for a quarter of a minute, she did not move. Then she reached out with her left hand and rested it lightly on Matthew's right hand.

Matthew let it rest there for a long time. Feelings he once thought he'd never have again, especially after the horrific loss he'd suffered, came back. With an effort, he kept his tears in check. But that didn't stop him from reaching up with his index finger and lightly touching hers.

Chapter 8

Matthew turned off the cloaking system long before Lieutenant Robinson's signal tower appeared. He didn't want to break this secret to anyone but Major Campbell and Captain Vincent—at least, not yet. Then he brought the LCG in the rest of the way and landed it in the recon camp.

Andrea and Barry climbed down from their perch in the signal tower to greet them. Steve Robinson came, too.

Matthew and Ayelet climbed down two ladders—flight deck, then boarding. When he reached the ground, he spoke rapidly. "Strike camp and prepare to move out," he ordered Lieutenant Robinson. "The SSF will likely come in force to investigate the sudden disappearance of their installation. I trust you know what it was?"

"Chief Sutton told me," said Robinson, almost turning green. "I gather…"

"It's true. And there's more. Your society has been compromised." Matthew explained about the VIP prisoners he and Jameson had taken. The revelations floored Robinson, who then said, "I've got to flag this to Major Campbell and Captain Vincent right away!"

"Where are they, if I may ask?"

"Back at Squadron HQ. In fact, the Major told me to send you there ASAP." He gave latitude and longitude of a position about five miles distant. And here, Matthew understood another virtue of the American Patriotic system: "nautical miles." Slightly longer than statute miles, they translated easily from minutes of latitude or longitude. At least, to two significant digits they did, and that was precise enough.

"I'm on my way," said Matthew. "Tell Major Campbell to expect me as soon as I can get there and that I recommend you stand down from your reconnaissance. The Major is your CO, not I. So ask him where to go. But I also ask, as a favor, that you detail two privates-first-class to fly with us and guard the prisoners we're carrying."

"Yes, Commander!" said Steve and turned immediately to bark orders to the Flag Team.

Matthew turned to Barry and Andrea. "Corpsman Riley, can you drive that van?"

"Yes, sir," said Andrea, confidently.

"Good. Work with Lieutenant Robinson to camouflage it as best you can. Where he goes, you go."

"Aye-aye, sir."

"Barry, you will come with me. Whatever your contacts told you about that other subject we discussed…"

"Which was plenty, sir. This goes all the way up to high command."

"Then Major Campbell and Captain Vincent will need to hear it from you. First-hand."

Lieutenant Robinson now asked, "What about Squad Two? And Fire Team Echo?"

"Corporal Jameson and his forces are on their way. They're bringing prisoners and more captured DEW weapons. He knows how to use them, by the way—I gave him a quick lesson."

"Don't you need to fly at night?"

"No, Lieutenant. We can manage," said Matthew, without explaining how.

* * *

"So that's how it is?" Major Campbell asked.

"So it would seem," said Matthew. "You know the value of these prisoners—four of them, anyway." He indicated the five men, still lashed to their chairs, with two Marine PFCs guarding them.

"That explains the excitement back in Cumberland," said the Squadron Commander. "You know I held A Troop back, along with the Intel Troop that consists of the HQ and recon platoons. Well, the Regimental Commander ordered me to send down those other assets. When I didn't, it let off a stink bomb. The Commandant of Marines reiterated the order. When I still refused, he threatened court-martial."

"That sounds serious," said Matthew.

"It was—until I mentioned Corporal Jameson's brother. That blew everything wide-open. Is he aboard?"

For answer, Matthew summoned Tom Jameson and introduced him to the Major.

"A lot of people will be glad to hear from you, young man," Campbell said when the introductions were finished. "It's well that I had a member of the Vincent family for an Ess-Two," he told Matthew next. "He got in touch with his uncle—the Director of Naval Intelligence himself. *He* briefed the Judge Advocate General, who, now, very much wants to see you. Now, I believe you said the President and Vice President are both suspect?"

"Yes," said Matthew. "Very."

"Which confirms an interesting impression the Judge Advocate General seemed to have. He told me the highest official to trust for the time being is the Speaker of the House of Representatives. Let's both hope he's right about him. Commander, I can't give you orders, so all I can ask is a favor. I'm asking you to proceed at once to the adit and introduce yourself to the JAG and the DNI. They'll tell you what to do next. And take Captain Vincent with you. He's familiar with the problem."

"I'll grant you that favor," said Matthew. "To which adit shall we proceed?"

"Harper's Ferry, Virginia."

* * *

"Apparently, a key incident took place there, having to do with an attempted liberation of slaves, five hundred sixty-five years ago," Matthew was saying. "When open war broke out, the town became Harper's Ferry, *West* Virginia. And, it changed hands eight times during that 'civil war.'"

"How appropriate," said Ayelet. "That must be a special memory for Lieutenant Robinson."

"Yes, and for every African we've met. And if I understand that civics lesson Major Campbell gave us so many days ago, Harper's Ferry is going to become famous all over again, and for a very similar reason."

The LCG flew on under cloaking. Matthew had started teaching Ayelet how to fly it—and she turned out to be a quick study. But Matthew also noted that she was as interested in studying *him* as studying how to fly a ship with a gravity drive.

At last, the time came to come out of cloaking and prepare to land. They were entering NRD-01-WV-Harper's Ferry.

And what a perfect spot for an adit. The Potomac River flowed here, of course—and from the south, another river, the Shenandoah, joined it. And at that junction, he spotted it: what must once have been a railroad tunnel portal, now cleverly hidden. The portal actually opened onto the northern bank of the Potomac, but this far away from the Civilized Footprint, NRD boundaries didn't always follow old political lines.

Next to this portal was an apparent Marine camp that the platoon leader must have erected in some haste. A small knot of people stood just outside this camp. Foremost among them, a man stood waving two brightly colored rods in the air, back and forth. *Some things, including a ground signal to approach, never change,* Matthew reflected. Carefully he set his craft down next to the portal, in a noticeable clearing.

Matthew signaled Ayelet to follow as they descended the flight-deck ladder. He briefly told Tom and Sandy to wait for his signal before disembarking. Only then did he,

Ayelet, Barry, and Captain Vincent descend the boarding ladder to the ground.

Three officers walked toward them, with an escort of white-clad uniformed men. The escorts each wore rank-and-rating insignia of various complexity, all sharing a shield-and-star device that Matthew assumed meant "master at arms." Behind them stood a man in a white smock over what looked like a Navy "pookie suit," in dark green. He stood at the head of a team of what looked like doctors, nurses, a corpsman or two, and some hospitalmen.

Two of the officers, one Caucasian and one African, were flag officers. In fact, they wore three stars each. The third wore Marine greens and lieutenant's bars.

"Matthew Morrow, I presume?" the African officer asked.

"You presume correctly, Vice-Admiral…"

"Leonard M. Smith, Judge Advocate General of the Navy, at your service. With me is Vice-Admiral Sean Vincent, Director of Naval Intelligence, and Second Lieutenant Ben Richardson, who leads this platoon. But I haven't had the pleasure of meeting your fellow officers—or this petty officer."

Matthew introduced Ayelet, who hastened to say, "Mine is a temporary commission, Admirals. I've just taken part in a very sensitive operation."

"I understand. The Commandant of Marines has briefed me as fully as he could."

"And this officer, *I* know," said the Caucasian. "How're you doing, Ian?"

"Just fine, thank you, sir," said the Marine Captain. "And how is Aunt Milly?"

"You know she's been dead these five years; bless her soul."

The younger man nodded—and Matthew understood. Passphrase and countersign. Briefly, he introduced Barry and explained about the intelligence Barry had to convey.

"I understand," said the JAG, "that you have some prisoners on board."

"Yes," said Matthew. "And forty-two children."

"All victims and witnesses?"

"Yes, sir."

"First, let's have those children disembark. We brought a medical team to evaluate them."

Matthew nodded to Ayelet, who disappeared up the ladder. A few moments later, she descended the ladder, with the children following, though with slight hesitation. The medical team leader had just arrived. "Captain Richard Morrison, United States Navy," he said by way of introduction.

"I am Lieutenant Commander Matthew Morrow, late of the United *Systems* Navy."

"And I," said Ayelet, "am Lieutenant Ayelet Cohen, now of the United States Marines. I also am a psychiatric nurse. These children have suffered abominably, and I must ask that you treat them with respect. In fact, you should treat them as combat veterans suffering from PTSD."

"I definitely understand," said Captain Morrison, who then started introducing his team. "Children," he then said, "if you will follow us, we can perhaps talk more comfortably."

Tom and Sandy looked up with slight fear in their eyes. Ayelet smiled and said, "It's all right. And I'll be with you."

Zach Radner, standing next to Ayelet, said, "She's right. They feel friendly. It's all right."

That was all the children needed to hear, so they went with the Ayelet and the team.

"And now," said the JAG, "we should take charge of those prisoners. Shall we board?"

Matthew led the party aboard the LCG. At the sight of the two officers, Averell Morton blurted out, "I want my lawyer! And I must emphatically protest the treatment I have received. Do you know who I am?"

"I do," said Admiral Smith. "I don't believe you know who *I* am. I am the Judge Advocate General of the Navy, and as such, I have the duty to advise you of your rights. You have the right to remain silent. If you give up the right to remain silent, anything you say can and will be held against you in a court of law. You have the right to speak with an attorney…"

"How dare you speak to me as though I were a common prisoner?"

"Do I take it that you understand your rights and require no further explanation?"

"I don't need a *flunky* to tell me my rights! I know my rights—and my privileges."

"And what privileges do you think you enjoy?"

"They include the *privilege* of having your stars and stripes for this outrage. I am under the protection of the President himself."

"Your privileges," said the JAG, coldly, "are terminated. You are under arrest on charges of treason and espionage against the United States, conspiracy to kidnap minor children, and aiding and abetting same. Senator Katzenbaum, Representative Porter, and Representative Shoemaker, those charges apply to you as well. And *you*," the Admiral said this to Captain Coleman. "Name, service rank, and identifying number, if you please."

"Coleman, Rodney. Captain, United Systems Special Security Forces." He then gave a ten-digit number.

"Captain Coleman, *you* are a prisoner of war. You will face a military tribunal on charges of aiding and abetting espionage against the United States."

Matthew interjected the charges he had already read out to Captain Coleman.

"Those charges," said the JAG, "will be added to your record. Chief Carter?"

One of the masters-at-arms, wearing a slightly more elaborate rank insignia than the rest, saluted. "Sir?"

"Secure these prisoners and take them below."

"Aye-aye, sir," said the Chief, who barked out rapid-fire orders. In less than a minute, the guards had unbound the prisoners from their chairs, handcuffed them, and led them down the boarding ladder. The JAG went with them.

"Admiral Vincent," Matthew asked, "may I ask what just happened?"

"What happened, Commander," said the DNI, "is that the JAG just confirmed how high this treason goes. The men in that Shore Patrol party are my men, whom I have vetted personally. And at the lower level of the adit hoist, another SP party awaits us. We should join them now. I will need you to give evidence before the House Judiciary Committee. They are, in fact, convening now."

"To hear what?"

"Evidence of treason on the part of the President."

"Don't forget the Vice President," said Matthew. "Mr. Morton boasted that he enjoys *that* civil officer's protection also."

"And your memory being fully admissible," said Admiral Vincent, "that should suffice."

But just then, the Shore Patrol leader strode up with a worried expression. Even before he spoke, Matthew knew the message would be dire. One look at the prisoners—all but Captain Coleman—told him that. They were positively smirking.

"What's the trouble, Chief?" asked Admiral Vincent.

"Sir," said the Chief, "we've got a problem below. I called down to the lower level, and I didn't get the right countersign."

Matthew, and only Matthew, heard the Admiral curse under his breath. "In other words," he said, "we're stranded."

"It certainly looks that way," said Admiral Smith, now joining them. "And the prisoners know exactly what's going on."

"Yes, I can see that," said Matthew. "But there's no use interrogating them. We haven't time. If I may suggest, let's take stock of other adits we can use and all our military assets."

"Good thought," said Admiral Smith. "Sean, this is more your territory than mine."

"Right," said Admiral Vincent. "Actually, Ian, you're the senior Marine present, so…"

"Aye-aye, sir," said the younger Vincent. "Lieutenant Richardson," he asked the platoon leader, "I assume you're with A Troop?"

"Yes, sir! Second Platoon."

"How are the other platoons deployed?"

"Cap'n Jellicoe is with First Platoon at Millville. Third Platoon is at Charles Town."

"Which means," said the Marine Captain, "that we have assets three and a half miles away and seven miles away. I see you have your flag tower up."

"Yes, sir. Do you need a dispatch sent?"

"Absolutely. Inform Captain Jellicoe of the problem—no, wait a minute. Let's decide exactly what to do first. Chief," he said to the lead SP, "this is important. Did you give any sign that you didn't recognize that countersign?"

"No, sir," said the Chief, looking only slightly irked. "I would never do that. Never let the enemy know they haven't got you fooled. Oldest rule in the book, sir."

"Good. That makes things easier—just barely. Here's my plan: send Second Platoon down this elevator. Yes, they'll be walking into a trap, but that's the point. When they get down there, they'll hold that position until relieved. In the meantime, we send First and Third Platoons down with orders to make their way to Harper's Ferry—pronto."

"What about this transport?" asked the elder Vincent. "Can anyone fly it besides Commander Morrow here?"

"Lieutenant Cohen can," said Matthew without hesitation. "I trained her myself, on our way here."

The DNI whistled. "You never cease to amaze me, Commander," he said. "Would she have a copilot?"

"That young man there," said Matthew. "His name is Zach Radner. He's a quick study and understands coordinated operations. After all, he just took part in one."

The Admiral grinned. "This is looking better all the time," he said. "Ian, this is still your plan."

"Right. We'll let Lieutenant Cohen fly it to Millville. Let Frank Jellicoe tell her where to fly next. Commander, will you take charge of this team?"

"With pleasure," said Matthew.

"Next question. We can work it one of two ways. One, you and your team give First Platoon, say, ten minutes to go down the elevator to Millville, then make their way back to Harper's Ferry. We're Cav, so we have our vehicles. *Then* you go down."

"No good, if I may, Captain," said Matthew. "The minute anyone uses that elevator, the enemy will know. I think you must assume some degree of reconnaissance to cover all nearby towns. It might take them a few minutes to suspect something amiss at Millville, but once they do, *you* will come under attack."

"Now, wait a minute," said the elder Vincent. "You don't propose to go down there now?"

The younger Vincent smiled. "Uncle Sean," he said, "I think that's exactly what he should do. You don't know how survivable this officer is. I've seen a demonstration— up close."

"I'll confirm that," said Matthew. "I ask you to take the word of an experienced combat officer. This is the only workable plan any of us can make."

"Well, at least have all platoons go down at the same time!"

"Wrong again, Admiral," said Matthew. "If I can draw their fire initially, First and Third Platoons will have better success going down unobserved and even unsuspected."

"All right," said Captain Vincent, swallowing hard. "How much lead time do you want?"

"One minute," said Matthew.

"I'll forward all this to Frank Jellicoe. Will you go down with only Second Platoon?"

"Best to take at least some of the others the enemy will be expecting," said Matthew. "Without them, they'll suspect a coordinated strike. With them, maybe not. Part of this shore patrol contingent to start with."

"I'll go, sir," said the Chief. "And I'm sure I can find enough volunteers."

"What makes you so confident, if I may ask?" said the Admiral.

"Sir," said the Chief, "this officer obviously knows what he's doing. We can do this, sir."

"I thank you for that vote of confidence," said Matthew. "You understand, of course, that you have just placed yourself under my orders—and I will be very strict."

"Wouldn't have it any other way, sir."

"And that goes for you, too, Lieutenant Richardson," he said to the platoon leader.

"Aye-aye, sir."

"There's one more touch we can add," said Matthew to the other officers. "We'll need some of the children."

"They're your witnesses," said Admiral Smith. "Are you sure you want to risk that?"

"I think some of them would be glad to take the risk," said Matthew. "Why not ask them?"

* * *

"Sir," said Tom Jameson, "I'll follow you straight to hell if I have to. You bet I'll go."

"And I," said Sandy Rossini.

"Are you two sure about what you're getting yourselves into?" asked Ayelet. "You haven't had the training Zach has had."

"Zach needs to help you fly that thing," said Tom, jerking a thumb back at the waiting LCG. "You're the only two who can do it besides Commander Morrow here."

Ayelet took the point. So did Zach, who nodded grimly.

Matthew nodded. "All right," he said, "it's like this. Tom, you and Sandy will be leading a squad of eight. So we need six more volunteers among you. I'll leave you to recruit them."

In less than five minutes, they had their recruits. It remained only to equip them with weapons they knew how to use. The DEW rifles were new to the Marines and the SP men, but Matthew spent a minute giving lessons to Chief Carter and the Platoon Sergeant. In the end, the two non-coms decided that half their forces should carry DEW rifles, and the other half should carry their familiar projectile rifles. Zach then suggested the children fight with the sort of weapons they knew.

For Tom and his three boy volunteers, it meant bow-and-arrows. For Sandy and the three girls who enlisted under her, it was knives. Sandy still had the ceremonial dagger she had used to kill the Elfin Ambassador. For the others, Matthew made this compromise: he used the ship's printers. As it turned out, the printers were still capable of producing decent throwing and slashing knives. Zach lent Tom the bow he had used during the operation. Ayelet lent her crossbow. For arrows and bolts, the boys quickly fell to carving them from the branches of nearby trees. The two boys who couldn't handle the longbow or crossbow would carry sharp wooden spears.

* * *

"Stand by for ingress," said Matthew to Lieutenant Richardson.

The Marines and the Shore Patrol party—about half its strength, the other half with a first-class master-at-arms with the rest of the party on their way to Millville—straightened up. So did Tom, Sandy, and their squad.

Matthew did not bother with a timepiece; he could manage a countdown just as easily without one. He waited for the last seconds to tick off. Then he said, "In three. Two. One. *Mark.*"

The Chief used an intercom and spoke the passphrase. When the "countersign" came back, the SP nodded. It was all the signal Matthew needed.

"Call the elevator," he said.

The Chief did. Matthew felt the elevator car come to the surface, then watched the doors slide open after the car had slotted in.

Matthew nodded. The Shore Patrol filed in first, weapons at port arms. The children boarded next, with the Shore Patrol closing ranks around them. Not only was this what the enemy would expect, but it would also protect the children—who were armed, but not as well as was the Shore Patrol—for a critical second or two. Last to file aboard were the Marines. It made for quite a crowd, but the car was big enough—albeit barely—to hold them all.

"Take her down," said Matthew.

The Chief nodded, then used the touch screen to give the command. The doors closed, and the elevator started down.

Matthew looked around for signs of tension in his team. The Shore Patrol actually felt it worse, for they knew the kind of forces they might be going up against. The children simply looked grimly determined. Fight or die. Zach had taken the same attitude. The Marines were— well, Marines.

The elevator reached the bottom. The doors opened a crack.

Matthew saw it before anyone else, of course. A black-clad section with guns at the ready. Not SSF, of course— but Matthew realized at once, likely having similar orders.

He gave an almost imperceptible signal. The SP Chief caught it, and Tom, Sandy, and Lieutenant Richardson took their cues from him.

As the doors opened fully, all the team members holding any long-range weapon opened fire immediately.

One SP went down, his AR-18 chattering on full-automatic fire before he died. The rest of the team instinctively took and held the best defensive position they could, while the black-clad force against them took their own cover. Matthew kept his eye out for the high-explosive canister—the word was *grenade*—that he fully expected the enemy to toss into the car. Sure enough, one came flying in. He caught it and threw it back. It made a most satisfactory explosion.

"Secret Service, sir," said the Chief. "That means the President's in on it, just like the JAG said."

"All to be expected," said Matthew, occasionally firing a DEW shot when he saw an opportunity. "How long can we hold this position?"

"It'll be a stretch, sir, no question," said the Marine Lieutenant. "But it's them or us. The stakes being what they are, those guys will likely take no prisoners. They'll *say* they'll take prisoners, but don't believe them."

Matthew took advantage of a temporary lull in the firing to reach for and grab the fallen SP's gun. He checked its ammunition clip. Empty. But three Secret Service men were down. So this master-at-arms had not died in vain.

Five minutes later, the Chief cursed. "Reinforcements!" he said. "And—what the …!? Some of them are carrying those new DEW guns! I don't know, sir; I've got a bad feeling about this."

"Don't talk that way, Chief," said Richardson. "Just tell me how much ammunition you have."

"I'll likely be out in another fifteen," said the Chief. "It might have lasted longer, but now there's more of *them*."

"Don't forget," said Matthew, "that the children have weapons and ammunition of their own."

"Pig stickers and darts?" asked the Chief. "Are you kidding?"

"No," said Matthew evenly. "Better that than nothing at all. And our irregulars have combat experience."

The time seemed to drag on for a very long period. The SP started to get even more worried. Not so the Marines; they seemed to take it in stride.

And then everything started to go sour, so fast, Matthew almost couldn't follow.

First, Tom Jameson stood up, nocked an arrow into his longbow, and let fly. As it happened, he scored a hit. As the target fell, Matthew leaped out, grabbed the body, and pulled it in. From it, he recovered another Armalite and several clips. They would hold out even longer, just for that.

Another Secret Service man had the bad sense to come charging in. Sandy threw a knife straight into his heart, which resulted in the capture of yet another gun and more ammunition. And yet, that acquisition had not come without cost; they lost a Marine in that mini-skirmish.

Now, a third Secret Service man rushed forward, firing at full auto. And Matthew, with his processing ability, saw at once that this man's aim was all too accurate. Bullets were flying straight toward young Tom Jameson, who had never taken cover! Matthew *refused* to let those bullets find their mark. He stepped out into the open and took the full force of the barrage on his chest.

It was like taking rapid-fire punches from a whole mob of pygmy bullies. That many projectiles overwhelmed his shields, tore his tunic to tatters, and made several dents in his chest. Just when he thought he couldn't take anymore, the barrage stopped.

The Secret Service man stared back at him in sick surprise. Then, in frustration, he threw his empty weapon at Matthew, who brushed it aside like a falling tree branch, took another flying leap, and bowled his enemy down. Now he had a live prisoner.

It made no difference at all. The prisoner's fellows riddled their own man with bullets in another attack on Matthew. *What would Ayelet think of this?* More bullets struck Matthew.

And then one of them struck him in the right knee. Pain such as he could not remember experiencing— ever—shot up to his brain from the stricken joint. Willing himself to stay calm, he shut off the pain pathway. Then he registered what must have happened: his artificial kneecap was shattered, and much of the complex joint was ruined. *So much for invulnerability!*

He couldn't help it—his knee buckled under him, and he went down. *This had been an exceedingly foolish maneuver,* he saw now. For he now had no weapon and now, no shield. And he could see several Secret Service taking aim ...

An arrow sang over Matthew's head and struck the leader in the heart, bringing him down. A throwing spear went next, striking another member of that squad in the belly. He went down, too. Then, the others started to aim at targets behind and to either side of Matthew.

All at once, the Secret Service men turned around to fire at another enemy hitting them from behind.

"It's First Platoon!" cried Richardson. "And there's Cap'n Jellico, too! Piece of cake now, sir. We've got 'em in a vise."

And they did. Not only that but First Platoon was armed with DEW weapons. Ayelet must have distributed the remaining DEW guns they had seized from the pedophile camp to Captain Jellicoe and the First Platoon. So the Secret Service had no more tactical advantages.

Matthew could only watch, with his right knee out of action, until Tom Jameson, longbow in his left hand, used his right to toss him a DEW gun. He used that to reasonably good effect, but the battle was nearly over anyway. By the time Admirals Smith and Vincent arrived—in commandeered AFVs—together with Ayelet and all the others, the last of the Secret Service contingent had surrendered.

Ayelet took a look at Matthew, lying in a heap with spent bullets scattered on the corridor floor around him. She gasped. And it actually sounded anguished.

"It's all right, Ayelet," Matthew said at once. "True, we've taken casualties. But I'd say we acquitted ourselves well, considering."

For answer, Ayelet threw herself to the floor next to him and then threw her arms around him. "Oh, Matthew, you're hurt!" she cried. "Are you in any pain? Talk to me, Matthew!"

Matthew cradled her in his left arm. "It's my right knee," he said. "But don't worry. Pain is discretionary for me. I need only to turn it off. And I'm sure these people can repair me."

Ayelet broke off and moved to where Matthew's extended right leg lay at a crazy angle. She drew her service knife and cut Matthew's trouser leg to expose the stricken knee assembly. Matthew looked—and confirmed—the assembly was severely mangled, no question. Ayelet knew it, too—was this how a "sinking heart" registered in someone's face? She looked up and shouted to anyone who could hear, "Could somebody get a doctor over here? No, wait … Nobody here would know what to do!" And she wrung her hands with that last word.

"We'll find someone, Lieutenant," said a man's calm but commanding voice behind her. Then that voice spoke directly to Matthew. "Are you Commander Matthew Morrow, formerly of the United Systems Navy?"

Matthew looked up to face the speaker. Out of the corner of his eye, he caught Ayelet standing up and managing her best try at a proper salute. That must have been all she needed.

The owner of the new voice returned her salute and nodded gravely to her. He was uniformed as a Marine officer, with two silver bars on each shoulder.

"I am Matthew Morrow," said Matthew. "And this is Lieutenant Ayelet Cohen of the United States Marine Corps."

"We've met," said the other. "Captain Frank Jellicoe, commanding A Troop, Third Regiment. I'm also Major Campbell's Ess-Three—Chief of Operations. I have orders to escort you, Admiral Vincent, and Lieutenant Cohen to an immediate meeting with the Speaker of the House of Representatives."

"Does that apply to me, too?" asked Admiral Smith, who now approached.

"Actually, Admiral, I have orders to lend you any escort you require to secure your prisoners. The House Committee on the Judiciary will want to hear from you. And you, Admiral Vincent—when the Speaker has a chance, to talk to you, too."

Matthew reached up to clasp Captain Jellicoe's hand. No unusual sweating, no palpitations, or rapid breathing. Matthew read puzzlement, not fear.

"Your pardon, Captain," he finally said. "I had to make sure of your *bona fides*. Yes, we will gladly accompany you. But I'm afraid I'll need—well, maybe not exactly an ambulance, but…"

Jellicoe took one look at Matthew's condition and nodded. "Got it," he said. "This might seem a foolish question, but can you stand?"

Matthew took a full second to calculate an answer to that. "Someone would have to lever me up," he said. "In fact, a whole fire team, at least. And then…"

"Never mind. You can't. We'll treat you exactly as we would a wounded soldier. And I'm afraid you'll have to coach us on the repair. We've never handled this kind of repair before."

"Not to worry," said Matthew, smiling ruefully. "Anyone who can handle fine tools, and follow instructions, can do this repair. Right, Ayelet?"

Ayelet smiled back, equally ruefully.

Chapter 9

Captain Jellicoe had some of his Marines put Matthew into the cargo bay of his commandeered AFV. Ayelet rode in the bay with him, along with most of a Marine squad. Captain Jellicoe, Admiral Vincent, and the rest of the squad climbed into the vehicle's cab, where a Marine proceeded to drive toward a curious sort of tunnel—a one-lane, one-way bore, like a pneumatic tube.

Matthew watched as the slatted bay cover rolled into place. Then he heard the sound of a pump and a hiss, like incoming air. Finally, the vehicle seemed to enter the bore, then accelerate to a speed Matthew put at around 150 miles per hour.

Four hours later, they emerged from the bore and slowed to a stop. Matthew felt the vehicle move on a level floor, make a few turns, then roll over a slight bump. It stopped, and Matthew felt a thud like double doors closing. Then Matthew felt the vehicle rise. He deduced the vehicle had entered a hoist. The hoist lifted them several deck levels, although Matthew couldn't tell how many. Eventually, the lifting stopped, and the lift doors rumbled open. The vehicle backed out then stopped again.

Finally, the bay door retracted. Matthew found himself looking into a space that looked as though it had always been a cavern, even before the Americans had re-established their society below ground. Several men in white smocks, carrying some *very* fine machine tools, greeted them. Wasting no time, they got to the repair.

In-between coaching this team of "surgeons," Matthew decided to ask about the cavern.

"You are correct, Commander," their escort said. "These are the Cumberland Caverns. Originally they were a drift mine. Then an accidental explosion at a nearby mill above ground brought local residents pouring into the adit, yelling at the mine crew, 'Get out of here, get out of here, this place is going to explode any second.' The crew literally left their equipment where it rested and rushed out. No one ever reopened the mine, so, for decades, it became a tourist attraction. That is, until the Re-Wilding War, when it became one of several places to which our ancestors fled from UNCLIFOR. That adit is sealed tight and camouflaged. We *rarely* use it for an exit."

"Do I take it you keep your seat of government here?"

"Absolutely," said the Troop Commander. "It's ideally suited. I won't say that our entire society spread out from here; that wouldn't even be accurate. But when the government needed to establish continuity, they set up here. The House of Representatives meets in the Hall of the Mountain King, and the Senate meets in a cave room nearby."

"Excuse me, sirs," said the Master Sergeant in charge of the surgical team. "We're just about done here, but our guest will need a more permanent repair later. The bullet got him right in the patella. We can make a replacement, but it'll take time."

"In my society," said Matthew, "someone would print the replacement. But just now, I don't think I would trust it. How do you propose to make the replacement patella?"

"We use an industrial press for that kind of work," the Sergeant said. "It'll have to cure overnight, in a brick kiln. But this repair should hold you until then. And by the way, your chest plate took a lot of damage. Maybe we can replace that, too, though that will take longer."

"Thank you," said Matthew. Then to Jellicoe, he asked, "And where are we going now?"

"To a room off the Hall, where the Speaker keeps his office."

The repair party bound Matthew's right knee in something that looked very much like a pressure splint. They then offered him something he had never used before: an adjustable crutch, complete with foot and shoulder pad! Matthew took time to finish adjusting it, then tried it. It would support him.

He climbed out of the bay, with Ayelet doing her best to help him up, then finally having two members of the surgical team finish that job.

Once on the ground, he first turned to the surgical team and said, "Thank you. For everything."

"Don't mention it, Commander," said the team leader.

Matthew nodded, then turned to Captain Jellicoe and said, "Lead the way, Captain."

The Speaker's room, actually a suite, didn't take too long to find. As they entered, Jellicoe flashed his ID at a waiting receptionist, who actually stood up to greet them. "Hello," she said, smiling. "Is this the Morrow party?"

"It is," Jellicoe said. "Is the Speaker in?"

"Oh, yes, and he said to go right in. He's been expecting you."

"Thank you," said Jellicoe, who then led the party through an inner door.

The room Matthew now entered had one wall that looked dated, and he could see it was part of the original cavern wall. Over it, someone had hung a detailed political map. But someone had added jaws, teeth, eyes, wings, and claws to the vaguely L-shaped area that, Matthew gathered, represented a legislative district. Matthew read the name *Andover* above a township near the base of the wings.

"Elkanah Tisdale's original Gerry-mander cartoon," said a man dressed as a civilian, behind the desk next to this wall. "Just as it appeared in *The Boston Gazette* on 26 March 1812. Let's see, in your dating, that would be…"

"Em-jay-dee-enn minus one seven zero three seven," said Matthew.

"You ran that off very fast, I must say."

"I have an on-board arithmetic logic unit to help me."

The speaker began laughing, then stopped short. "I didn't know you'd been wounded!"

"I took a bullet to the knee," said Matthew. "Your people should give yourselves and your industries credit; you make fine battlefield weapons. And they are equally adept at repairing damaged equipment. I have spare parts on order."

"I assume, Captain Jellicoe, that this officer is in for a Purple Heart?"

"Yes, Mr. Speaker," said the Marine officer without hesitation. "The Commander is being too modest. He's no machine. It's just that every part of his body that you can see is prosthetic. But a wound is a wound."

"Then you definitely are that Commander Matthew Morrow I've heard so much about. Frederick V. Howland, at your service."

Matthew extended his hand, and Mr. Howland shook it warmly—and sincerely. "Nominally, I represent a district that includes a cavern named after the original township of Andover, Massachusetts," he went on. "But for our purposes, I am the Speaker of the House of Representatives. And as such, I am the senior civil officer who can deal with the crisis we are now facing."

"Then you know," said Matthew, "that the President and Vice President have both been compromised. Your Secret Service would never have attacked us otherwise."

"I was afraid of that," said the Speaker. "Fortunately, we already had the Seventh Cav topside, and I see they came through. Boy, the President certainly stepped in it. Have we prisoners?"

"Yes, Mr. Speaker," said Jellicoe.

"Among the Secret Service?"

"Yes, and also, as I understand it, from a pedophile game preserve on the original site of Lucketts, Virginia."

"And what has that to do with this?"

"That, Mr. Speaker," said Matthew, "is where I can testify." He started to tell his story.

The Speaker, cutting him off, said, "Save that for the Judiciary Committee. In fact, I need to call its chairman right now. I'll have to ask you all to allow me complete privacy, since I expect you all to testify before that committee, and…"

"It would not be proper for a witness to meet the judge, even indirectly, before testifying," said Matthew. "I understand. May I assume you have some accommodations arranged for us?"

"Absolutely. In fact, Vincent Neurological consulted on this, which means we can even accommodate you personally, Commander. Jennie, outside, will fix you up."

* * *

The accommodations turned out to be at least as good as his stateroom aboard *Bonaventure VI* had been. *Bonaventure VII* had been smaller, since the Ganymede Navy Yard had built it for speed and fighting strength, not exploration and diplomacy. Capt. Jellicoe led them to this room. "I'm sorry that we have just this one room to spare, but…"

"This is perfect," said Ayelet, smiling. "Give our profuse thanks to the Speaker and tell him we'll be waiting."

As soon as Jellicoe left, Ayelet closed the door and came back into the center of the room. "You, Commander, simply must sit down," she said, leading him to a table. "Come now; I'm still a nursing officer by training, and I know you said you can turn off the pain, but that's all the more reason to be careful. Have you any idea what can happen to an organic who uses his limbs without the sensation to let him know when he's injuring them?"

"Yes," said Matthew. "Dr. Girard, the Ship's Surgeon aboard *Bonaventure VI and VII*, once apprised me of the consequences. Amputation, for one."

"Which *you* cannot risk. And your system is almost as intricate as … well, mine, for that matter. Now sit down, big boy."

He did, taking a seat at a small round table in the middle of the room.

"Matthew, this is all happening so fast," she said as she took another seat at the table. "Are you sure we can trust these people?"

"I once told you I could tell instantly if you were lying to me," he answered. "That goes for anyone whom I can touch, including Captain Jellicoe."

"Well, I know you can normally charge up, and, in fact, I see they fitted out an alcove for you. Can you use it with your knee banged up like that?"

"Fortunately, this crutch can support my weight, I know how to lock the knee, and this bandage will certainly hold."

"Well, I can't do any of that, and I'm starving. How do you get anything to eat here?"

"Have you queried the local computer servers?"

"Good idea," she said and moved to the small desk along one wall. That desk had a computer console built into it. While she did that, Matthew started to get up.

"Oh, no, you don't!" Ayelet said. "You just stay where you are. Tell me what you want checked out, and I'll do the checking-out."

"That closet there," said Matthew, pointing the way.

Ayelet checked it out. Then, in a delighted voice, she said, "Well! Someone's provided Class A uniforms for us both. A Navy uniform for you, and a Marine uniform for me—and a few other kinds of clothing you probably wouldn't know about. I can help you change into your uniform if you'd like."

"First, query the computer for a meal," said Matthew. "You do have your own needs to see to."

A minute later, Ayelet said, "Oh, no! Matthew, I don't know what to do! I see a menu for ordering meals, but they want some kind of money for that. And I can't make out what it is."

"Let me query the system," he said.

"Oh, no," said Ayelet, holding both hands up. "I told you: you stay there."

"I don't need the console," he reminded her. "I can connect to the network from here." Once he had connected wirelessly, he saw the problem. "You're right," he said. "All the meals available are offered, not *gratis*, but in exchange for a precious-metal coin." He queried further, then smiled. "Not to worry," he said. "Speaker

Howland has thoughtfully provided us with twelve silver 'dollars' and one-half gold ounce on our account."

"Excuse me ... 'dollars'?"

"One *dollar*, or originally one *thaler*, originally stood for one Troy ounce of silver. Today it does once again, in this society—and for that matter, in the State of Israel. In fact, the Speaker left a file for our perusal explaining the American and Israeli monetary systems. You might like to know that the dollar and the *shekel* are interchangeable. The gold ounce is worth forty-eight dollars—four Troy pounds of silver."

"Seems awfully complicated."

"Not really," said Matthew. "Didn't ancient Israel have silver coins, at least?"

"Oh! Of course. And the ratio you mentioned was at the low end when everything went to pieces. Now let me look again at those prices." She did, and her face brightened. "Why, we can eat like generals and admirals at these prices! A single meal—a modest one, but still a good meal—can be had for one-tenth of this 'dollar.' And they gave us an amount worth *thirty-six* dollars!"

"Obviously, they want us—well, you, anyway—to eat well. Why not order a meal for yourself while I study the other files in the system?"

So she ordered a meal of venison stew, priced at fifteen "cents," while Matthew studied the file explaining American money. He saw that the monetary system included amounts as small as a "mill," which was one-thousandth of a dollar, or one-twentieth Troy ounce of copper, and as high as a gold talent, one hundred Troy pounds, or twelve hundred Troy ounces. Israeli money was much the same.

Then he reached out beyond the small data server in this room to the larger network that connected most computers in these undergrounds. The results were a revelation. Morton Enterprises, of which Averell Harriman Morton was president, was worth *one thousand gold talents*. A man with that much specie at his disposal could well believe that he *ought to* have the privilege of telling presidents what to do—because a president typically received an annual payment the Americans called a *salary*, after the *salt* with which ancient Rome paid its infantry, of a mere fifteen silver talents. That was enough to let anyone live like a king in this society but paltry in comparison to the worth of that company.

Matthew shared these insights with Ayelet, who interrupted him. "We've let far too much time go by," she said. "And we both need to change. Here," she said, reaching for his new Naval uniform. "Let me help you with this."

"Won't you find that awkward?"

"Not at all," she said, smiling. "In fact, I think I like the idea."

It could have been a struggle, but Matthew had gotten used to his crutch and could help far more readily than either of them supposed. While they set to the task, he continued with his insights about American money—and the temptation it risked. "It occurred to me," he said, "that we see corruption of a sort new to both of us. I can understand how the Five Ladies persuaded so many followers to embrace a society without money. They abolished the kind of venal corruption that created the present scandal. But they replaced one kind of corruption with the kind we know."

"Yes," said Ayelet. "Power lust. I wonder which is really worse?"

"The power lust, I think," said Matthew. "One who lusts after money is a mere thief. But one who lusts after power is at best a bully, and at worst, a tyrant. Far more dangerous."

"Except," Ayelet reminded him as she now swiftly changed into her Class A Marine greens, "that the money-grubbers often play with the power freaks. As I'm sure this Averell Morton did, in this case. Oh, when I think about what those children suffered for that, I could kill him myself."

A soft chime sounded.

Matthew glanced at Ayelet, who was just fastening the last of the buttons (*What an odd invention!*) on her Marine uniform tunic. She nodded. So Matthew reached out to the automatic systems and unlatched the door. "Enter," he commanded.

Capt. Jellicoe waited outside. Drawing himself up to full attention, he said, "Commander Morrow, Lieutenant Cohen, the Chairman of the House Committee on the Judiciary requires your immediate presence in its hearing chamber."

"I just ordered a meal," said Ayelet. "What will happen to that?"

Jellicoe relaxed. "I can give orders to delay delivery until after you return." And he did. After which, Ayelet and Matthew followed Jellicoe outside.

* * *

"The committee will now come to order." So saying, a middle-aged woman picked up a gavel and rapped the dais with it. On a black background, a black nameplate bearing the legend "MRS. EWER" in white text identified her.

"For the benefit of the witnesses," she went on, "we are hearing evidence for possible Articles of Impeachment against the President and Vice President of the United States, charging them both with treason, espionage, bribery, extortion, kidnapping, criminal endangerment of minors, and accessory-to-murder of some of same. I understand that these witnesses can testify directly to these matters. Accordingly, the Chair calls Lieutenant Commander Matthew Morrow, late of the United Systems Navy, to testify."

Matthew Morrow, still wearing his new American Navy blues, levered himself up and half-walked and half-hopped to a green baize table. He was wondering how he would raise his right hand and stay supported when Mrs. Ewer said, "The Chair takes cognizance of the witness' wound and grants him permission to give the oath with his hand on a Bible."

The committee clerk stepped forward and held out a bound codex-style volume labeled HOLY BIBLE in both hands. The last time he'd seen anything like that was in the library Captain de Grasse had kept on *Bonaventure VI*. That library had held a volume labeled *Sacré Bible, Édition Louis Segond*. "I keep it," the Captain had once said, "because it has such beautiful language in it."

But these people obviously took it very seriously. Matthew rested his right hand on the volume now before him.

"Do you solemnly swear," the clerk said, "that any testimony you may give in a cause now pending before this committee be the truth, the whole truth, and nothing but the truth, so help you, God?"

That concept again. Matthew would have to ask about that. For now, he said, "I do."

"Please be seated, Commander."

Matthew took his seat, an operation that came more easily with the practice he'd had.

"State your name, rank, and serial number, for the record, please," said Mrs. Ewer.

"Morrow, Matthew. Lieutenant Commander, United Systems Navy." And he gave his serial number.

"Now, then, Commander, it is customary at a hearing such as this to ask the witness to recite any prepared statement he might have. I realize you likely did not have time to compose one, so if you would like to open with some remarks, please do so, and then we will question you in detail."

Matthew told the story of his escape into Protected Wild Space, his falling in with the Recon Platoon, the attack on the Marines' camp by the SSF, overhearing the withdrawal order—and then his reconnaissance of, and subsequent raid on, the pedophile camp. The Members seated before him seemed to take an avid enough interest in his story. But when he named some of the prisoners he took, and mentioned their boasts about having the ears of the President and Vice President, it was as if he had riveted them to their seats. His account of the attack on him and his party by elements of the Secret Service drew a murmur of outrage, which the Chair checked.

One or two members tried to shake his testimony but could not, especially when Ayelet took the green table and backed him up completely. Matthew had found it interesting to note the clerk had offered her a slightly different volume on which to take the oath: a volume written right-to-left and bearing Hebrew words on its cover: *Torah, Nevihim, Kethuvim.*

And when the JAG and the DNI took the green table to tell of their own investigations into Morton Enterprises and the Senator and Representatives Matthew named, their evidence cut all arguments short.

The session took a total of three hours. And at the end of it, the committee voted almost unanimously to impeach the President and Vice President on all the charges Chairman Ewer named.

After the committee adjourned, several of the members wanted to shake Matthew's hand—and Ayelet's, too. But Admiral Smith whispered in Matthew's ear, "We should leave right away. At least two other committees need to hear evidence from us."

Matthew whispered back, "Admiral, this might sound vain, but I should go through this—to make sure of these people."

Admiral Smith opened his mouth to object, but Admiral Vincent said, "He's right, Len. I can explain as we go down the passageway to the House Ethics Committee."

The JAG shrugged and let his colleague lead him away while Matthew and Ayelet did about ten minutes of meet-and-greet. Afterward, the party left the hearing room to walk down to their next committee meeting.

"Well?" asked Ayelet, smiling.

"They're good," said Matthew. "Most of them are. But two of them are plainly worried."

"The two who cross-examined you?"

"The same."

When they arrived at the hearing room of the House Committee on Standards of Official Conduct, Admiral Vincent was just finishing his opening statement. He named ten members of the House who had taken part in activities that merited expulsion. Representatives Porter and Shoemaker led the list. But Matthew heard two other names that he recognized—the two worried members of the Judiciary Committee.

And so, when he and Ayelet gave their evidence, the committee took it as confirmation of what the Admiral had said. More than that, Matthew heard mention of *more* pedophile camps. Matthew recognized the likely NRD's: ID-Boise, AB-Calgary, NV-Las Vegas, KY-Lexington, MO-St. Louis, and SD-Keystone.

Nor was that the end of Matthew's testimony. He and Ayelet then had to appear before the *Senate* Committee on Standards of Official Conduct to give evidence against Senator Katzenbaum.

When that committee dismissed him, Admiral Vincent said, "You two might as well return to your assigned billet. Things are still going to happen, all right, but they'll happen in the full House and Senate. The Senate never lets anyone attend its sessions, except in the gallery. And, in any event, the time for testimony from witnesses is passed."

"What exactly can we expect?" Matthew asked.

"The House will meet; first, to consider the report of its Ethics Committee and, we presume, to expel those ten members," said Vincent, ticking off a point on his index finger. "And, also, to hear the *Judiciary* Committee's recommendations to impeach the President and Vice President. While that is happening," he said, ticking off a point on his middle finger, "the *Senate* needs to hear the report of *its* Ethics Committee and expel a few Senators. By then, the House should have Articles of Impeachment ready for the Senate to consider. Finally," and here, he ticked off a point on his ring finger, "the Senate must meet, with the Chief Justice sitting in the chair, to *try* those impeachments."

"That would seem to require several days," said Matthew, feeling dismayed.

"Not this time," said Admiral Smith. "Those guys are furious and intend to move fast. But while they're doing that, we can look over some of the intelligence take from that raid you laid on."

"Why not now?"

"Because some of us need some sleep to look at it with fresh minds. Don't worry—we'll have the full day tomorrow to draft a briefing for the new president when he is ready to take office."

"Let me guess: that will be Representative Howland from Andover."

"Correct!" said Smith, grinning. "As Speaker of the House, he's next in line. But come; your friend needs sleep, and I would imagine you could use a recharge. We'll see you tomorrow."

* * *

It wasn't until 0200 hours when Matthew and Ayelet returned to their billet. Ayelet was still hungry, but, to her delight, her meal order arrived immediately after they did. "Why, this is fresh and warm!" she said. "It tastes almost as good as what we had in camp! And, all this without a printer!" she said in wonderment. "Why would any society even bother with such things?"

"Sheer laziness," said Matthew. "At least, that's the appeal of a technology like that. But we both know that technology is doomed to fail. You'll recall, I said I wouldn't trust a spare part that came from my own society? That's why."

After Ayelet finished her meal, she drew out another item from the closet: nightclothes. While she excused herself to the bathroom to change, Matthew did his best to inspect the charging alcove in the far wall. Remarkable—someone had correctly guessed that he could charge wirelessly. Captain Vincent must have been very busy—and as explicit as he was thorough.

After Matthew made a few minor adjustments, the alcove was ready. Matthew stepped into it at the moment Ayelet emerged from the bathroom, wearing the nightclothes. She actually stared at him for a good long time before she caught him looking at her with a curious eye. Then she climbed into the bed and composed herself for sleep.

Matthew, drawing the charge from his new alcove, watched her for fifteen minutes. He noticed her expression: peaceful, yet, anticipating something more. Then he commanded himself to sleep. His brain, being organic, still needed it from time to time.

* * *

Morning came. First to arrive was the Sergeant who had taken charge of repairing him the day before. He had the spare part for Matthew's knee. After inspecting it, Matthew said, "I'm tempted to ask you to order a second one for my left knee. This is true workmanship, something I'm not used to seeing."

"Well," said the Sergeant, "what we could do is place a more extensive order for spare parts of all kinds. But let's see to installing this, and then you can walk without that crutch."

The "operation," as they called it, took half an hour, during which time Ayelet ordered breakfast for herself. Then, shortly after the Sergeant and his party took their leave, the meal arrived. To Matthew's surprise, it was two meals.

"Won't you join me?" Ayelet asked, smiling up at him.

Matthew paused a moment. "Thank you, Ayelet," he nodded. He had momentarily thought to decline when he suddenly decided, *Why not? If she's going to treat me as a real person, I should act like one. Besides, she is excellent company.*

As he sat with her, he thought, *What a relief to sit down without a crutch!* Then he noticed at once her continued fondness for venison. Both meals consisted of venison strips, an egg boiled very soft, and sliced bread, browned to a crisp with a small bowl of olive oil to dip it in. He remembered many of his fellow officers would order a dairy-based spread with such a meal when he was on shipboard. He decided to ask about that.

In answer, she smiled that rueful smile again. "That's because," she said, "your shipmates were Gentiles. Gentiles do not know how particular we Jews can be about what is fit to eat and what is not."

"Do I take it someone has taken pains to observe your dietary specifications?"

"I think it more likely that whoever designed this menu consulted long ago with that 'State of Israel' community. This little card tells the tale."

She held up a small white placard that bore a curious symbol of the Roman letter U inside a circle—or maybe a capital O. Beneath this, he read three Hebrew letters. From right to left, they were the *koph*, the *shin*, and the *resh*. Transliteration: *kosher*. The Hebrew word meaning "fit."

As they started to eat, Matthew did what he had always done whenever eating organic comestibles: he analyzed them. Dr. Frankel had managed to replicate the taste buds as well as the olfactory chemosensors. So he could taste food as well as could any organic—and appreciate flavors.

This food tasted good, better than anything that came out of a printer, certainly. Obviously, these foodstuffs were free of the drug he had identified in printed food. But more than that, he could readily appreciate that food like this would be more easily digestible for an organic and was even slightly more efficient for him to process for energy.

He said so, and asked, "Where do these *kosher* regulations come from?"

For answer, Ayelet described passages out of a book she called *Vayiqra*. "The Gentiles call it Leviticus, meaning 'of the Levites,' I suppose." It described the dietary regulations in some detail.

"I'm not quite following, Ayelet," said Matthew. "That is, I understand where the—what does this symbol stand for? The capital 'U' inside the capital 'O,' that is?"

"'Orthodox Union,'" she said. "It's a wonder that organization still exists."

"As may be, I understand where the Orthodox Union derived the regulations. But how did they get into this work—the *Vayiqra*? Why would they write regulations that are more appropriate to … Wait a minute. I think I see it."

"See what, Matthew?"

"Your ancestors crossed a desert, didn't they?" he asked.

"Yes, they did."

"And they had to subsist on wild game and fish. One would expect them to take caution in the kind of game they took and the fish they caught. But how would they know to take such caution?"

"They had the Eternal to tell them," she said, smiling at him almost as she would smile at a small boy who asked such a question.

"The Eternal … Is that another name for the concept of *God?*"

"Oh, yes," said Ayelet, her eyes beginning to shine a little.

"But what does it mean?" he asked. "I learned that God was an obsolete concept. The Five Ladies went into it in detail. Their writings were required reading when … Well, for as long as I can remember, anyway. But you take it seriously. And not only you but our hosts. Why?"

"Well, after all, He only did a little thing like create the Universe, this world, and all the life on it. Including human beings."

"I could almost ask who created Morgens and Neo-Inuit and, for that matter, the Elves," said Matthew. "But that wouldn't suffice, either. Had your people invented an all-wise commandant, ruler, and adviser, as they taught me, at least at the Galactic Institutes of Psychiatry and then at the Academy, that I could understand. But that doesn't explain how your ancestors knew in advance not to take wild game or catch wild fish that were any less particular about what *they* considered fit to eat, as you are. That passage you described to me reads like a field manual for camp management in the wild. It doesn't describe any of the science that we might put in if we were writing it. But the advice is sound."

"I should think so," said Ayelet. "All the *Tanakh* is a manual of instructions for human behavior. And a history book, too."

"That word, '*Tanakh*'—what does that mean?"

"It's a letter word, from the three letters *tav, nun,* and *koph*. Which are the first letters of…"

Matthew finished it with her: "…*Torah, Nevihim, Kethuvim*. And these words mean?"

"Law, Prophets, and Writings."

"Ayelet," Matthew said after a moment's reflection, "you now have me profoundly curious. I want to know more about this … Eternal, as you call Him. So I should start by reading the *Tanakh*, cover to cover."

"I would be glad to procure a copy for you," she said, even more warmly than before. "Would you like it in Standard?"

"No, I would prefer to read it in the original," he said. "Early in my education, I realized that Hebrew was the root of all human language, so I studied it as well as I could. I'm sure I'll be able to read the *Tanakh* in

Hebrew—and you know as well as I that translation is never exact.

"I do have one other question," he went on. "Those two committees offered me another volume, called '*Holy Bible*,' to swear on. What might that have to do with the *Tanakh*?"

Ayelet looked a little uncomfortable—but only a little. "Actually," she said, "that other work you mentioned contains the *Tanakh*, or most of it, anyway, along with another body of work, which we Jews have some contention. That other body refers to a certain historical figure who claimed to be our—the word is *Maschiach*, or 'anointed one.' True enough, he satisfied an incredible number of prophecies about the actual *Maschiach*. But he ended up going to his execution. It didn't make any *sense* for him to be the *Maschiach* if the Roman Army could treat him that way."

"A debate for another time," said Matthew with finality. "Perhaps someday you and I can sort it out. But first things first."

They finished their meal in relative silence, then put on those Class A uniforms again. But just before they left their quarters, Ayelet reached for Matthew's hand. He let her hold it for what seemed an age, though it was only a few seconds. She also looked him in the eye. Her expression … *Oh, how it reminded him of a distant memory … Natalya.* Ayelet's look was not unlike the look she had once given him. But then the moment was over; they had to leave. It left a lingering impression on Matthew, though.

* * *

Matthew, Ayelet, Barry, Captain Vincent, Captain Jellicoe, and the two admirals convened in a conference room in the Speaker's suite of offices. All the officers, Matthew saw, wore the Class A uniform, which meant that actual medals dangled from the ribbons they normally wore. "The Speaker sends his regards," said the receptionist, "and says he'll likely return by noon today. The House will be in emergency session all morning long."

"We understand perfectly," said Admiral Vincent.

As the receptionist closed the door to the conference room, everyone started poring over some of the intelligence take from the pedophile game preserve. This took the form of computer records that went a lot further than personnel records. And they confirmed every suspicion he had—including the guilty knowledge of Matthew's own capabilities, though, certainly not all of them. Barry also briefed the officers in detail about what his contacts had turned up.

"Shall we brief the Speaker about this?" Vincent asked.

"Brief me about what?" said a new voice, which was that of Frederick Howland.

"Mr. Speaker," said the Admiral, "we have some information you are likely going to want to act upon very rapidly."

"I don't doubt that ... Excuse me. Yes, Miss Tompkins?"

"You're wanted in the Senate chamber, sir," said the receptionist. "As quickly as you can get there."

Howland smiled a wan smile. "I think I know why," he said. "Gentlemen, and Lieutenant Cohen, I'd like you to come to the Senate with me. If the Senate wants what I think it wants, I can think of no better witnesses I'd like to have on my behalf."

Matthew nodded to Ayelet, who said, "I would be honored to attend."

"As will we all," said Admiral Smith. "Shall we go?"

The large party left the office and instantly fell in with a Marine honor guard. Then, with them as escorts, they walked rapidly down several hallways.

As they entered the Senate chamber, the Senate rose as one to greet them. At the bottom of the cup-like well of the Senate, a man in a black robe with three felt chevrons on each sleeve rose from a great chair at the central desk. At the same time, a Senator rose from his small desk and made his way quickly to the party.

"Hello, Sam," said Fred Howland to the Senator.

"Hello, Fred," said the Senator. "A helluva way to proceed. Have you got your credentials?"

For answer, Mr. Howland drew out a piece of paper and handed it to the Senator.

From his place at the desk, the robed man asked, "Senator Adams, have you a presentation to make?"

"Yes, Mr. President—your honor…"

"Mr. President will do here. You may proceed."

"Mr. President, I present the credentials of the Honorable Frederick V. Howland, Representative from the Andover Cavern in Massachusetts. He has lately served as Speaker of the House of Representatives and now is tendering his resignation from that position, pursuant to the Presidential Succession Act of 1947, as amended."

"The acting President-designate—along with what I presume are his witnesses—will present himself at the desk, where the Presidential Oath of Office will be administered."

At a nod from Senator Adams, Fred Howland stepped forward along the center aisle. The two admirals followed next after him, and then Matthew, Ayelet, Barry, and Captain Ian Vincent.

The party formed a semicircle in front of the desk, where the robed man—who Matthew now realized must be the Chief Justice of the United States and *temporary* president of the Senate—remained standing and drew out a leather-bound book. Another Holy Bible.

"Raise your right hand," said the Chief Justice.

Howland did so.

"Do you solemnly swear that you will faithfully execute the office of President of the United States, and will to the best of your ability preserve, protect, and defend the Constitution of the United States, so help you, God?"

"I do."

"You may lower your hand—Mr. President."

The new acting President did so, then glanced at the small table next to the Senate presidential desk for the first time. That table held an ornate spring-loaded case. Resting within it, Matthew spotted a prominent medal: a gold heart shape, with a left profile of a very high-ranking general, wearing a uniform that was obsolete but which these people still respected. This object hung from a simple purple ribbon with silver-gray borders.

"Mr. President," Howland said, "I thank you for your consideration in another small matter. I see no reason not to attend to that at once. Will Lieutenant Commander Matthew Morrow please step forward?"

Matthew did.

Taking the small medal out of its case, the acting President said, "For having been wounded in an action against persons guilty of treason against the United States, who were, therefore, its enemies, and for sustaining said wound while preserving and protecting a citizen of the United States whom allies of those same enemies had unlawfully abducted from us, I have the high privilege and distinct honor of bestowing upon you the Order of the Purple Heart."

And with that, Howland pinned the medal on Matthew's chest. With that done, Matthew raised his right hand in salute. The President gravely returned it.

* * *

The new acting President's next task was to nominate one, Jesse H. Lyman, as his vice president. The Congress confirmed him in that office even more swiftly than it had dealt with the Articles of Impeachment against his predecessor.

On that same day, the Recon Platoon finally returned home with the rest of the prisoners. After which, the treason trials, and the expulsion proceedings, began in earnest.

Chapter 10

I need not tell you, I'm sure," said acting President Howland, "that our society is in turmoil. No other word does justice to this appalling state of affairs. Of all the ways I imagined becoming president of this republic, I never imagined this."

Matthew, Ayelet, Andrea, and Barry sat in quite comfortable chairs in a room the acting President called "The Oval Office"—modeled, apparently, after the original office of that name in the building that had been as close to a presidential palace as the United States had ever had, before the Great Climate War. He glanced at his companions and noted that they were finally growing accustomed to the relatively low overheads in these underground spaces. They were comfortably high enough—seven feet, in United States Patriotic units—but still cramped to one accustomed to overheads of three and a half meters. Their host sat behind a mahogany desk and wore an expression as grave as the situation they were all meeting to discuss.

As if to underscore that gravity, four *very* high-ranking military officers were also attending. Vice-Admirals Smith and Vincent were both present, along with a five-star Admiral introduced as Fleet Admiral Jack Scott, and General Josh Painter, Commandant of Marines. Major Campbell and Captains Frank Jellicoe and Ian Vincent, looking to Matthew as if they felt very out-of-place, were also present.

All wore the much simpler uniform, called "utilities," of the kind that Lieutenant Robinson had first worn when Matthew had met him in camp. Matthew now wore a similar uniform. The simple ribbon of his Purple Heart was still fixed in place on his left chest. Of course, he still would need a new chest plate assembly. But technicians from Vincent Neurological had already examined him and said they could commission a replacement. That replacement would be ready within a week.

"Mr. President," Matthew began, "I certainly never imagined, during all my education, training, and career, coming to such a pass as this. And I am immensely gratified that your society could move so quickly in correcting a very serious error in the choosing of its leadership. But, you and I need to discuss a situation far more urgent than the one with which your Congress has lately dealt."

"You refer to our existence being known to your former government?"

"I do." Matthew quickly explained his spotting of an anomaly in "Protected Wild Space," his arrest, Ayelet awakening him from a fifteen-year coma, then his escape, and why he chose to enter Protected Wild Space. "I entered this space," he said, "searching for answers to the question of my arrest and why a very secretive authority was pursuing me. Imagine my surprise to discover the continued existence of a society I had thought extinguished. Now imagine my outrage upon discovering that the object of my search was a pedophile game preserve. And in my investigation and subsequent raid of that preserve, I found evidence of something much worse.

I did not fully appreciate that until after Captain Vincent, Lieutenant Cohen, and myself had an opportunity to examine copies of specific computer files seized at that preserve. Those files tell a very dire story.

"Mr. President, first, I thank your Director of Naval Intelligence for allowing me to examine those files closely. I can now tell you what they mean, in light of my memory of my cyborg life and records pertaining to the project that led to my construction. And I doubt that you will like what I say.

"Mr. President, your society is in serious, perhaps imminent, danger. In point of fact, the intelligence services of the United Nations and United Systems have, for the past fifty years, suspected your continued existence, centuries after they thought they had wiped you out. *Also,* fifty years ago, they began a secret program to construct an army of ultimate warriors, to quote Major Campbell's turn of phrase. Five years into their program, they abandoned their first paradigm: constructing man-like artificial intelligences, or *'androids,'* as they called them. I imagine that Dr. Erich Frankel, the lead project scientist, finally concluded what any physician could have told him: cramming the intelligence, rationality, *and self-awareness* that distinguish rational from non-rational beings into a space no larger than a human or humanoid cranium was physically impossible.

"So he settled on the next best idea: construct a total-body prosthesis, having all the capabilities the ultimate warrior should have, and install into it a complete central nervous system.

"Mr. President, *I am the first prototype*. I might not even be the only one. And the timing of the project and the first suspicion that you existed and had eluded the earlier efforts of the United Nations Climate Force to destroy you absolutely precludes any coincidence. I now conclude that the object in constructing me was to develop a model for building similar cybernetic organisms with one mission: to destroy your society once and for all."

The President, and the other attendees, sat in silence for half a minute. Finally, the President asked, "Why wouldn't they simply bombard us with missiles? Put several vessels in geostationary Earth orbit and fire away?"

"They don't know how far down you are," said Matthew, echoing Barry's intelligence. "Some of your caverns lie as deep as two and a quarter of your *miles* beneath the surface. I can only marvel at your achievement in this regard. More to the point: if my society's intelligence apparatus has any hint of the maximum depth of your settlements—and I would repose about ninety percent confidence that they have at least a working hypothesis to that effect—then they know that any bombardment intended to destroy any settlement as deep as that would be worse than futile.

"Nor do they want to risk collapsing an aquifer. They severely weakened the Great Plains Aquifer with their action against the Hoover Dam. Most of your settlements lie *beneath* aquifers. Far beneath them. Correct?"

"Correct," Howland said.

"Third," Matthew went on, "they want to hide their intentions from the general public. They fear the people as it is. Did Major Campbell brief you on the printers my former society uses?"

"Yes, and the abandonment even of farming and animal husbandry, and the introduction of a major tranquilizer into everyone's food and drink."

"Just so. That alone tells you that they fear the people. Add to it that they have been involved in numerous wars—they seem to have a penchant for making enemies. So they could scarcely afford having real or potential enemies watch as they dealt with a possible rebel society on their very homeworld—or as close to a homeworld as the United Systems has. And last: they are, quite simply, bullies. They would never attack you until you had already lost."

"Which, maybe they tried to make happen by subverting our institutions and striking terror into many parents' hearts by kidnapping some of our children."

"That, Mr. President," said Matthew, "is a highly probable scenario. May I ask what sorts of products or services the corporate group known as Morton Enterprises provided?"

"You mean before we shut down that company and all its subsidiaries, pending multiple civil and criminal indictments? Why, they operated in a wide variety of industries—education, entertainment, computer software…"

"And full-object printing?"

The President looked to Admiral Vincent, who said, "We've only just begun to look into that aspect, but yes,

Mr. President. Not only that, but we seized quite an arsenal—and armory—of those fancy new DEW weapons."

"And there, Mr. President," said Matthew, "you have it."

"Just what do you suppose they were doing with DEW weapons?" Howland asked. "They're the last thing I would expect our apparent enemies to trust them with."

"Not if a palace coup against your predecessor was part of their plan," said Matthew.

"What need for that if they were going to build a force of ultimate warriors like you?"

"Any war plan has Plans A, B, C, and so on," said Matthew. "I represent Plan C."

"And what do you suggest we do about it?"

"You have no choice, Mr. President. You must declare war against the United Nations and Systems. I can help you fight them, but only after you commit yourselves to fight."

"And what do you get out of it, Commander Morrow?"

"My own survival and service of the cause of justice."

"Which you would serve by treason against your people?"

"Not treason, Mr. President. Revolution."

"But why revolution? You've talked a great deal about our *casus belli*. What's yours?"

"Mr. President, my society *used me* as a prototype to attack an inoffensive target—you. People like that will attack other targets just as easily. And they placed me under arrest after I discovered an even more disgusting practice of theirs. Now I find that what I, at first, took to be a technical malfunction—the promazine derivative—was a deliberate design. *Of course,* I have *casus belli.* I have to think not only of myself, and of you, but of ordinary people in my society who labor under the kind of regime that has no respect for life or liberty. And which abolished property, which I see as just as much of an injustice as anything else they've done."

The President leaned back in his leather swivel chair. Then he turned to his right. "Major Campbell," he said, "your thoughts?"

"My analysis is the same as his, Mr. President," said the Squadron Commander. "We are in trouble—bad trouble. We have to fight. And if I may suggest, sir, we bring the Israelis into this. They have a stake in this, too."

The President leaned forward and sat where he was, looking at his hands for five seconds. Then he said, "I agree. I called this meeting to get everyone's opinions before I called the Prime Minister of Israel. Without objection, I propose to do precisely that. Does anyone object?"

Silence.

"Very well, then," said President Howland. "This meeting is adjourned. We will reconvene in the Cabinet Room this afternoon—as soon as the Prime Minister can get here, with whatever team he wishes to assemble."

* * *

The Cabinet Room was much larger, with a long table running the length of the room. Matthew saw at once that it was the one room in this mini-complex that could seat everyone present.

Three newcomers had joined this conference. One wore civilian clothes, as did Howland. The other two wore a uniform strikingly different from the typical American Naval uniform. The shoulder boards of one of them displayed a crossed sword and olive branch and two olive-tree drawings above this. The other officer had shoulder boards displaying only one olive tree.

"Ladies and gentlemen," Frederick Howland said, "let me introduce to you—Prime Minister Yitzhak bin Avram of the State of Israel; Marshal Caleb Marcus, Commandant of the Israel Defense Forces; and General Salmon Levi, Director of the Israeli Institute for Intelligence and Special Operations."

General Levi smiled and said, "Our host is so long-winded. We just call ourselves The Institute—or *Mossad* in Hebrew."

The President went on to introduce the Americans, and Matthew and his companions, to the Israelis. When General Levi heard the name *Ayelet Cohen*, he started. "One of your companions is Jewish, *Rav Seren* Morrow?"

"Yes, indeed, *Aluf* Levi," said Matthew, giving the Hebrew version of the general's title. "Ayelet," he went on, "perhaps you can introduce yourself more fully."

She did.

General Levi beamed. "So a movement of *Zealots* has formed in UN country?"

"Perhaps," said Ayelet, "our *zeal* derives from our shame since our ancestors failed to join yours."

"The record of your service in the latest surface operations belies your modesty, *Segen* Cohen," Levi said. "But come. I understand that we are met in a council of war. Yitzhak gave me only a sketchy briefing. Naturally, Caleb and I need to hear more."

It fell to Matthew to deliver the briefing, which he did—all of it, including his own origins and capabilities. And then it fell to General Levi—*Aluf* Levi—to ask the obvious question: "How extensive *is* the knowledge of these 'United Systems'? And how widely are we known?"

"I doubt anyone suspects your people, *Aluf*," said Matthew. "But the Americans are certainly known to the race called the 'Elves,' that advised the United Nations Climate Force."

"Naturally, we are curious about them," said the *Mossad* Chief. "Especially about a vessel that is stealthy even against visible light. Have you photographs of that vessel to share?"

For answer, Fleet Admiral Scott placed a briefcase on the table, opened it, and extracted several photographs that Naval Intelligence had taken of the Elfin VIP transport, which now rested at an adit more closely above their heads. It was very well hidden indeed; Matthew had figured out how to adjust the cloaking system to project an image of a low-lying hill.

"We haven't yet figured out these markings on this vessel," the Admiral was saying.

Aluf Levi grinned. "Oh, come now, Yacov," he said, "Are you sure you don't catch the little hint of Hebrew in those markings? Though, I admit, I have a little trouble translating it."

Hebrew? Matthew took another hard look at the photographs. "But that's Elfin script," he said, failing to notice the resemblance to Hebrew. "The ship's name would mean little to you."

Levi's eyes bulged. "An extraterrestrial civilization speaks a variant of *Hebrew?*"

"General—excuse me, *Aluf*—didn't I tell you?" asked Matthew. "You are looking at a ship's name legend in Elfin. Where did you develop the notion that this is Hebrew?"

Then Ayelet abruptly blurted out, "Matthew! He's right! Those markings *do* look like Hebrew letters—very ancient letters. Or maybe they just aged in a different way."

"Ayelet, how can you know this?"

She grinned. "Didn't I tell you that the Dead Sea Scrolls have been in my family since I was a child?" she asked. "I *lived* with letters like those! Of course, you're right; that ship's name wouldn't translate into any Hebrew equivalent. I'm sure it's a proper name, but with roots no one ever spoke on Earth."

"We must get my friends, the Academicians, in on this," said Levi. "If they can translate that language directly, then…"

"I can show everyone how to access the operating, tactical, and maintenance manuals." *And if Ayelet and this Intelligence Chief were even halfway correct, those should translate easily.*

For five minutes more, Matthew described the vessel further. He did not question Levi's interest; absolutely anything might be important in building defenses. Naturally, he laid special emphasis on the cloaking system and the ship's weapons.

"A formidable foe, to be sure," said *Rav Aluf* Marcus. "But if we once start imagining him to be invincible, we have lost before we begin." That provoked a chorus of hear-hears.

The discussion then turned to the physiology and origins of the Elves. Matthew speculated that they arose on a desert world, or maybe a world that was first jungle and then desert.

"That's what your Elves want you to think," said Levi. "But they definitely speak Hebrew or a variant of it. Therefore they must have originated on this world— perhaps even before the Deluge."

"Deluge, *Aluf* Levi?"

"*Oy, gevalt!* Can you have never learned that this world suffered a great flood that once covered all land areas?"

"If I may, *Aluf* Levi," said Ayelet, "he received his education from people who have consistently denied both the Deluge and the Eternal One who brought it about. He did express interest in reading our *Tanakh*, however."

Obviously, that struck a chord with the *Mossad* Chief, for he took his time answering. "Excellent," he finally said. "You will find in that work a full description of the Deluge. But we have a more immediate problem. I can well believe, from the description of their technology, that they intervened in the Great Climate War. Or perhaps more accurately, ran that war."

"At first, I didn't know whether to believe it," said the President. "Even though Major Campbell and Captain Vincent are trustworthy officers. But Commander Morrow shows up in a classic flying saucer that looks like the one from the Roswell incident. Or do you know what I'm talking about?"

Of course, Matthew did and shared how. The President objected that the LCG was much larger than the two-man coracle of Roswell. But Matthew then explained the basic stealthiness of the hull shape, even without its cloaking system. With that, no one wanted to argue.

"Let's discuss our more immediate concerns," the President said. "We know now that this was not the only installation on this world, or even above us. Testimony before our Congress has disclosed the existence of *six more* such camps. We now know where to find them—and our liberation of them must be our first priority. More to the point, our examination of records we have seized from the offices of Morton Enterprises and their subsidiaries sheds more light on those camps. Ladies and gentlemen, those camps served for more than twisted entertainment. Each and every one was a spy center, as well."

"Which gives you two motives to move against them," said Matthew. "In addition to the obvious ethical motive, you must shut down those spy centers, and now."

"Just one more thing," said Admiral Vincent. "Something's been bothering me since you said it—that the air on Earth was more polluted than you remembered."

"Yes, it is," said Matthew. "That's definite. But the pollution, such as it is, is less noticeable here than in the Civilized Footprint."

"Then the UN has something secret going on," said the DNI. "Something military. There is no consumer economy—your consumers print everything they want, on-demand. But printing isn't enough for what they're cooking up, which makes it a gilt-edged priority to find out what that something is."

"I can give you a detailed chemical analysis," said Matthew. He gave all the details he could deduce on exactly what trace chemicals he smelled in the air of Earth.

"Sean," said Admiral Scott, "do you recognize those chemical signatures?"

"They sound like the kind of noxious pollutants common to the twentieth-century industry," said the Intelligence Chief. "We haven't used that for years. If someone is building polluting smokestack factories again, that's more than hypocritical—it's desperate."

"The quality of printed goods," said Matthew, "has declined significantly since my arrest, fifteen years ago."

"And I told you," said Ayelet, "that Bethesda Naval Hospital was talking about re-establishing their central supply room. I thought that was just talk, but maybe it's more."

"All of which suggests," said *Aluf* Levi, "that *Rav Seren* Morrow's assessment of the UN economy is correct. The system is breaking down. These printers are overtaxed and accumulating too many replication errors. And now the UN is trying to re-create the industries they insisted on destroying so many centuries ago.

"Gentlemen, the opportunity is clear. We've been waiting for more than three hundred fifty years for an opportunity like this. We must strike, and strike now."

"Weaker they might be," said the President. "But are they really too weak to win?"

"Three points, if I may, Mr. President," said Matthew. "One: if you don't strike now, you will face an army of cyborgs, like me, but with far less scruples. Second: if this were their only problem, they might not be too weak to win. But they also are at active war, even now."

"You're right, Commander," said Admiral Vincent. "Consumer goods and light-grade supplies are running short, and they also need munitions to fight a war about a quarter of the way across the galaxy. General Levi's right; they're not only weak but sorely pressed. Mr. President, we not only have an opportunity, we have an imperative. If we don't strike now, we never will."

"Commander," said the President, "you mentioned three points. What's the third?"

"The so-called 'American Reservation' on Botany Bay—or Australia, as you call it."

"Then that decides it," said the President. "I will go to Congress and ask for a declaration of war. In fact, Commander Morrow, I would like *you* to address the Congress also. You can explain it with far greater urgency than I."

"And I also would like you and *Segen* Cohen to address the Knesset, and for the same reason," said Prime Minister Ben Avram. "And not the Knesset only—but the Sanhedrin also."

Ayelet gasped. "You mean you re-established the Priesthood?"

"That we did," said the Mossad Chief.

"Do I presume correctly that you mean the Orthodox Union?" asked Matthew.

"Where did you hear ... never mind. But the Union of Orthodox Rabbis is much larger than the Sanhedrin ever could be. And though the Sanhedrin recruits from them, neither body speaks for the other. More broadly, only those of us who take our faith seriously accepted the hospitality of the Patriotic Americans. The Knesset and the Sanhedrin need to hear about you and these Zealots."

"And why, if I may ask, did you re-establish your ... Sanhedrin, as you call them?" Matthew asked.

"Because," said Levi in a more solemn tone, "we had just suffered tremendous losses, in death and injury, from a 'modern medical' preparation we ought never have accepted. Almost the only rabbis who survived with their minds intact, it seems, were those who definitely refused the preparations."

"Immunizations against the coronavirus?"

"The same. They told the rest of our people that the 'Second *Shoah*,' as they called it, to say nothing of the Second Diaspora, was the Eternal's punishment for 'burning incense on the *bamot*'—by which they meant 'high places.' And they had one high place in mind: the 'high place of technological solutions' in preference to prayer, faith, and obedience."

"To your dietary regulations?"

"That and much more," said the intelligence chief.

"About that vessel up there," said Admiral Vincent, "my cousins at Vincent Aerospace would love to examine it. Especially with its active stealth system. I wonder whether we can adapt it for our two *Zumwalts* to use."

"If you mean your two more modern surface ships, perhaps," said Matthew. "Especially if everything I heard about their deceptive radar signature is correct. I can explain the theoretical principle behind the cloaking device, but not the practical application."

"The more reason to start translating the Elfin language," said Levi.

"We've taken a great deal of time," said the President. "Major Campbell, before we adjourn, I have something very special to say to you. You should know that your Regimental Commander turned out to be compromised, along with so many Senators and Representatives."

"In fact," said the Commandant of Marines, "he's in the brig, pending court-martial."

"Major," said the President, "I'd like you to take his place. It would mean an immediate promotion, by two grades. Will you accept?"

Joe Campbell smiled broadly. "That, Mr. President, would be an honor! Yes, I accept. May I name my own staff?"

"Actually," said the President, drily, "you have to. His entire staff is compromised."

"Then I'll make two staff appointments right now, with everyone's permission," said Campbell. "One: that Frank Jellicoe take over the Seventh Cav for me and continue as my operations officer. Two: that Ian Vincent stick with me as my intel officer and take over the Third Regiment's Intel Squadron."

"I'll be glad to attend to all of that," said the Commandant.

"Good," said the President. "Then let us adjourn."

* * *

Matthew reviewed—again—the speech that had become his labor of love. As he stood outside the Hall of the Mountain King, he reflected again on the marvelous things he had seen. But everything depended now on this speech. To deliver it, he had donned the Class A uniform again. The Purple Heart medal dangled from it, as did another medal: the Distinguished Service Cross. Colonel Campbell explained that those medals would carry much weight with Congress. Matthew was inclined to agree.

"Madame Speaker," the House Doorkeeper intoned, "Lieutenant Commander Matthew Morrow, late of the United Systems Navy!"

He walked along the now carpeted trail, conscious of the applause, the loud cheers, and the curious stares that greeted him. With few exceptions, he knew where each of these people had come from. They represented caverns today but once had represented territory that now lay above their heads. But he could tell: they wanted that territory back! The acting President had done an excellent job of convincing these people—the decision-makers for war—that he could help them get it back.

He walked on, climbing the incline, then the steps that led to the high-level shelf that overlooked the Hall. Once, President Howland had said, it held a control console for a narrated light show. Now it held a three-tiered central podium, where now sat the Speaker of the House, the new Vice President of the United States, and several other officers. Before him, sat the House of Representatives. To his right, in two long columns, sat the Senate. Matthew counted seventy-seven Senators and five empty chairs. Blame the recent scandal for that.

The applause died down. Then, Ann Archer Ewer, now Speaker of the House, began to speak. "Ladies and gentlemen," she said, "today we greet a most unusual visitor, one from beyond the barriers that enclose what is left of our territory. We meet in joint session because he has an equally unusual proposition for us, one that you all must hear. Ladies and gentlemen, I present Lieutenant Commander Matthew Morrow, formerly of the United Systems Navy."

Again the applause; again, the cheers. Something made Matthew look up at two windows in a narrow passageway that overlooked the hall. In one, he spied Ayelet, waving at him and smiling broadly. He inclined his head toward her as he waited for quiet to return to the vast chamber.

"Madam Speaker, Mr. President, ladies, and gentlemen of the Congress," he began, "I come to you, not presuming to lead you, but definitely to warn you—and to petition you. I recognize the serious nature of my petition. For nearly four hundred years, you have looked outward and seen the United Nations as a great power, which drove you into caverns like this, then *pretended* you no longer existed. I come before you as a defector from that power.

"The *warning* I give is this: that power *does* know you're still here and now seeks to destroy you. That, in fact, is why they built me and intended to build many others like me—which leads me to my petition: that you support me in making a revolution against a society that no longer knows whether to use me or destroy me—and which is systematically and stealthily oppressing its people.

"Five hundred years ago, your ancestors intervened in a war that convulsed the then center of civilization on this world, in the name of justice, and in the name of a much-abused concept called 'democracy.' Twenty-four years later, your ancestors were intervening again—this time to strike back at an alliance that had struck a cowardly blow against yourselves. And *while they were doing that*, some of your ancestors made the mistake for which you would eventually pay with your liberty and your territory: the founding of the United Nations."

An angry murmur erupted from the crowd until the Speaker picked up her massive gavel and rapped it on her desk. Quiet returned.

"As you might well guess, the United Nations, and the United Systems of which it is a part, now betray even the lofty goals to which they pretend." He listed the two worst injustices: the introduction of a major tranquilizer into everyone's food and the pedophile game preserves. His description of the last provoked even angrier murmurs. Again, the Speaker had to gavel the chamber to silence.

"Any one of you would have a perfect right to ask: what is that to us?" Matthew now took a deep breath—strictly for effect—and raised his voice: "Ladies and gentlemen, *that's* not why you should go to war! You have another, much plainer reason. Nearly four hundred years ago, the United Nations stole your land and even kidnapped most of your people! But now they are weak—and at the same time, they are hard-pressed. What better time, then, to take back what is rightfully yours?"

"No time like the present!" shouted a voice from the right-hand side of the center aisle. And that provoked more applause and cheers. This time, the Speaker left her gavel where it rested. Matthew simply waited for a minute, then raised his hands. Silence descended yet again.

"Your colleague speaks correctly," he said. "No time, indeed, like the present. And here is why!" He went over the reasons to suspect weakness, beginning with the return, however slight, of the air pollution that had long since cleared. Then he described Ayelet's Zealots. Last, he described the Metamorphic War and the apparent fresh outbreak of hostilities in the Nine-o'clock Quadrant.

"You understand what I am saying, do you not?" Matthew asked. "Those settlers in that far-off part of this galaxy are following an example. *Your* example! I now stand before you to ask you whether you will remember—and follow—your own example, just as those people are doing! *Will you?*"

"YES!" thundered nearly five hundred voices.

He turned quickly to the Speaker, who was about to raise her gavel again. "Madam Speaker," he said quickly, "I yield back the balance of my time and offer to withdraw."

"Are you sure, Commander?" the Speaker asked. "You've barely touched on your most important point."

"Do you suppose you will have a better opportunity to obtain the declaration we both seek?"

The Speaker smiled a feral smile. "No, Commander, I do not," she said. "Thank you." Now she did pound the gavel. The House—and the Senate—gave her its full attention.

"This Chair thanks our guest, who has graciously yielded back the balance of his allotted time," Mrs. Ewer said. "The chair will hear a motion to adjourn, after which we can consider immediately a joint resolution declaring war against the United Nations and United Systems!"

"Madam Speaker," called the Representative (who had shouted "No time like the present"), "I move to adjourn this joint session and that the House convene immediately!"

"So seconded!" agreed someone sitting next to him.

Everything moved swiftly after that. The joint session adjourned, and the Senate quit the vast hall for its own, smaller cavern. The House passed the declaration of war in not more than two minutes. A young page took the message out of the hall. He was back within fifteen minutes and walked rapidly up to the podium.

"Madam Speaker, Commander Morrow," he said, "the Senate has just acted. The declaration of war has passed. The Vice President also said to tell Commander Morrow that he has his treaty."

"I'm curious," said Matthew. "How many Senators voted in favor? Of the resolution and of the treaty?"

"Sir," said the solemn eleven-year-old boy, "it was unanimous. Both votes."

"Congratulations," said the Speaker. "Just give me a few minutes to conclude here."

This meant "hearing a motion" to adjourn the House for the day. After which, it seemed, every member of the House wanted to shake Matthew's hand—a request he granted. Last to shake his hand was the Speaker, who said, "Sir, I have just one favor to ask."

"I shall grant whatever is in my power, Madam Speaker," Matthew said.

"Just this," said Mrs. Ewer. "If your travels ever take you to Western Australia, and if you happen to run into any of my relatives, greet them for me."

"I shall do that with all my heart," he said.

The Speaker smiled, gave him a friendly wave, and turned away, leaving Matthew alone in the great hall.

He didn't have to wait long before he had company. Ayelet entered the hall, with Andrea and Barry following behind.

Ayelet rushed up to him and seized both his hands. "Oh, Matthew," she said with a broad smile, "that was—that was magnificent. We were watching in the gallery, and we all agree."

Andrea and Barry gave enthusiastic nods.

"I have two favors to ask you. Will you at least consider them?"

"I'll likely do more than that, Ayelet," he said. "Are you going to tell me what they are?"

"Yes," she said. "First, *Rav Aluf* Marcus just sent me a message—actually, orders. I applied for transfer into the *Tzahal*—the Israel Defense Forces. The message was my acceptance—and orders to report at once to Mara Yerushalayim in Mara Israel for formal induction."

"Congratulations," said Matthew, offering his hand for a shake, which she took. "The United States Marines just lost a fine officer, but the IDF just gained one. May I ask what the favor is? As if I couldn't guess."

Ayelet smiled even more warmly than before. "*Rav Seren* Matthew Morrow," she said in a not quite formal tone, "I have a message for you." And she handed him a piece of paper with Hebrew script on it.

Matthew unfolded it—remarkable, how the people in these two underground societies seemed to embrace centuries-old technologies. Well, why not? They certainly made better weapons than he would have given them credit for! To say nothing of the inarguable wisdom of retaining their farming, animal husbandry, and industry.

Matthew quickly translated the script: "The Chief of Staff of the Defensive Army of Israel requests the honor of your presence at the formal induction of *Segen* Ayelet Cohen as its newest officer." It continued with a date and a time—two days from now—time enough for Matthew to travel to the Caves of Israel if he started within the hour.

"I will gladly attend," he said. "May I assume that Chief Sutton and Hospital Corpsman Riley received similar invitations?"

The two smiled and nodded.

"I invited *Rav Seren* Campbell—no, *Aluf Mishne* Campbell," Ayelet went on. "But he declined. He said he would be awfully busy doing something else."

"Of course," said Matthew. "He will be moving against those other pedophile game preserves, about which the House Judiciary and Ethics Committees lately heard. These United States Marines move swiftly, as we all know. What, then, was the second favor?"

"Matthew," she said, lowering her voice only a trifle, "will you address the *Knesset*?"

"To petition them also to go to war? Of course—if they'll consent to this."

"That shouldn't be a problem. You're already quite famous in the Caves of Israel."

"Which I ought to tour more extensively in any case," said Matthew. "Yes, I will address them. As you know, my kit is lightweight, so I can leave whenever you're ready."

"I'm ready now," she said. "In fact, we all are." Andrea and Barry grinned at that.

"I assume you two have leave," said Matthew. "In that case, shall we go?"

With that, Matthew led the way out of the Hall of the Mountain King toward the hoists to the deep underground tube station. But as they reached the hoists, Ayelet turned to Matthew and said, "Matthew, may I have a word with you?"

Matthew turned to Andrea and Barry and started to speak. But Andrea said, "Commander, as I understand it, we can all reach the deep station a lot faster if we use personal hoists only. Except, they're a little cramped, so maybe we should split up. You and Ayelet can go first; we're sure to catch up very quickly."

"Thank you," said Matthew, who pressed the appropriate call button. In another minute, a narrow double door opened into a tiny hoist car. Matthew and Ayelet climbed aboard—and Andrea was right. This car wouldn't hold more than two. Matthew nodded to Andrea and Barry, who saluted. Matthew had just returned their salute when the doors closed. Then the car began to drop. Rapidly. Matthew and Ayelet each found a handhold.

"Matthew," Ayelet said, "there's so much I want to tell you, but I don't know how."

"We can trust each other, Ayelet," Matthew said. "We have to—we have a war to fight."

"And I can't imagine going into that war without you," she said. "I don't know what thrills me more: joining the army of a society I had thought wiped out, or having you there to watch me join it."

"I'm sure we'll be more than thrilled when the fighting starts in earnest," Matthew replied. "You do know, if you didn't before, that war can be nasty."

"Nasty or not, I know we can win—with you as part of it."

He reached for her hand. She raised her hand and clasped his.

At that moment, the hoist car reached its stop. The doors opened, and Matthew saw the IDF honor guard out of the corner of his eye as they all snapped to attention and saluted.

THE END

Matthew's War

The Terra Prime Series

Book Two

Terry A. Hurlbut

Chapter 1

"**M**r. Prime Minister, Members of the Cabinet, *Rav Aluf* Marcus, *Aluf* Levi, and Members of the *Knesset:*

"I am here, at the invitation of the newest officer in your Defensive Army, to tell you what you already know—and, I hope, tell you something you did *not* know.

"Allow me to introduce myself. My name is Matthew Morrow. Until recently, I held the permanent rank of Lieutenant Commander—that's *Rav Seren* in your rank structure—in the United Systems Navy. I have defected from that power. Today I am an officer without a country. Before, I was one of my society's most promising officers. In fact, I was, and am, the prototype of what was to be an army of invasion. And now I am in exile—a state you know only too well."

Murmurs began until Prime Minister Yitzhak bin Avram raised his gavel and brought it down.

Matthew Morrow, wearing a lieutenant commander's uniform of the United States Navy, regarded his hosts for several seconds. "I am in that exile for two reasons," he said. "One, I discovered a very ugly secret of the security services of my society. Two, I discovered my true purpose. My society intended that I eventually lead an army of invasion against the United States—and against yourselves. Either that or they intended that someone else assume that leadership role. They are very patient, these planners. I have worn this body of metal and plastic for, to the best of my knowledge and recollection, fifty years, to one significant digit. I have had a career in my Navy that originally seemed to hold great promise. Then, fifteen years ago, I made the discovery that led to my arrest, imprisonment, and languishing for fifteen years in a medically induced coma."

That provoked, not murmurs, but gasps. Again the PM brought down his gavel.

"Happily, for me and, I hope, for all of you, a striking young lady brought me out of that coma and helped me to escape. That young lady is, in fact, your newest officer. Give your hand to *Segen* Ayelet Cohen of the Defensive Army of Israel!"

Applause broke out. Beside him, Ayelet, looking as lovely as ever, though now she wore the dark khakis of the *Tzahal,* stood up and waved her right hand. Her raven-black hair caught the lighting of the cavernous meeting hall. This time, the PM let the applause continue for half a minute before once again gaveling the assembly to silence.

"I do not exaggerate," Matthew went on, "in saying that she saved my life. Only later did I come to appreciate that fully. Since then, she and I have taken part in three major actions. These included the liberation of a 'game preserve' in which children were the game." Angry murmurs greeted that, but, as before, only for a moment. "The last operation was the decisive battle that led to the removal from office, on impeachment for and conviction of *treason,* of the President and Vice-President of the United States." More gasps.

"The United States is in the hands of an acting president," Matthew went on. "And—more to the point—

the United States is now at war with the United Nations and the United Systems."

More angry murmurs broke out but didn't last long. Matthew could tell that these parliamentarians were hanging on his every word now.

"I need not tell you how the United Nations betrayed you," he said. "I suspect I need not tell you, either, how the United Nations betrayed the very nation-state that founded it. But I *do* need to tell you that, in these treasons, the United Nations had help. *Extraterrestrial* help. For the race we call the Elves, who hail from the planet Tau Ceti e, intervened in the war that is variously called the Great Climate War, the Re-Wilding War—or the Second War of *Diaspora*, as I believe you call it."

The gasps now were of sheer surprise.

"It has taken me a relatively short time span," he went on when the PM had restored quiet yet again, "to realize that the Elves *are not* the friends of humanity they pretended to be. They have willfully withheld from the nominal leaders of my society—leaders they themselves installed—several technological secrets. *And they are responsible for that pedophile game preserve. And at least six others,* which the Third Cavalry Regiment of the United States Marine Corps is now attacking."

A second round of applause greeted that announcement. Matthew waved both hands for silence, and this time the PM didn't even need to move his hand toward his gavel.

"Your Prime Minister, your Chief of Staff, and your Director of Intelligence have all received full briefings on this matter," Matthew went on. "I attended, and indeed took part in, many of these briefings. Much of what I have told you, I have shared with them. They agree with me that you, too, ought to declare and wage war against the United Nations and Systems.

"But what they could *not* tell you, because they might not grasp the implications themselves, is that your position is far more advantageous than you suppose.

"No doubt you are asking yourselves, 'But what can we do, with the relatively primitive weapons we know how to make, against a society that boasts directed-energy weapons and bombs that could create magnitude-ten or stronger earthquakes?' Well, let me answer. They *dare not* use the second sort of weapon, else they would have done it long ago. This happens to be the headquarters world of the United Systems. It would not do to start seismic or even tectonic events on this world. *Especially* not when they recently fought a long, bitter, and costly war against an enemy halfway across the galaxy, and *now* must fight some of their own colony worlds, who have declared their independence! And *that's* why they built me, and hoped to build hundreds of others like me, to come down here, into these Caves, and into the American caves, and root you all out.

"But what, then, of the powerful energy weapons they possess? Well, I could say that your friends, the Americans, have by now acquired samples of these weapons and are working out how to duplicate them. I could say that, but that would be of no moment. *Because you, and they, already have far superior battlefield weapons!* The simple method of projecting an object by expanding gases from a chemical explosion in a confined space was one method upon which they need never have tried to improve. Energy weapons are *highly* overrated on the battlefield. In a space battle, maybe they have their place. On land, they perhaps have greater range. But at close range—ladies and gentlemen, I took part in three battles after my defection and escape. In the last action, friendly and enemy forces used both kinds of weapons. And I can tell you straight: yours are the better weapons. And as for the energy weapons, I can give you the secret of an absurdly simple defense against them—an electromagnetic force field, like the one I personally can generate at need.

"All of which to say this: *fear not!* I have taken the measure of your enemy, and I tell you, he is weak, hard-pressed, and his soldiers would crumble in an instant when facing your weapons. A great flash of light is *nothing* compared to thousands of tiny metal shells flying at them." *As I know only too well,* he didn't say. His body shield proved too weak against an onslaught of such tiny shells. If Ayelet had delayed a second longer with the reinforcements she had brought, he would be dead. The repairs his generous hosts had made shortly afterward did not erase the memory of that event.

"So as you deliberate, as you ponder how much longer your exile need last, remember the example of the many leaders who have vanquished seemingly superior foes. Otnyel. Yehud. Devorah. Gideon. Yiftach. Shimshon. And, of course, the incomparable David."

That name brought the *Knesset* members to their feet or set them drumming on their desks for a full minute.

"Will you, therefore, follow their example?" he cried out to them. "Will you take back what is rightfully yours and help restore freedom and justice to this world, and, by extension, to a galaxy?"

"*Ken! Ken! Ken! Ken! Ken! Ken! Ken!*" The chant went on for a full three minutes until the members ran out of energy. The Prime Minister then took over and called for an immediate vote. Matthew didn't have to guess: the vote was unanimous: for war.

After that vote came another unanimous vote to adjourn. And, after taking that vote, someone broke out in song. Quickly the other members took it up.

'Kol od balevav panimah, nefesh Yehudi homiyah,

'Ulfa'atey mitzrach kadimah, ayin le-Tzion tzofiyah.

'Od lo avda tikvatenu, ha tikvah ha noshana,

'La'shuv le-eretz avoteynu, le'ir ba David, David hana.

'La'shuv le-eretz avoteynu, le'ir ba David, David hana."

* * *

"And where did you learn all those names?" asked *Rav Aluf* Caleb Marcus, the chief of staff.

"You may thank your newest officer, *Segen* Cohen, here," said Matthew. "She introduced me to your *Tanakh.* A most inspiring work. My society has nothing like it."

"Or perhaps they have forgotten it," said Ayelet. Then, to the chief of staff, she said, "I can assure you, sir, that my Zealots have the *Tanakh*."

"They have a digital copy of the Dead Sea Scrolls," the lead General said. "Thanks to you and your family, of course—and for that alone, I ought to decorate you. But *Rav Seren* Morrow, here, did not know it—until, if I understand him correctly, you introduced him to it."

Matthew and Ayelet both nodded.

"And I *still* don't know this work," said Hospital Corpsman Andrea Riley. "I can see how important it is to everybody, and now I'm frightfully curious."

"So am I," said Chief Information Technician Barry Sutton. "Is this history, or philosophy, or what?"

"A little bit of each," said the General. "And more to the point, *Rav Seren* Morrow, you spoke those names as though they were your own heroes."

"They are," said Matthew. "Each of them fought a war similar to the one I wage. I noticed that at once when I read of the *Shoftim*."

"But how could you possibly read a work as complex as the *Tanakh* so quickly?"

"My auxiliary processors, to say nothing of my secondary memory, allow me to read any bound volume as quickly as I can turn its pages," said Matthew. "But I take your point. You ask how I could come to such an understanding so quickly. I will say only this: stories of heroism and strategy against impossible odds have always resonated with me. I've never known why, but that is the truth."

"Well," said *Aluf* Levi, head of the Institute for Intelligence and Special Operations, "I never met a *goy* who understood our *good book* half as well. As much as our American friends tell me how much they revere it, with you, it's different. You treat it with a respect with which I could wish our own, younger generation could treat it."

"You flatter me, *Aluf* Levi," said Matthew. "Though, I still don't *quite* understand all of it. The Deluge, for example. For what can that possibly be a metaphor?"

"I assure you, that's no metaphor," said the Intelligence Chief. "Oh, I suppose everything in the *Tanakh*, even events, are metaphors for something or other. The Eternal is like that—symbolism means everything to Him. But if you're wondering whether the Deluge ever took place—I assure you, it did.

"But perhaps I am not the one to educate you along that line. You really need to talk to those who can."

"The Academy of the Hebrew Language?"

"As good a group as any—though, I definitely would recommend the Sanhedrin to you. I don't suppose you have with you the photographs of that Elfin transport you stole?"

"Don't forget, *Aluf* Levi, that I need no photographs," said Matthew. "I have graphics processors that can help me render into graphic-file form the image of any person or object I see. I can record everything I see and hear—as still pictures or as motion pictures. And store any text I read as machine-readable text."

"Remarkable," said the General, almost in a whisper. "I look forward to receiving the Academicians' report. But first: we have been remiss as hosts. You and *Segen* Cohen will, of course, join us for dinner."

"Almost a *state* dinner," said the Prime Minister, speaking for the first time. "For *I* shall play host. Though, I have never played host to a … Forgive me…"

"Machine?" Matthew smiled a crooked smile. "Well, strictly speaking, I *am* mostly machine, except for my central nervous system and spinal and cranial nerves. Nevertheless, my builders did not neglect any of the senses. They left me taste and smell, as well as touch, sight, and hearing. I shall very much enjoy your dinner—especially since it doesn't come out of a printer."

Matthew's last remark actually set everyone else present to laughing.

* * *

"And what exactly is this 'printer' that my husband was trying to tell me about?" asked Leah bin Avram, the Prime Minister's wife.

"I'm not sure you would wish to know, ma'am," said Matthew to his hostess. "I certainly would not deliberately insult such a good cook as yourself."

"Now, don't you hold back on me, my good man. I still want to know what a printer is."

"Well, I don't think you would care to imagine a machine that can prepare a dinner plate, laden with food, almost as quickly as any of your own printers reproduces a document."

"Ugh," she said, her face reflecting a moue of disgust. "How can your people so degrade themselves by eating a meal that comes out of a machine like that?"

"By sacrificing quality for convenience," said Matthew. "And that's even allowing for this being a *kosher* meal, fit to eat by a higher standard than most I've seen."

"I'll vouch for that," said Andrea Riley. "Everything at your table has been excellent, and much easier to digest."

"Furthermore," Matthew went on, "the printers cannot last in our former society. They are making mistakes. Already it is making food taste a little worse every day."

"Tell them about the promazine derivative," said Ayelet.

"Oh, yes," said Matthew. "The printers leave a foreign substance in all food and drink they produce. And that substance is an antipsychotic medication."

"*Oy, gevalt!*" cried the Prime Minister. "Why didn't you mention it at our conference with the American acting President?"

"It did not seem to matter then."

"But I should think it does! If we're going to face an enemy with their bodies full of something like that, then we have even *less* reason to fear."

"Not after I send out a virus to cancel that part of every printer's program."

"Eh?"

"That's right, Mr. Prime Minister," said Barry. "Matthew wants to stop the printers in our society from drugging everyone's food. Because he wants the people themselves to rise up in revolt."

"That's very wise, Prime Minister," Marcus said. "Remember that it is not war only that *Rav Seren* Morrow wishes to wage. It is revolution. That means defeating the enemy from within. And rousing the people themselves to take up arms. Those people will be our allies."

"I still don't understand," said bin Avram. "Why do you want to make revolution? What drives you?"

"Simply this, Prime Minister. I cannot trust the leadership of my society any longer. They built me to attack an inoffensive target. They arrested me when I discovered something about their activities they wished to keep secret. And, several times, they have tried to destroy me. Now, I can either try to make my case to a sympathetic authority—which is useless because we have no separation of powers like what you, Israelis, have, or the Americans have. Or I can make revolution. I choose revolution."

"Your service rank name does not do you justice, Matthew Morrow," said the Prime Minister. "Even though it is the rank you had achieved, or as near enough to it as will translate into Hebrew. I would like to propose a higher title for you. You ought to call yourself *Shofet* Matthew."

The comparison actually shocked Matthew. Could he really compare himself to a *judge*? And not just any judge at that. The *Shoftim* were more than judges. They were great heroes and military leaders who rose to challenges almost none of them thought they could meet.

So he asked the obvious question: "Can I truly take my place beside men like Otnyel, Yehud, Yiftach, and the other leaders I named?"

"Why not? You have a strength that Shimshon himself would envy, and a self-restraint he never had. You have the dedication of Gideon and the heart for justice of Yiftach. And, you have the matter-of-fact directness of David. True, they called him *Melech*, not *Shofet*. But Shmuel, last of the *Shoftim*, declared David for what he became, so David did have a connection to the *Shoftim*. And believe me, young man—for you *are* a young man in my eyes, even with your machine body—you are everything an ancient *Shofet* was and embody everything the *Shoftim* were all about."

"You have paid me a great many compliments, Prime Minister," said Matthew. "I'm not at all sure I deserve them. I began my warfare, if you will, to ensure my own survival—and happen to have met a lot of friends along the way. Like Ayelet here, and Chief Sutton and Corpsman Riley. And some very brave children whom I helped liberate from … Well, perhaps I oughtn't to mention that in front of a lady."

"Don't worry about that," said Leah. "My Yitzhak told me all about those horrible places."

"Then you understand," said Matthew, inclining his head to her. "In any event, Prime Minister, I'm only trying to do justice as best I can. As I told you, the stories of the *Shoftim* resonated with me. I'm not sure I'm entitled to have you remember me as one of them. Not yet. Not until I can earn it."

"And when might that be?" asked Yitzhak bin Avram, suddenly sounding more solemn.

"I might not be able to tell you that," said Matthew, "until the war I must fight, is over."

The group finished the meal in silence, after which everyone agreed that they should rest. Matthew retired to a room that had a makeshift charging alcove—another favor everyone seemed to know to do for him. But it also had a regular bed—and sure enough, Ayelet joined him in that room.

"I trust this arrangement won't be awkward for you?" Matthew asked.

"Of course not!" said Ayelet. "Why should it be awkward? You're a very special friend to me. In fact: *Shofet* Matthew—the more often I repeat it, the better I like it."

"Please don't repeat that," said Matthew. "I do take your point. But can you take mine?"

She opened her mouth—closed it—and finally said, "I do, Matthew. If not for the modesty you are now showing, you wouldn't be the special friend that you are."

"Thank you."

"But seriously, your own history matches so many of those of the *Shoftim*. For example, Yiftach lost out of his share of his father's estate because his mother was … well…"

"Not his father's lawful wife?"

"Yes. And Gideon had to face the resentment of his own people after he took action against a practice he saw and recognized as wrong. And the Prime Minister was right—you are far superior to at least one of the *Shoftim*—Shimshon. You have his strength but none of his weaknesses."

"But as I say," said Matthew, "I can only hope to distinguish myself half as well as did any of those ancient leaders."

"You already have—at least in my eyes."

"Now *that* is quite a compliment, coming from the leader of the Zealots."

Ayelet suddenly frowned.

"Did I say something wrong?" Matthew asked.

She stayed quiet for five seconds. Then she said, "No, Matthew. It's just that the Zealots haven't actually done more than recruit up to now—and provide intelligence for at least one of those operations you mentioned in the *Knesset*. Now they have to do much more. And … Oh, Matthew, you worry about deserving an ancient title? *I* worry about whether my movement will be worth anything—now that the time has come for action!"

Matthew needed only a split second to know what to say. He moved toward her and took both her hands—and felt the tension in them as he did. "Ayelet," he said, smiling, "look at me."

She did.

"I'll repeat to you what I told the *Knesset*," he said. "You saved my life back in the Harper's Ferry cavern. Before that, you made the difference between mission success and failure at the pedophile camp in the Lucketts District. More than that, you took on a challenge, not even knowing whether you would succeed or fail, but because it was the right thing to do. That was true of most of the *Shoftim*, and of *Melech* David, too. *You* deserve the title of *Shofet* more than I. And you shall have it. Your Zealots will rally to you when the time comes—and you, and they, will know it."

He felt a slight change in the conductivity of her skin—not the mark of a liar, but the effect of one realizing something new and amazing about herself. She smiled back at him—a warm, radiant smile. "For one who never heard of our law, prophets, or writings," she said, "you have paid me the most profound compliment you could have paid. And I believe you meant it."

"As surely as I stand here, in Mara Israel."

"Thank you, Matthew," she said. "And you're right. I will do what—well, what *Shofet* Devorah did. Wait for my opportunity, knowing it will come."

He released her hands. And before he could react, she reached up with her right hand, cupped the back of his head, and brought his head down so she could touch her lips to his.

The kiss lasted only a fraction of a second. But in that moment, he remembered again the last woman to kiss him. *Natalya.* With an effort, he stopped the flow of tears to his eyes.

Then it was over. Ayelet stood before him, displaying her usual mild impudence. "Come," she said. "We both need sleep—even you, as I know perfectly well. We have a big day tomorrow."

"Oh?" he asked. "And what have you planned for tomorrow?"

"First, I need to show you at least two places that hold some of my people's memories—not all of them pleasant. Then we will meet a delegation from the Sanhedrin. And *HaAkademiyah LaLashon HaIvrit.* Members of both these organizations definitely want to talk to you. And you should talk to them."

"I look forward to that. All of it."

The rest of the evening didn't last too long. Matthew prepared himself for the charging alcove, while Ayelet disappeared into the bathroom attached to their room and emerged wearing what appeared to be makeshift sleeping fatigues, for lack of a better term. They said little to one another—besides wishing each other a good night. As she had when they had shared a room in the Cumberland Caverns, Ayelet composed herself for sleep—but Matthew read the odd mixture of peace and anticipation on her face. Then he willed himself to sleep. At least he could do *that*, knowing that it was only temporary. He had no wish to return to the enforced sleeping state in which he had languished for fifteen years.

* * *

"As I'm sure you've heard many times before, welcome to Mara Israel," said the leader of the three-man group who greeted Matthew and Ayelet. Each of these men wore the same kind of civilian dress to which Matthew was still trying to accustom himself to seeing. Except, all three men wore black-on-white outfits, topped with black broad-brimmed hats. They also sported full beards and moustaches. "These two gentlemen are Rabbi Reuven Lapid, Vice-Chairman of the Sanhedrin, and Eliezer Perel, Dean of the Academy of the Hebrew Language. And I am Rabbi Shmuel Govan, Chairman of the Sanhedrin. And on behalf of all of Israel, we offer you our profuse thanks."

"And I thank you," said Matthew. "Now, I hope I can earn your thanks. Thus far, I have done little but make speeches."

His three hosts laughed. Rabbi Govan said, "Your reputation for modesty precedes you," he said. "And what impression have you formed of us?"

"You are certainly a very brave people," said Matthew. "No one should underestimate you. I have just come from a tour of Yad VaShem. A most enlightening display—and a tragic one. I have seen very few stories of wrongdoing on such a massive and ugly scale. And I commend your people for preserving historical evidence."

"We tell ourselves, 'never again,'" said Rabbi Lapid in a solemn tone. "But I have to observe: our ancestors of the twenty-first century did succumb to a false sense of security. As tragic as the Shoah was, the Second Shoah and Diaspora were even more tragic—and infuriating. First, our people had to burn incense on the *bamah* of high technology—true enough, that was our chief export in those days, but it was as seductive as a priestess of Astarte in the days of *Aluf* Joshua. And I refer, of course, to the 'immunizations' against the novel coronavirus. One-third of our people died that way, and another third were so befuddled in their brains that they could not fight the United Nations Climate Forces when the time came.

"And yet, the Eternal has heard our cry and raised Him up a *Shofet* for our modern age. It hasn't been quite as long as was our time in Egypt, but long enough."

He felt Ayelet take his hand and give it a quick squeeze. It was on the tip of his tongue to tell these men that they should honor Ayelet with that title, not him. However, he sensed Ayelet wouldn't consider herself ready for that. But someday…!

Aloud he said, "Yes, I've read your *Tanakh*. And was able to confirm much of it at the Israel Museum, which I have also seen."

"I must say," asked Dean Perel for the first time, "that your Hebrew is *mo'ed tov*. Where did you have time to learn it?"

"Oh, as to that, I studied that early in my career, and have studied it all my life."

"Really?"

"Why not? Don't you know that Hebrew is the root of all human language?"

"And who among the *goyim* would admit such a thing?"

"No one, of course," said Matthew. "But it's only logical. Every root in every other language traces back to Hebrew, directly or indirectly. That's the simplest theory I could construct for the similarities I observed. But I did make one oversight."

"And what might that be?"

"Failure to notice the similarities between Hebrew and Elfin."

"Ah, yes," said the Dean. "*Aluf* Levi of *Mossad* told us about the extraterrestrial race that actually speaks a variant of Hebrew, which is why I was so glad to receive the invitation of these two learned men to meet you. Have you a sample of Elfin writing that you can share?"

"Let me interface with one of your network consoles," said Matthew, "and I can at least share part of a document I have seen."

"We have one right here," said Rabbi Govan. "By all means, proceed."

Matthew did so. When he did, the Dean took his time to read it. Then he said, "*Aluf* Levi is correct! This isn't *exactly* Hebrew, but it is a variant. A branching that has simply 'aged' in a different way. A very early branching— earlier even than the Sanskrit and Oriental branchings."

"About how early, would you say?"

"Why, I wonder whether this branching came earlier than the Deluge! But if it did, it would be literally fantastic. No one is supposed to have survived that, except Noach and his family."

"*Aluf* Levi mentioned the Deluge," said Matthew. "He insists that it took place, exactly as the *Tanakh* describes it. But he also suggested that you could enlighten me further."

"Indeed I can!" said the Dean with an enthusiastic air. Then more soberly, he said, "I suppose we are the only ones left who keep that legend alive. According to it, the Eternal was sorry He had made human beings and also had to scour the earth of a hybrid human-demon race that was abroad in those times. So He released a flow of water that drowned every land animal, and every human being— except for a family of eight, and several breeding pairs they carried." Having warmed to his subject, the Dean narrated in detail a passage from the *Torah,* describing the event. Matthew recognized it at once.

"You do realize," he said to the Dean, "that this passage you just quoted reads exactly like a ship's log, as I should know. I signed hundreds of them as the second officer on two Navy ships."

"Really!?" cried Rabbi Lapid, delighted to hear the comparison. "But of course. This is the log of the *Thevah*—the Life-ship. Noach, the Shipwright, built and commanded her, and his three sons kept this log."

"About those 'hybrids,'" Matthew asked next. "What did they look like?"

Rabbi Govan cradled his chin in his right hand for a few seconds. Then he shrugged. "No one knows," he said, "apart from pure speculation. Noach never drew any pictures. Neither did his sons. Or if they did, those pictures are lost. Even *Yovhelihim*—Jubilees—doesn't have them."

"But surely a flood of that magnitude would have crushed all the plant life beneath it," said Matthew. "I don't understand why we don't see its evidence today."

"Are you sure?" asked all three men in chorus.

"Well, you tell me," said Matthew. "How did the plants grow back? How did an olive tree grow back so that a turtledove could pluck off a compound leaf and bring it back to Noach's ship?"

"Reseeding, of course," said the Dean. "And as for the pressure you mentioned ... Tell me this, *Rav Seren* Morrow—or I should say, *Shofet* Matthew. Does any civilized world, besides this one, have such abundant quantities of petroleum, natural gas, or coal?"

Matthew didn't even have time to reflect embarrassment at these men urging that title on him, yet again, for what he felt was utter astonishment. Because he realized that no other world had anything like the "fossil fuels"! They didn't even have deposits of radioactive ores, nor did their crusts exhibit background radiation. And the only isotopes of lead or any lighter metals were the most common that one could find on Earth. The dizzying variety of light, heavy, and even radioactive isotopes was unique to Sol d. After a considerable silence, he admitted as much.

"Of course," said the Dean. "I would expect the Deluge also to be unique to this world. The fossil fuels are its products, as are the radioactive substances in this world's crust. The crushed forests and jungles of the world of the Deluge became coal. And the dead animals, some of which were very large, became petroleum and natural gas."

"And the radioactive and other odd isotopes?"

"Products of piezoelectricity. Centuries ago, an American engineer named Walter T. Brown worked this out. You see, the Deluge involved the escape of an ocean from beneath the crust—more than sixty miles deep."

"I thought only the Americans used the mile as a unit of great distance."

"We use it, too, and have ever since the Second Diaspora. The only difference is that we describe it as three thousand five hundred twenty cubits, not five thousand two hundred eighty feet."

"And that subcrustal ocean—would that be the 'fountains of the deep'?"

"Just so. And this event produced earthquakes the like of which had never happened before, and never happened again. And when they acted on the buried quartz deposits, they produced electromotive potentials measurable in billions of volts—SI volts or American Patriotic volts, which doesn't matter much. Enough to produce elements with atomic numbers greater than 180. These split at once to form the two most abundant radioactive elements, uranium and thorium. And in that highly charged environment, these would decay—very rapidly—to produce all the other radioactive elements heavier than lead."

"And the light isotopes?"

"Beta decay products from radioactive isotopes of the next lighter elements, of course."

"And where did all these come from?"

"From the same source that produced the heavy isotopes. All that activity I mentioned, the formation of such incredibly heavy elements, followed by their fission or cluster decay, released uncountable neutrons. If the *Thevah* hadn't been floating on the water that now covered all the land, those neutrons would have killed Noach, his family, and all their specimens. As it was, the cluster decay created an isotope of carbon that pervades all life, and shortens all life spans."

"Yes," said Matthew. "I had wondered why, beginning with Shem, the life span of human beings declined ninety percent in eleven generations. The Elves, I note, did not have this problem.

"And it explains something else. Ayelet, maybe you know what I mean. On every origin world of every species except humanity, industrial development went directly from beasts-of-burden to biofuels, and from there to hydrogen-oxygen and eventually to photovoltaics and solar-thermal. With no intervening step using fossil fuels—because those societies never had them. Nor nuclear fission, for that matter, and by reason of a similar lack. I'm surprised they developed nuclear fusion."

Ayelet nodded. "And that's how the Elves could have their appeal to the original UN," she said. "They didn't have to pretend to be disdainful of a fossil-fuel-based economy or nuclear reactors. Because they never had either."

"The Elves might be a special case, however," said Matthew.

"What makes you say that?"

"First, as I told you, they live longer than any other hominid race. Second, their technology has always been vastly superior to that of any other race. And their physiognomy is significantly different from that of the others. Their pointed ears set them apart from everyone else. And their anatomical dimensions are up to one-half larger than those of any other race."

"One-half larger?" asked one of the rabbis.

"Does that suggest something to you?" asked Matthew.

"If not for those pointed ears, I could almost take them for … No. Too fantastic."

They said no more about it. But Matthew noticed that the two rabbis left that meeting with more than usually thoughtful expressions.

"Ayelet," he asked, as they took a taxi back to a tube station that would take them back to the Prime Minister's residence, "do you have any idea what the Dean might have been talking about?"

"You mean, about who the Elves might actually be?"

"Yes."

"There *is* one possibility, and I'm almost afraid to mention it. But you have to go back to the *Tanakh* to find it. The *Tanakh* might have two names for them."

"And those would be?"

"*Anakim*, and *Nephilim*."

"The 'mighty men of old, men of renown'? But I thought the Deluge destroyed them."

"Maybe ... or maybe not. The verse you just quoted said the *Nephilim* were abroad in those days, *and even afterward*."

"Dean Perel is right," said Matthew. "Too fantastic, and those pointed ears tell against that. But still ... Why should they speak a variant of Hebrew that is older even than the Hebrew you and I speak now?"

"That's the central riddle, isn't it?"

"Yes," said Matthew. "But it's also another riddle to solve another day. All I know, especially after what you and I saw in that second operation we fought together, is that they are enemies pretending to be friends. If that theory is at all correct, then it might explain their enmity. But, since I already know all I need to know, that can wait."

"For what?"

"For me to acquire any more evidence on this point. That is, when I'm not fighting a war ... Excuse me." The Personal Digital Device the US Navy had issued him had just throbbed. He pulled it from a pocket of his uniform and answered it. "*Rav Seren* Morrow here," he said by force of habit.

"Here, Yitzhak," said the voice on the other end. "I just had a message from your acting President. He requires your presence back in the Cumberland Caverns as quickly as we can arrange it. It seems certain persons are about to come to trial, and he requires your testimony. Yours, and that of *Segen* Cohen."

"We're on our way back to your compound, Prime Minister," said Matthew. "I apologize for having to depart on such notice, but duty does call."

"All of us understand perfectly. Your other companions will be waiting for you when you return here. And again, from all of Israel, thank you."

"And I thank *you*, Prime Minister, for the welcome and the opportunity. I'll see you later." He closed the contact, then turned to Ayelet. "Thinks are moving fast back in the American caverns," he said. "Trials, the Prime Minister said. I can well imagine—treason trials, criminal trials, and courts-martial. They'll want our testimonies. You, Andrea, Barry, and me."

Ayelet stiffened—only slightly, but still. "I'll be ready, Matthew," she said.

Chapter 2

"**W**hat is your name, rank, and affiliation?" asked Rear Admiral Sean Vincent.

"Captain Rodney Coleman, United Systems Special Security Forces," said the defiant prisoner. "And you, *sir*, are in deep…"

Before he could utter what obviously was on the tip of his tongue, the American Director of Naval Intelligence brought his gavel to the table with a loud *crack*. The prisoner fell silent.

Admiral Vincent, sitting at a broad table with Matthew Morrow to his left and his nephew, Major Ian Vincent USMC, to his right, regarded the prisoner with a quizzical eye. Matthew, wearing the blue suit of the United States Navy, complete with ribbons representing the Purple Heart and the Distinguished Service Cross, could guess what his newfound friend was thinking. Here was their prisoner, lashed to a straight-backed armchair, telling his *captors* that *they* had reason to fear. Of Matthew himself, the prisoner had taken no notice at all, thus far. More futile defiance, Matthew knew. After all, Matthew himself had captured this man and brought him here, though it had been … difficult.

Admiral Vincent resumed his interrogation. "You would do well," he said, "to take better stock of where you sit."

"And *you* would 'do well' to let me go while the letting-go is good!"

"And if we don't?"

"Then you will die—all of you!"

"Who is Captain Folsom?" asked Vincent abruptly. *Good*, thought Matthew. *Change the subject.*

"She is none of your business!" snarled Captain Coleman. Then: "On second thought, maybe I'll make her your business. She's the one who will lobotomize all of you. Except for you, *Matthew Morrow*. Of you, she will take a *very* special interest."

"And what interest would that be?" Matthew asked, deciding to join the conversation.

"That's for me to know and for you to find out."

"No, Captain Coleman, it is for you to tell us," said the younger Vincent, speaking for the first time. "Again: you would do well to take better stock of where you sit— literally and figuratively. A military tribunal has just convicted you, on the testimony of unimpeachable witnesses, of aiding and abetting kidnapping, aiding and abetting criminal endangerment of minors, accessory to attempted murder—and crimes against nature involving minors. Not to mention espionage against the United States."

"Convicted, hell! By a kangaroo court, with no counsel of my choice…"

"You will not speak without permission. The tribunal offered you counsel, but you refused. You chose to act on your own behalf, which is never wise. A court consisting of officers similar in rank to yourself convicted you.

"And then the court granted you a singular mercy. Offenses like yours once rated life imprisonment without the possibility of parole. You *have* the possibility of parole. And your parole board could, in theory, release you to a place of relative freedom, though, also, a place of exile."

"But there are two catches," said the elder Vincent, resuming control. "The first is that *I* will run your parole board—I, the Director of Naval Intelligence. The Judge Advocate General of the Navy has signed off on that. Second, you will never see that exile until *all of us* can leave these Caves any time we please. That will require victory in the war that, as we told you, the United States Congress and the Israeli Knesset have now declared against the United Nations and United Systems. So it's up to you, Captain Coleman, but in your place, I would help us prosecute that war. Because you don't go free until we win—or you die a natural death—whichever happens first. Do you understand?"

The prisoner hawked up and spat across the room. The wad didn't land very far—six feet, and he was fifteen feet away. How odd, thought Matthew: I can actually *think* in these "American Patriotic" units of measurement my hosts use. Before today, I would have judged that distance to be two meters—not that it matters very much.

But the prisoner wasn't done. He cast a baleful eye on Matthew. "Traitor!" he shouted. "Is this what you signed on for?"

"I did not *sign on* for being *used,*" said Matthew, slowly and deliberately. "I did not *sign on* to have my central nervous system transplanted into this body of metal and plastic I now wear, just so your superiors could eventually have an 'ultimate warrior' to attack these people for no good reason. And I certainly did not *sign on* to be subject to arrest, imprisonment, and a fifteen-year medically induced coma after spotting that little 'recreational facility' of which you were chief of security. So don't you *dare* talk to me about treason."

The prisoner, wearing a sullen face, said no more.

Admiral Vincent spoke to the helmeted Shore Patrol Chief—whom Matthew remembered. This was that Chief Carter who had led the SP Squad that helped Matthew face down an attack by the corrupt former President's Secret Service contingent. "Unbind the prisoner and escort him to his cell," the Admiral ordered. "This court will now go into executive session."

Chief Carter escorted Captain Coleman out, whereupon the DNI looked at his two companions in turn. "Well, gentlemen?" he asked. "Your opinions?"

His nephew threw up his hands and sighed. "We told him," he said. "He's been under confinement for a week and a half now. I thought it rocked him when we tried him as swiftly as we did—I think that's one of the fastest courts-martial on record, and that's saying something. But it's almost as if he thinks this is an elaborate game."

"Which, apart from the deaths of his men, his commanding officer, and the Elfin Ambassador, it would be," said Matthew. "What do you think I concluded when the Seventh Cav Squadron's Recon Platoon discovered my fellow escapees and me from Bethesda Naval Hospital? *I* thought it was a game. In his service, they play that kind of game all the time. He has simply raised his psychological defenses."

"I asked for your recommendation, Commander," said the Admiral. Then he added, "My apologies. I did not intend to speak to you as I would to a subordinate." He meant, of course, that Matthew now had a remarkable distinction—that of a military ally. That came with his defection to this underground society, its declaration of war against the United Systems, and the treaty he now had with his hosts. And now, of course, with the Israelis.

"That's of no moment, Admiral," said Matthew. "In fact, I *do* have a recommendation."

"And that would be?"

"Expose the prisoner to something he would fear greatly. Specifically, sudden changes in acceleration."

"I don't follow."

"Admiral," said Matthew, "our society has total gravity manipulation. He's used to riding in a conveyance that adjusts itself so well to changing acceleration that he feels as though he's sitting still. He's never experienced the slightest stress from launch or braking. So let's expose him to these things."

"Where?"

"Your society has an abundance of amusement centers," said Matthew. "Use one of them."

The two officers at the table next to him stared at him in openmouthed astonishment. Then the younger man asked, "Are you sure it can be that simple? After all, our citizens and lawful residents enjoy such facilities all the time, and they don't have problems of that kind."

"That's not exactly true, son," said the Admiral. "You wouldn't catch *me* on any roller coaster at my age. And I speak for a lot of adults."

"More to the point," said Matthew, *"he* has never done so. He has probably filled his head with lurid visions of the stress of abruptly changing acceleration, and the harm such stress can bring."

"And where might he have visited, to do that?"

"The United Nations Educational, Scientific, and Cultural Organization took over several amusement parks on the surface. These parks belonged typically to some very large joint-stock corporations with names like Walt Disney Enterprises, Six Flags, Anheuser Busch, and Cedar Fair Entertainment. Today UNESCO maintains them as museums, all to show the people how 'profligate' you Americans were before the Great Climate War."

Instantly Captain Vincent's eyes lit up. "Would that include Kings Dominion, in Doswell, Virginia?"

"Yes," said Matthew. "You know about that installation?"

"I should hope so! Kings Dominion is legendary in Virginia. But you're sure Captain Coleman knows about it?"

"Considering where we captured him, he's probably toured that facility often. But he would never dare or even imagine taking any of its rides. No one in my former society would."

Even as he said that he knew it was not true. For another memory came to him—a memory of an earlier visit he had made to the Kings Dominion Amusement Museum. Only, he wasn't on shore leave at the time. In this memory, he was just *a boy of four.* His parents had taken him—so he *did* have parents once. They had spent their time in the children's area of the park, a place named after a character in a twentieth-century comic strip. Every attraction in that area repeated the theme. But in the distance, he had seen another attraction—a very tall double-tracked red arch resting on yellow columns. As he watched, a train of ten cars, each black as jet, rode up to the top of the arch at a forty-five-degree angle—then plunged down the other end at an eighty-five-degree angle. He had stared and breathed two words. "Some day…" But he then had turned to look at his mother—and caught a look of white-hot fury tinged with terror in her eyes.

Then the memory cut out, and he was back in the present day, just in time to see Ian Vincent grinning wolfishly and saying, "Then let's oblige him."

"Now hold on a minute, Ian," said the Admiral. "Do you seriously suggest capturing the original Kings Dominion and subjecting the prisoner to 'enhanced interrogation' there?"

"You betcha—sir."

"But why? Why not simply strap him onto a roller coaster down here?"

"It wouldn't be as effective, sir. He knows Kings Dominion but *doesn't* know any of our facilities. He's had time to scare himself about Kings Dominion's roller coasters, which in any case are probably a lot taller than anything we've ever been able to build. Right, Commander?"

Matthew answered, "I can't vouch for how tall your tallest roller coaster is in these Caves. But in Kings Dominion, the builders had the advantage of the open air—and one coaster, in particular, rises to a height of three hundred and five feet."

"Which is half, again, as tall as the tallest coaster we've got in the Caves."

"We'd have to crash the barrier, wouldn't we?" the elder Vincent asked.

"That would not present a problem," said Matthew. "Chief Sutton could get us in." That, of course, would be Chief Information Technician Barry Sutton, one of his three original fellow escapees. "Besides, I know the layout. I, too, have visited the Kings Dominion Amusement Museum, and often, on shore leave. It cannot have changed much since my last visit. UNESCO makes no attempt to redevelop it. When I last visited it, it was at the same state of development as when UNESCO took it over, in…" (here he paused to convert to the Gregorian Calendar the Americans used) "…2035.

"Furthermore, the Barrier near the Museum has a gate. We will 'crash' it."

"I take it you have a particular program of enhanced interrogation in mind."

"Indeed I have, Admiral. And there's more. Kings Dominion's communications center has a direct connection to the main information network. That makes it the perfect place from which to distribute propaganda videos—or the software 'upgrades' I talked to your nephew about, to stop the printers my society uses from drugging everyone's food."

"It's still a hair-raising campaign," the Admiral went on. "Such a thing should be a diversion for a much larger operation."

"I cannot recommend that at this time," said Matthew. "But I *would* remind you that this operation will inspire Ayelet Cohen's Zealots, and anyone else willing to make revolution."

"Let's ask Colonel Campbell in for a conference," said the DNI.

* * *

"It's crazy, sir," said Colonel Campbell. "In fact, it's just crazy enough to work."

The conference had moved from the interrogation room to another room much better suited for planning a battle. Those in attendance now included the Marine Commandant, the Marine G-3 (Chief of Operations), and the staff of the Third Cavalry Regiment, including Major Vincent and Major Frank Jellicoe, the Regimental S-3 and commander of the Seventh Cavalry Squadron.

It also included Matthew, the DNI, and all three of Matthew's companions. These last included Chief Sutton, now of the United *States* Navy instead of the United *Systems* Navy; Hospital Corpsman Andrea Riley, now transferred to the United States Navy; and *Segen* Ayelet Cohen, now of the Israel Defense Forces.

The G-3 asked, "Then you approve of Commander Morrow's battle plan?"

"Without reservation, sir," said Colonel Campbell. "And to the point Admiral Vincent raised, as I understand it, about diversionary tactics: as a matter of fact, I *have* been thinking about a main action we ought to think about taking. Commander Morrow, am I correct in assuming that, pursuant to the Great Environmental Reset by UN Secretary-General Gunilla Thorsell, the UN truly did eliminate all uses of—do you understand what *aircraft* were?"

"Craft that used their bodies, or some parts of them, to generate aerodynamic lift?"

"Correct. Well, did they eliminate such craft from use?"

And Matthew saw the point at once. "Indeed, yes, Colonel Campbell," he said. "And if your next question is what do they use instead: well, they *don't* use gravitomagnetic transports as a rule. They transport everything by rail, in underground evacuated tubes. The UN built several, following, as nearly as possible, great circle courses."

"As I thought!" cried Colonel Campbell, warming to his subject. "And where do those tubes run?"

"The longest, and perhaps the backbone of the tube system, runs from Rio de Janeiro in Amazonía, then northwest toward the narrow strip connecting that continent with the larger continent of Aztlán, and from there through Antigua (which they once called Guatemala Ciudad, as I understand), Mexico Ciudad..."

"And then through Los Angeles, San Francisco, Portland, Vancouver, Juneau, and from there across the Bering Straits and through Siberia, Manchuria, and then...where?"

"To Ho Chi Minh City in Vietnam, by way of Beijing," said Matthew. "Branch lines from this line serve all the major population centers. The one of your former States that this network does not serve is Hawaii—which the UN reorganized as the Kingdom of Hawaii, transformed to *status quo ante* the arrival of the first American settlers, and left to its own devices."

"Commandant, do you understand the opportunity we have?" said Campbell. "Can you imagine what we could do if we tapped into those tubes, anywhere between Los Angeles and San Francisco? We'd have instant access to all their population centers! But to do that without detection, we need to distract the enemy. And that's easiest done at Kings Dominion. We stage an overland assault, capture it, and defend it with what looks like everything we've got. Of course, we really mean to abandon it. But while we're doing that, we press toward our underground objective— which is probably at or near our level anyway—and, well, I'll let you guess what we do next."

"Now you're talking about an even more hair-raising campaign," said the G-3. "You're saying to expand this to more than just a brief expedition. And to begin with, you want to capture this amusement park with just *one* squad?"

"Yes," said Matthew. "The pedophile game preserves were each better defended than Kings Dominion will be. Strictly speaking, I captured the Lucketts preserve with the aid of two archers."

"Yes, I heard about *Private* Zachary Radner," said the Operations Director drily. "But you won't have him at your side this time."

"Why not?"

The G-3 almost choked on his coffee. "Are you … *serious!?*" he blurted.

"I am," said Matthew.

"But he's just a kid!!"

"This *kid* has accepted Marine training." Out of the corner of his eye, Matthew noticed Colonel Campbell nodding and the Commandant smiling. "Besides, I want him. And several of the others."

"You want to use kids on a major military operation!? What the … for!?"

Calmly, Matthew explained: "To interrogate Captain Coleman effectively, I will need a staff of adolescents, or pre-adolescents, uniformed as twenty-first-century Cedar Fair ride operators and attendants. And those 'kids' would be just the cadre I need. They might not all have been old enough three hundred eighty years ago. But they certainly look it and act it today."

"You'd ask *them* to take part in a thing like that?" asked the G-3. "After all they've been through? To say nothing of their lack of training for an intelligence operation?"

"General, if I may," said *Segen* Cohen. "I think you'll find those kids would jump at the chance. Sweet revenge. And it might give them just the catharsis they need."

"She's right, sir," said Major Jellicoe. "I remember how well some of those kids fought at the Battle of Harper's Ferry. Two of them saved the Commander's life in that engagement."

"Yes, after Commander Morrow here took a fusillade of bullets for one of them," the G-3 answered. "As I recall, that particular kid was standing way out in the open. Bad form, to say the least. And Private Radner didn't even fight at Harper's Ferry."

"But that's only because he was awfully busy doing something else: helping *Segen* Cohen here fly that Elfin VIP transport to deploy my platoons to two other adits. He'll want that catharsis as well as anybody. It's not exactly pleasant to remember this, sir, but I attended some of the courts-martial and treason trials and other criminal trials, at which he and others testified to what they endured."

"And I," said the G-3, "presided over many of those courts-martial, as you know very well. *Segen* Cohen, you were originally a psychiatric nurse. Will you give me your professional opinion that those children will benefit from taking part in this operation?"

"Without hesitation, sir," said Ayelet.

The G-3 paused. Finally, he said, "All right. Against my better judgment, I agree to this plan."

"Good," said the Commandant. "And you and I need to start drawing up plans for a wider assault against the

UN. For now: Colonel Campbell, the assault on the KDAM will be your baby. You will coordinate with Commander Morrow and his staff."

"And I," said the DNI, "would like an interview with *Private* Radner and anyone else whom you recommend take part in this operation."

"I'll arrange that," said Ayelet.

"But I also want to repeat to you, Commander, my invitation to avail yourself of the services of Vincent Neurological. If they can enhance you—as my nephew thinks highly likely—you're going to need all the enhancement you can get."

"I'll accept your invitation."

"Good. Then I'll leave you other officers to it. I have some reports waiting for my attention."

With that, the Admiral, the Commandant, and the G-3 excused themselves. Colonel Campbell took over the meeting and called it to order. "We will now take up operational planning," he said. "Hospital Corpsman Riley, you're excused—unless you feel you can contribute in any way."

"I took a few shore leaves at Kings Dominion myself, sir," she said. "I'd like to contribute a few mites if I could."

Ayelet smiled. "In my new country," she said, "a *mite* is actually worth something,"

"Yes, I've read," said Andrea. "One Troy pennyweight of copper. But yes, if I may remain?"

"I'll vouch for her," said yet another voice: that of Captain Stephen Robinson USMC. He was now the S-2 of the Seventh Cav. "Her service was invaluable during the Lucketts raid, so she definitely knows her stuff. And, for that matter, those kids."

"Then that's settled," said the Colonel. "Let's begin with the lay of the land, as it were."

Matthew called upon one of his favorite sets of "extra circuits" that enabled him to draw free-hand as precisely as a draftsman might draw with table, drafting arm, compasses, and so on. *Remarkable that this society has revived the use of such tools. A good thing,* Matthew thought, *it gives their industries greater precision.* Within five minutes, he produced a full and accurate map of Kings Dominion. This included the backstage area that would be their immediate objective.

Chief Sutton confirmed Matthew's precision. "That gate will yield easily," he said, grinning.

"And my old Recon Platoon can take care of that guard force with no problem," said Captain Robinson.

"I hope," said Colonel Campbell, "that your replacement as leader of that platoon will do half as well as you might have done."

Suddenly Steve Robinson felt a little uncomfortable. "Well, sir," he said, "I'm counting on the new Platoon Sergeant to lead that platoon. I agreed to break in a new warrant officer, under instruction from the Officer Candidate School."

"You're telling me that you're going to send that platoon in, with an untried, not-quite officer, to lead it?"

"Actually, if I may, Colonel," said Matthew, "command of this operation will effectively fall to me. So three points. One, I'm confident that I can handle any senior officer candidate whom the OCS cares to send. Two, as is true in my old service, sergeants have as much to do with leading platoons as their nominal leaders. To this same point, I know Sergeant Jameson from our earlier operation together. I will personally vouch for *his* ability to lead that platoon, with or without a nominal leader. Three—and possibly most important—I know the members of that platoon. That will be vital in bringing this operation off. If I have to go in with an 'untried' platoon leader, with as good a platoon sergeant as Peter Jameson to back him up, that's a small matter."

"You are correct," said Colonel Campbell. "This will be your operation, just as the Lucketts raid was your operation. So let's get down to detailed planning. How do you plan to go in?"

"Through the barrier gate, with Chief Sutton's help, then through the delivery gate here, and then to capture this blockhouse." Matthew pointed to the single blockhouse that, he knew, housed Park Operations, Communications, and First Aid. "That's where the guard force has its headquarters."

"How big a guard force do they have?"

"Six altogether," said Matthew.

"*Six?* That's not even a squad! How do they cover all that terrain?"

"With wireless networked cameras."

"Cluster…! Where's your element of surprise?"

"That's another place where I come in," said Chief Sutton. "I can spoof those cameras to light up their screens with perfectly ordinary and unoccupied vistas. Those guards won't even know we're there until we hit the blockhouse. Piece of cake."

"'Funnel cake,' Chief?" asked Matthew, unable to resist that bit of wry humor.

Major Vincent and Captain Robinson both burst out laughing.

"What's so funny?" asked Campbell.

"Sorry, sir," said Robinson, still smiling. "But 'funnel cake' is a signature Kings Dominion confection. Obviously, Commander Morrow, here, knows the objective very well."

"I take the point," said the Colonel. "Apart from that guard force, do you expect to find anyone else in the park?"

"No, Colonel," said Matthew. "It's off-season, so the guard force will be the only ones present when we make our assault, which I plan to make at two zero hundred hours. By then, the sun should be well set. In the original period during which the park operated, that might not be true this time of year…"

"But since we abandoned Daylight Saving Time, having no use for it in these caverns, that will definitely hold," said Campbell. "What other resources and personnel will you need?"

"If I may suggest," said Matthew, "we'll need at least two autonomous omnibuses. Do you have a cavern under NRD-01-VA-Doswell?"

"We have, if I understand that Nature Reclamation District reference correctly."

"Then let's bring those buses up from there. We'll use that as our primary staging point."

"We can do better than that," said Campbell. "If we start now, then in four weeks, we can bore an adit to pop out not far from that gate. Right into the I-95 depression."

Matthew knew that depression well. In fact, it ran next to the park, on the associates' parking side—right where he would need to be. Remarkable that the depression still remained after all these centuries. Thank lazy UNCLIFOR for that—for though they had torn up the highway, they never filled in the depression. Vincent Tunneling should easily be able to bore a ramp to come out into it. Matthew wouldn't care to drive a bus up the embankment. But one of their AFVs could make it easily, even with one of those buses in tow.

"I'll agree to it," said Matthew. "That will definitely make logistical support easier."

"Now, once you get in, you want to stage a scene, right? That means you'll need a ride crew, and they'll need outfits."

"I'll ask Cedar Fair Properties to help us out," said Matthew. "UNESCO still maintains the old post-exchange-cum-quartermaster store called 'KD Central' in the old Human Resources building, right here, next to the Team Check-in Gate. They'll have most of the uniforms in all the old color schemes. HR will have the equipment for forging authentic-looking employee identification cards and magnetic name tags. I'll also want Cedar Fair to lend us some ride trainers. My younger force needs to operate at least two of the rides in a realistic manner appropriate to the twenty-first century."

"That," said Major Vincent, "will make quite a show. But we have another thing to consider now, don't we?"

"We certainly have," said Major Jellicoe. "Now that we've broached the subject of using this as a diversionary action, we have to defend Kings Dominion. I'm sure those Special Security Forces will respond as fast as they can to take it back, right?"

"Right," said Matthew.

"Then your command will need to mount an effective defense, but not *too* effective—and still manage to evacuate. Quite a tall order, wouldn't you agree?"

"Not necessarily," said Matthew. "Chief Sutton and I could, I'm sure, collaborate on how to create a fully automatic defense and an equally automatic means of recording everything that happens."

"Recording? What's the point of that?"

"Not only recording," said Matthew. "Streaming it out from the communications center. It will have propaganda value."

"To whom?"

"To my Zealots," said Ayelet, now grinning like a she-wolf. "They will definitely draw the moral. But I'd like to suggest something else, and I hope you won't mind."

"Go ahead," asked Jellicoe.

"When I was last in Mara Israel, I had time to examine some of their battlefield weapons. I don't know how to say this, sir, except straight-out, but…"

"I'll say it for you," said Jellicoe. "You're wondering whether the Israelis make better weapons than we do. Well, it's always been an open question, whose weapons would be better. Suppose the three of us—you, Commander Morrow, and I—make some direct side-by-side comparisons. Then we'll select the best weapons we can get from American and Israeli armorers."

"Agreed," said Ayelet.

"Then that pretty well covers it. All that's left are details."

That discussion took another hour, after which the meeting adjourned.

* * *

"I'm starving," said Ayelet when Matthew and his three companions were alone. "Can any of you suggest a good restaurant? Or do they have those here? I've eaten nothing but commissary food since I came back to give my evidence. Good food—better than anything I ate at Bethesda. But still.”

“They have restaurants here,” said Matthew. “Unlike our old society, these Americans did not get rid of their restaurants. They almost did—during the SARS-CoV-2 affair.”

“Don’t remind me,” said Andrea. “I’ve just got through a lecture on that—about how the infamous Dr. Ottavio Fausto engineered that virus, with help from the Wuhan Institute of Virology. And how half the governors of the original United States accepted his recommendations—with disastrous results. If they had followed the example of the Swedes, they wouldn’t have suffered as they did. As it is, it’s a wonder any of their travel service industries survived.”

“But of course, these Americans revived their hospitality industry as soon as they established these undergrounds,” said Matthew. “And yes, I know a place where we can all go to eat discreetly. In fact, it’s a kosher restaurant, too.” Out of the corner of his eye, he saw Ayelet’s face light up at that prospect. So did Andrea and Barry.

Reaching the restaurant didn’t take long, and the restaurateur knew Matthew by reputation, as nearly every American did, especially here in the Cumberland Caverns. Within minutes he had seated the four at a private table; within a few more, they had given their food orders.

As the table waiter left with their orders, Ayelet said, “And to think that these people are all used to waiting for someone to prepare proper food. In the good old United

Systems, only the elite eat anything like that. And even that was a compromise by the Five Ladies and the foundation for a New World Community."

"I heard about that, too," said Barry Sutton. "'You will own nothing, and you will be happy,' they said. And they got their wish—but only when the Elves came to this world. I still have trouble wrapping my mind around what the Elves did. I grew up thinking they were *friends* of humanity."

"Which they clearly are not," said Matthew. "Without the Elves, UNCLIFOR could never have prevailed; the Five Ladies would be political also-rans…"

"And ironically, human society would have achieved a lasting prosperity while *still* addressing the environmental concerns they *thought* people were neglecting," Barry finished. "Look at Leon Vincent, whose name is so famous down here. That guy even *believed* their hype about how a 'runaway greenhouse effect' would turn this world into another version of … well, Elfhaven, where the Elves come from, though no one knew it at the time. Leon Vincent changed the world's automotive industry all by himself, producing vehicles that could use the energy they had more efficiently and without polluting the air around them. These Americans *still* use his ideas because they're ideal for this kind of underground living. The Israelis, too. But look at what the Five Ladies nearly did to him. *And* how the Americans took care of him. He wasn't even a natural-born American citizen, and yet these Americans rescued him after Francisca Ordoñez-Pizarro had him thrown into … What was the name of that prison?"

"Sing Sing," said Matthew. "In what is now NRD-01-NY-Ossining. They didn't even retain all the cities in the polity that became Nuevo Aztlán. Only the academic and major sympathetic administrative centers remained. But enough of that. Barry, how are your studies coming at the Naval Technical School?"

"Fantastic," said Barry. "And thanks for thinking of me for the assault on Kings Dominion and those programs for automated defense and camera feeds. I already know my professors at NTS will be delighted to have me work on that."

"Maybe you'll have another project," said Ayelet. "Vincent Neurological is going to enhance Matthew here. In fact, I think I'll suggest that I second myself to them as a staff nurse. They'll need somebody who knows you."

"Thank you, Ayelet," said Matthew. "I'm sure that will be very helpful."

"While you're getting enhanced," said Barry, "get them to move some of your fighting skill and other routines onto permanent Read-Only Memory chips."

"I'm not sure my body can hold much more."

"Matthew," said Barry, grinning, "you don't know the half of what these people can do. They can pack ten times the information we can into a ROM chip. While you're at it, get a full listing of their *Encyclopedia Patriae.*"

"Their equivalent of the *Encyclopedia Galactica?*"

"You got it," said the Chief. "Among other things, it will come with a full set of values for the Seven Constants of the Universe. Remember the trouble I had using one of their multimeters? It's because when they decided to get away from the metric system, or *Système International d'Unités…*"

"Which we now know as *Système Interstellaire,*" Matthew said, interrupting.

"Right. Well, these Americans wanted even to get away from using the first units for electrical and magnetic quantities, plus chemical quantities and those having to do with light. So, in addition to going back to the foot, the slug, and the Rankine, for length, mass, and temperature, they *also* redefined the units of electric current, which they call a franklin, after Benjamin Franklin, plus amount-of-substance and luminous intensity. Ayelet and Andrea, you might as well know: they use a much larger Avogadro number than we're used to. I'm having to learn all new units and variations for physical quantities like electromotive potential—that's voltage—electrical resistance, power, capacitance, inductance, magnetic flux—all across the board. And all new chemical units, too."

"Why'd they bother with all that?" Andrea asked.

"Are you kidding?" said Ayelet. "After the way the UN did them, they'd want no part of the old units."

"But still, electric current and amount-of-substance don't have anything to do with time, length, mass, or temperature."

"Actually," said Barry, "they do. The original definitions the UN used, back before the Great Convention of 2019 that gave us the Seven Constants, derived the last three base units from the first four. The original unit of electric current, the ampere, depended on lengths and forces, expressible in SI units. One mole of a substance was originally its 'formula mass' in grams. In the American Patriotic system, it is the formula mass in drams."

"I see," said Andrea, her face registering her enlightenment. "They did that to maintain coherence."

"Coherence?" asked Matthew. "What's that?"

"Coherence is when you can derive a unit from others without having to use some arbitrary multiplier as a constant for no better reason than the historical. In this case, if the Americans had merely retained the old ampere, mole, and candela, they would have had to use arbitrary constants to bridge the gap between these quantities and the other four fundamental quantities. To avoid that, they created new definitions of current, amount-of-substance, and luminous intensity."

The conversation had to break off then; their food orders had arrived. Even Matthew had ordered a meal. Besides his being able to appreciate taste, he found it much easier to partake of a meal in the presence of others while having a dinner table conversation with them.

As they started to eat, Barry said, "I did notice one thing. Their 'foot' is a lot smaller than our 'meter.' That's quite an exception to our finding that their units are larger than ours."

"Not entirely," Matthew reminded him. "The Rankine is a smaller increment of temperature than the kelvin in SI."

"True. But the length unit might be significant in another way. The meter was originally one-ten-millionth of a half-meridian on Earth. Which, come to think of it, makes it specific *to* Earth—not exactly appropriate for the *United Systems,* is it? I wonder why people missed that."

"That kind of hypocrisy is rampant in the United Nations and Systems," said Ayelet.

"Yes," said Barry slowly, "I can see that. But the point I wanted to make is that the foot derives from the average length of a person's foot. Yours, mine, anyone's. And for that matter, a morgen foot, or a Neo-Inuit foot—just about anybody's average foot—except one species."

"The Elves," said Matthew. "We go right back to them. I wonder what Dr. Girard would say?"

The Chief laughed. "You have to remember, Commander, sir, that we lowly chiefs don't get to speak to Surgeons General, even if they have offices in the same building."

"I might, someday," said Matthew. "Because she was once my ship's chief surgeon."

"Really?" asked Andrea. "Débora Girard was the ship's surgeon on *Bonaventure VI?*"

"Yes," said Matthew. "I'm surprised she didn't intervene in my case."

"Maybe they keep your presence secret from her," said Andrea. "Remember, that was a Special Security Forces operation. And we know how chilling they can be. By the way, this meal tastes very good. Even by the 'real food' standard in this society. Where'd you find this place?"

"After Ayelet introduced me to kosher food—shortly after the Harper's Ferry incident—I made sure to find a restaurant she and I could both enjoy."

"Speaking of enjoyment," said Ayelet, "I can't wait to talk to you about what I have discovered."

"What time is it?" Barry asked abruptly.

"Thirteen-twenty-three hours Central Standard Time—or thirteen-twenty-three Sierra as we say in the Navy."

"Sorry that I have to eat and run," said Barry. "But I should be getting back to the NTS."

"And I have my own school to go to," said Andrea. "Chief Hospital Corpsman's School. They want me to help run Sick Bay on one of their old battle destroyers— USS *Elmo Zumwalt* DDG 1000. A lot of new things to learn." She stood up, as did Barry. "Ayelet, Matthew, it was lovely seeing you again."

"Likewise," said Barry. "Now, where do I 'settle up'?"

"I'll take care of it," said Matthew.

"Maybe someday you can brief me in greater detail on this thing called *money*," said Barry. "These people are like Merchantmen, except a lot more honest. Anyway— permission to leave?"

"Granted," said Matthew.

After Barry and Andrea left, Ayelet smiled. "That was awfully considerate of them, giving us this time together. How've you been, Matthew? I find it so hard to go without seeing you."

"Is that why you volunteered to sign on the Vincent Neurological during my enhancement?"

Ayelet smiled more sheepishly. "You can always see right through me," she said.

"And you," said Matthew, smiling back, "are far more obvious than you know. But that's part of your charm. You told me I was your special friend. Well, the feeling is mutual."

"Thank you," she said. "And that still goes." As if to reinforce the point, she reached across the table and put her hand on his.

* * *

For the next three weeks, Matthew put in full days. Vincent Neurological gave him something very like a private hospital room while they examined him every day. Ayelet did sign on as a staff nurse, an arrangement to which the *Tzahal*—the Israel Defense Forces—readily agreed.

Gradually the examinations gave way to discussions, and after that, some interesting repair sessions and even two neurosurgeries. Among other repairs, Vincent Neurological's engineers followed Barry Sutton's advice to move as many of his capabilities as possible to ROM chips that would hold them, even if the worst happened to his memory. And he did receive the *Encyclopedia Patriae*, in parallel to the *Encyclopedia Galactica* he already had on board. The Library of Congress expressed immediate interest in receiving copies of the Galactic Encyclopedia, for historical curiosity and the other information it held, to which the Americans, being underground, would not have access.

And every late afternoon—for him, neurosurgery was an outpatient procedure—Matthew would talk earnestly with engineers from Vincent Aerospace. They were, of course, most interested in duplicating his body shield—and the Elfin cloaking device from the captured Elfin ambassadorial transport that now rested on the ground above them, still projecting the image of a low hill.

Once, Matthew, Chief Sutton, and Hospital Corpsman Riley traveled to a *very* secret installation, the location of which their hosts did not reveal. There, they saw the two modern ships of the American Navy—USS *Elmo Zumwalt* DDG-1000 and USS *Michael Monsoor* DDG-1001. When he saw these two vessels, with their inward-sloping hull designs, Matthew agreed: these two ships could definitely use the cloaking device and the electromagnetic shield.

And on another occasion, Matthew, Ayelet, and Frank Jellicoe traveled to Mara Israel, bringing several American weapons along and some of the best Marine weapons instructors to test them. The Marines and the IDF held a series of "meets" because all agreed the only way to test battlefield weapons, apart from actual battle, was in competition. To no one's great surprise, the Americans conceded the advantage to the Israelis. Jellicoe ordered three mortars, eight Israeli-made UZI submachine guns, and the latest IMI Negev mounted machine gun from Israel Weapons Industries for use in the upcoming Kings Dominion operation. He also said he would ask the Commandant of Marines to talk to *Rav Aluf* Marcus about active IDF participation in the other operation he was planning, namely, the breach of the Great Spinal Four Bore Line.

And in the evenings, Matthew enjoyed the company of Ayelet Cohen. Part of that included frequent tours of some of the more interesting "attractions" in the caves. These mainly included many museums of art, including life-sized sculpture and statuary, and the natural and political history of the United States of America. Most of these, Matthew's hosts told him, their ancestors had relocated to the Cumberland Caverns from many places above ground where they once stood. Sadly, his hosts told him of incalculable losses of some of those works of art, even more than a decade before the Re-Wilding War had finally broken out. It gave Matthew a fresh appreciation for the value of art.

In the third week, Chief Sutton turned in his greatest "special student projects." These included a routine Matthew could use to crash the gate at Kings Dominion, and the "autonomous television director" and "autonomous company commander" programs he would use to direct the propaganda feeds and automatic defenses once he held Kings Dominion.

In the fourth week, Rear Admiral Vincent asked to see Matthew—and Zach. In private.

"Good news and bad news," he said. "The *good* news is that we do have an upsloping tunnel that opens into the I-95 Valley. Really, every time I think about that, I wonder why a river doesn't run through it."

"Neither source nor adequate depth nor outlet," said Matthew. "And several real rivers cut the depression in several places. In Virginia alone, you have the James, the North and South Anna Rivers, the three tributaries to the Mattaponi—all of which required bridges to cross them, and those bridges are now gone. So—no water channel."

"As may be. Now the bad news. There's something we three have to face right now. You two cannot afford capture. Or rather, *we* cannot afford to allow your capture."

Matthew didn't need the Admiral to tell him why. "Betrayal of information?" he asked.

"Correct. And you each have to face what you will do in that event."

"I will die first," said Zach, lips tight. "I told Commander Morrow that when I first met him."

"That," said Matthew, beginning to feel the odd glow from having a new idea, "might not be necessary." He went on to explain what he had in mind.

The Admiral swallowed hard. "I've often wondered," he said after ten seconds, "how it would feel to send a man into … well, never mind. Who else has to know about this?"

"A very select cadre at Vincent Neurological," said Matthew. "But if I may suggest, you should brief General Levi at Mossad. Before he tries to find out for himself."

"Why the … would he do that?"

Matthew shrugged. "General Levi once shared with me the story of Jonathan Pollard," he said.

Admiral Vincent winced. "You're absolutely right," he said. "That aside, our Israeli friends have a right to know. I'll brief him myself. How about you, young man? Do you understand what you're getting into?"

"Yes, sir," said Zach Radner. "I'll take the risk."

"For the record," the Admiral asked, "why?"

"Anything to help a friend, sir," said Zach. "Or, as in this case, a lot of friends."

* * *

A knock on his door made Matthew look up. Odd. He'd left orders that no one disturb him. He crossed to the hallway door and put his eye to the small eyepiece in the centerline of the door.

Ayelet stood outside. But he could plainly see she was upset. Her hazel eyes were bloodshot, and that raven-black hair he liked so much was matted. Quickly, he opened the door and let her in.

She came in, but did not speak. He reached for her, and she flinched and drew away.

Matthew closed his door. "All right, Ayelet," he said directly. "Just tell me what the problem is."

She didn't answer.

"You must know," said Matthew, "that I will wait as long as I must before you tell me."

She turned and looked at him—just stared, without speaking. And then she did speak—or rather, shouted. "How can you men be such *jerks!?*"

He smiled—and quickly raised a hand to intercept hers gently. "At least you tell me I *am* a man," he said. "I greatly appreciate your regarding me as a man, not a machine."

"Oh, I wish you *were* a machine just now!" cried Ayelet—and she really *was* crying. "Then it wouldn't hurt so much! But you're *not* a machine. You have a man's brain, so you're a man. A man I … I…" She broke off.

"What exactly are you trying to tell me?"

"Oh, as if you didn't know!" she shot back—and now he saw the tears in her eyes. "I'm in love with you. Andrea knew it, that first day. That's how she could goad me into switching you on. And now you've set yourself up so that I might never see you again!"

That made Matthew angry clear through—but not at Ayelet. "Did *Aluf* Levi talk to you?"

"Is *that gonif* involved!?" she fairly shouted. "No wonder the doctors made me sign a Non-Disclosure Agreement!! Oh, Matthew, did you forget that I was on the staff at Vincent Neuro? Do you really think they could keep a secret like that from me? They didn't even try! They told me what they're going to do, and…" And she covered her face with both hands and sobbed.

Matthew had never known the meaning of the word "awkward" before tonight. He said, "Ayelet, you are an officer. You've joined the IDF. You know the risks if I should fall back into enemy hands."

"Oh, how can you be so *cold* about it?"

"That kind of coldness keeps me alive," he said. "It has saved other lives, and missions, and too many to count."

"That's not it, Matthew," she said, lowering her hands. "You can't fool me. You've had some other woman in your life. A woman you lost—and you still feel that loss. I know the signs as well as anyone. But do you have to take your sorrow out on the living? Is that fair?"

He turned to stare directly into her eyes. The tears flowed more freely than ever. And he found himself moved as he had never been before. "Sit down," he finally said.

That seemed to make her angry all over again. "Don't you dare try to con me…"

"Sit down, Ayelet. Please. What I have to tell you, you need to be sitting down to hear. I speak from experience." For that matter, *he* had to sit down to tell it.

She sat at the small table holding the laptop the company had lent him. He sat down next to her, pushing the laptop aside.

"Her name was Natalya Fyodorovna Bronskaya," he began. "I first met her when we were both assigned to PCU-81, the future CV-81, USS *Bonaventure VI*."

"*Bonaventure VI*? Then would that be the Marine Lieutenant who died in action on Rigel g?"

"The same. I was second officer aboard *Bonaventure*, as you know. And she commanded the strike force. Which, again, as you know, is a full company of Marines for ships of that class. The strike force commander is *also* in charge of security for the ship—because when they're not fighting an action on the surface, a ship's Marine strike force doubles as its security force. And, given that role, the strike force CO has access to the 66-1 and other files on nearly everyone aboard.

"And *I*, as second officer, had access to *her* 66-1. Some very interesting information in that file. Do you remember I told you that I once knew a witness to the failure of the Novy Mir colony on Kepler-438 b?"

Ayelet gasped. "She was *there?*" she asked.

"Yes, and she was that witness," said Matthew grimly. "Born on that world, raised on it—and a child of sixteen when the colony degenerated into an orgy of looting, gang warfare—and some other things that Natalya kept hidden behind a privacy block.

"Anyway, USS *Napoléon Bonaparte* drew the assignment to pacify Novy Mir. Her Marine contingent practically rewrote the book on urban ground warfare in that action. They found Natalya, and had more than a little trouble getting her to trust them. She must have made an impression that was at least halfway favorable because they actually sent her to Marine Base Quantico. Where, to the surprise of a lot of people, she enlisted."

"Probably wanting to be as strong and skilled as possible," said Ayelet, who was actually starting to relax—somewhat. "So she could take care of herself. I assume you later found out what else happened to her on Novy Mir?"

"Yes," said Matthew. "Things I'll never tell a living soul."

"You don't have to," said Ayelet, with feeling. "We, psychiatric nursing officers, learn all about Novy Mir as a model for post-traumatic stress disorder. But please—go on."

"She graduated near the top of her class. After three years, she'd made sergeant, then was selected for Officer Candidate School. She finished in six weeks and then, as a fresh second lieutenant, was leading the platoon tasked to guard the Ambassador Extraordinary/Plenipotentiary of the United Systems in his peace negotiations with the Morgenetic Empire. Her file is sketchy on this next point—but you might recall that someone tried to assassinate the Ambassador. She figured it out and stopped it. For that, she received a decoration and a promotion—and her assignment to *Bonaventure VI*, moving up from platoon leader to company commander."

"Quite a service record," said Ayelet. "But how did you two become—do you understand what 'being an item' means?"

"I can guess," said Matthew. "It happened on a shore leave we took together—not at any fleet base, but in a liberty port. Not just any liberty port, either—it was a Merchantmen's world. You understand the sort of establishments the Merchantmen like to build to gain the confidence of United Systems Naval and Marine personnel on shore leave. For reasons I never did learn, she took me to a casino. We didn't gamble, but she did order several rounds of double drinks. I remember getting seriously intoxicated. So did she. The only other thing I remember was that we somehow wound up in bed together."

Ayelet stared back in openmouthed astonishment. Then she said, "I've heard of women trying something like that to get over that kind of trauma," she said. "But this is the limit! I hope you didn't put her on report?"

"And compromise myself?" said Matthew, smiling an ironic smile. "I'll tell you this much, though: she taught me, in that one episode, more about women than I had ever learned before. I'll confess something to you: I was still an adolescent—in fact, I think a pre-adolescent—in an adult body before then. After that, I knew what it felt like to be a man. But she found the episode dreadfully embarrassing. Do you know what she told me the next morning?"

"What?"

"She said, 'About last night—it never happened.'"

"*Never happened*?" said Ayelet. "Whom was she kidding? Did she *want* to go on report?"

"For disrespecting a superior?" asked Matthew. "Odd—that never occurred to me."

"Why not?"

"Because the entire wardroom treated me that way. Sure, I had the nominal permanent rank of lieutenant commander. But my fellow officers, I must tell you, did not all treat me as someone having authority over them. The Captain certainly treated me with the respect and expectations due to and from an officer. But the others … It was almost as if I were their special project."

"Sounds disgustingly condescending," said Ayelet. "No wonder you didn't want to carry the title of *Shofet*. Did you ever get past that condescension?"

"Actually, yes," said Matthew. "The ship went on other missions, and gradually the condescension went away. In fact, I made four very good friends. I won't say that of the Captain—because ship's captains can't afford to be 'friends' with any of their officers. But the exec officer, the ship's surgeon, the ship's psychiatrist, and the engineering officer all became my fast friends.

"Natalya, though, was a special case. We drew another special assignment together—one that the JAG Corps handed to us, in fact. On that occasion, she finally apologized to me.

"Then she said … sorry…" Matthew apologized to Ayelet as tears, coming back afresh, blinded him.

"Take your time," said Ayelet—and not sounding like a psychiatric aide, either. "I told you—I know the signs."

"Thank you. I … I'm all right now. Anyway, she said she still had feelings for me, feelings she hoped I would understand. I didn't, of course—I still had an emotion-blocking chip in my brain. But I could still feel respect, and treat her with the respect she deserved. And that's when she told me those other things she had suffered on Novy Mir."

He paused for fifteen seconds. Then he said, "I'll likely never know why she, herself, had taken such an interest in me. Nor did we ever have time to explore any possibilities. Because—well, you see, Rigel g happened not long afterward. And I ... I was not able to mourn her passing for another six years. That's when Dr. Girard and engineer Shaka worked out a plan to remove my emotion-blocking chip. *Then* I could mourn—and I did. Not only losing a friend—but losing an opportunity she and I could never have again."

"You didn't try to drown your sorrow in alcohol, did you?"

"Oh, no," said Matthew. "That would have been impossible. You see, after that shore leave—after she said 'it never happened'—I asked Dr. Girard to enhance my organic intake processors. I was never going to let ethanol, or any other intoxicant, affect me that way again."

"I don't blame you," said Ayelet. "Oh, I can't imagine what you've been through. All your adult life, you've been someone's science project—first this Dr. Frankel, who put you together; then the Naval Academy; then the officers of *Bonaventure VI* and *VII;* then the psych department at Bethesda—and now those people at Vincent Neurological. And ... me. Oh, may the Name help me, I've done it to you, too." And she turned away from him.

"Don't blame yourself for that," he said, turning her back to face him. "After all, I consented to most of it, especially from you. You did me a great favor. I have a high ideal to serve, higher than I've ever had before. And I have you to thank."

"How can you brush it aside so easily?" she asked. "Matthew, there's a human being under that golden shell you wear. I have come to know that man. Sure, you can be hard—when you have to be. But you can also be kind and gentle—and you can enjoy being alive. All those trips we've taken since we came to this underground—I know you enjoyed them as much as I did.

"And I have this horrible feeling that it's not going to end well for you this time."

"Your … concern for me touches me greatly," said Matthew. "You were telling the truth, then."

"Matthew," said Ayelet, "I do not lie about such things. And I will never, never lie to you."

"I thank you for that," he said. "That means more than you know."

She suddenly seized both his hands and held them tightly. "Then know this," she said. "I don't care, just now, about missions, or protocol, or any of it. I care about the man I have come to love. And if it wouldn't break discipline, I would very much like to … to … Oh, please, Matthew, do I have to say it out loud?"

"No," he said. Then he stood up, drawing her up with him.

And at last, she smiled. She was still smiling as she let go of his hands and slowly put her arms around him. Her starting to remove his tunic was all the clue he needed.

Naturally, Ayelet stayed the night. The next morning, they said goodbye to one another. He could see the tears in her eyes again. Just barely—because tears filled his own.

"Thank you—for one thing more," he said.

"What's that?"

"For not telling me 'it never happened.'"

"I would never say a thing like that to you," said Ayelet. "Especially after last night. Oh, Matthew, if you knew how badly I've wanted that experience, you'd probably write me up yourself. And it would have been worth it. If we never see one another again, last night was the most wonderful experience I ever had."

Matthew could only nod. They embraced one last time and then left, each going his and her separate way.

* * *

When Matthew joined the Recon Platoon of the Seventh Cavalry, Sergeant Jameson winked at Matthew. Chief Sutton, who accompanied Matthew, wore a more solemn expression.

What Did You Think?

Enjoying *Matthew's War?* Head on over to Amazon to follow me so you can pick up your copy. And, please leave me an honest review on Amazon, letting me know what you thought of *Matthew's Run.*

Thank You For Reading My Book!

I really appreciate your feedback about my books; your reviews make my books better!

Visit my online store at https://www.cnav.store/ to purchase patriotic gear and see my latest books and merchandise.

Thanks so much!
–*Terry A. Hurlbut*
www.conservativenewsandviews.com
https://www.cnav.store/

Acknowledgments

First and foremost, the character of Matthew Morrow has its basis, not in "case histories" of "persons on the Autism Spectrum," but on my personal experience. In that light, I couldn't possibly acknowledge everyone in my life who taught me a valuable lesson on what neurotypicals really think of persons on The Spectrum. Some of those lessons have been positive, some negative—but all have been valuable. In addition to which I acknowledge God, Who never fails in love or honor.

Next, I must acknowledge the "giants" on whose shoulders I have the privilege of standing. They start with men like C. S. Lewis, H. G. Wells, and Jules Verne. But they also include some less obvious names—like William Shakespeare and C. S. Forester. And perhaps even less obvious names, like Julius Caesar.

I must also acknowledge many, who would ask me not to identify them, who have apprised me of certain evils in the world in which we are now living. This applies equally to the ugly side of modern allopathic medical research, education, and services, as it does to certain criminal activities.

Next, I must acknowledge Jeannie Culbertson, who served as an invaluable guide through the weeds which every writer must travel.

And last, I must acknowledge my dear friend Andrea, without whose guidance and inspiration this work would not have been possible.

Terry A. Hurlbut
March 7, 2022
(MJDN 59645)

About the Author

Terry A. Hurlbut has been a student of politics, philosophy, and science for more than 45 years.

He is a graduate of Yale College and has served as a physician-level laboratory administrator in a 250-bed community hospital. He also is a serious student of the Bible, is conversant in its two primary original languages, and has followed the creation-science movement closely since 1993.

For more information and to read more of his writing, please visit Conservative News and Views at this link:

https://www.conservativenewsandviews.com/author/temlakos/.